The Children of Alsace

Les Oberlés

René Bazin

Alpha Editions

This edition published in 2021

ISBN : 9789355118233

Design and Setting By
Alpha Editions
www.alphaedis.com
Email – info@alphaedis.com

As per information held with us this book is in Public Domain.
This book is a reproduction of an important historical work. Alpha Editions uses the best technology to reproduce historical work in the same manner it was first published to preserve its original nature. Any marks or number seen are left intentionally to preserve its true form.

PREFACE

René Bazin is already known to the English public as a writer of exquisite charm and wonderful sensibility. "The Nun," "Redemption," and "This My Son" have revealed his powers to appreciative readers. Bazin is not only an original writer, a charming story-teller, but also a deep thinker, a clear delineator of human character and life, a wonderful landscape-painter, and a bold realist. For it is real life, humble, poignant, palpitating, which we meet in his stories. Life, full of misery and suffering, but also of pity and charity, of self-sacrifice and heroic traits. Bazin is a passionate admirer of Nature, and this admiration and love manifest themselves in his preference for pastoral and rural scenes, and his description of nature and peasant life.

Nature and climate, M. Bazin thinks, exercise a paramount influence upon the soul, and produce deep and permanent impressions.

But in none of his books has he laid so much stress upon this mysterious influence of a country upon the soul of its inhabitants as in "Les Oberlés," which is now placed before English readers under the title of "The Children of Alsace." For it is the country of Alsace, with her woes and sorrows and sufferings, her aspirations and hopes and dreams, which speaks to us through the mouth of Jean Oberlé, the hero, who mysteriously feels the influence of soil upon his soul, and is drawn to France, since Alsace is sighing under the German yoke, and her weeping soul has fled to France there to wait the day of delivery and freedom!

"Les Oberlés," or "The Children of Alsace," possesses all the elements necessary for a real drama, for a great tragedy, namely, the clash of conflicting passions, emotions, and duties. And these conflicting passions arise where one has a right to expect peace and goodwill. The author introduces us to a divided family, and we see the husband rise against his wife, the son against his father, and the brother against the sister. Their different modes of thinking and of feeling, their ambitions and dreams, turn these beings, united by the ties of blood, into enemies. But "Les Oberlés" is not only a family drama, tragic, irreparable, but also depicts the love of the native soil, a love almost physical, in conflict with the love for the Greater Fatherland. It also shows the clash of two civilisations, the Latin and the Teuton, which for forty years have now been waging war on the soil of conquered Alsace.

All these elements make "Les Oberlés" a really tragic novel—a novel full of dramatic incidents, of poignant scenes, but also full of life and love.

A. S. RAPPOPORT.

LONDON,
November 1.

CHAPTER I
A FEBRUARY NIGHT IN ALSACE

The moon was rising above the mists of the Rhine. A man who was coming down from the Vosges by a path—a good sportsman and great walker whom nothing escaped—had just caught sight of her through the slope of forest trees. Then he at once stepped into the shadow of the plantations. But this single glance through the opening, at the night growing more and more luminous, was sufficient to make him realise afresh the natural beauty amidst which he lived. The man trembled with delight. The weather was cold and calm—a slight mist rose from the hollows. It did not bring with it yet the scent of jonquils and wild strawberries, but only that other perfume which has no name and no season—the perfume of rosin, of dead leaves, of grass once again grown green, of bark raised on the fresh skin of the trees, and the breath of that everlasting flower which is the forest moss. The traveller breathed in this smell which he loved; he drank it in great draughts, with open mouth, for more than ten strides, and although accustomed to this nocturnal festival of the forest, to these lights of heaven, to these perfumes of earth, to these rustlings of silent life, he said aloud: "Bravo, Winter! Bravo, the Vosges! They have not been able to spoil you." And he put his stick under his arm in order to make still less noise on the sand and pine-needles of the winding path. Then turning his head:

"Carefully, Fidèle, good friend. It is too beautiful."

Three steps behind him trotted a spaniel, long-limbed and lean, with a nose like a greyhound, who seemed quite grey, but who by daylight was a mixture of fire-and-coffee-and-milk colour, with fringes of soft hair marking the outline of his paws, belly, and tail. The beast seemed to understand his master, for he followed him without making any more noise than the moon made in passing over the tops of the pine-trees.

Soon the moonlight pierced through the branches; breaking up the shade or sweeping it away from the open spaces, it spread out across the slopes, enveloped the trunks of trees, or studded them with stars, and quite cold, formless, and blue, created out of these same trees a new forest, which daylight never knew. It was an immense creation—quick and enchanting. It took but ten minutes. Not a tremor foretold it. M. Ulrich Biehler continued his downward path, a prey to growing emotion, stooping sometimes to get a better view of the undergrowth, sometimes bending over the ravines with beating heart, but watching with head erect, like the roebucks when about to leave the valleys for the upland pastures.

This enthusiastic traveller, still young in mind, was, however, not a young man. M. Ulrich Biehler, called M. Ulrich throughout the countryside, was sixty years old, and his hair and beard, almost white, proclaimed his age; but there had been more of the sap of youth in him than in most, just as some possess more bravery or more beauty, and something of this youthfulness he had retained. He lived in the middle of the mountain of Sainte Odile, exactly twelve hundred feet in the air, in a forest-house without any pretension to architecture, and without lands of any sort except the sloping meadow on which it stood, and at the back was a very small orchard, ravaged periodically by hard winters. He had remained faithful to this house, inherited from his father, who had bought it for a holiday residence only, and here he spent the whole year alone, although his friends, like his lands, were plentiful in the plains. He was not shy of men, but he did not like to give up his own way of living, consequently there were some fanciful stories told about him. They said that in 0 he had gone through the whole campaign wearing a silver helmet, from the crest of which hung, instead of horsehair, the hair of a woman. No one could say if this legend were history. But twenty good people from the plains of Alsace could affirm that there was not among the French Dragoons a more indefatigable horseman, a bolder scout, a more tender companion in misery, or one more forgetful of his own suffering, than M. Ulrich, proprietor of Heidenbruch, in the mountain of Sainte Odile.

He had remained French under German rule. That was at once his joy and the cause of the many difficulties which he tried to surmount or to endure as a set-off for the favour they showed him in allowing him to breathe the air of Alsace. He knew how to make himself respected in the rôle of a man vanquished, tolerated, and watched. There must be no concession which would show forgetfulness of the dear French country, but there must be no provocation; he had no taste for useless demonstration. M. Ulrich travelled much in the Vosges, where he possessed forests here and there, which he looked after himself. His woods had the reputation of being among the best managed in Lower Alsace. His house, shut up for thirty years because of mourning, had, however, a reputation for comfort and refinement. The few persons, French or Alsatians, who had crossed the threshold spoke of the graciousness of the host and the art with which he made his guests welcome. Above all, the peasants loved him, those who had gone through the war with him, and even their sons, who took off their hats when M. Ulrich appeared at the corner of their vineyard or of their lucerne-field.

They recognised him a long way off because of his slim, tall figure and his habit of wearing only light clothes, which he bought in Paris, and invariably chose in shades of brown, varying from the dark brown of the walnut to the light brown of the oak. His pointed beard, very well kept, added length to a face which had but little colour and few wrinkles; his mouth smiled readily under his moustaches, and his prominent nose, with its fine outline, showed purity of race; his kind, intelligent grey eyes would quickly become haughty and defiant if one spoke of Alsace; and the wide brow, which imparted a touch of dreaminess to this face of a fighting man, seemed larger still because of two bare patches extending into the thick growth of stiff short hairs.

Now, on this particular evening M. Ulrich had returned from visiting the wood-cutting going on in the mountains of the Valley of the Bruche, and his servants were not expecting him to go out again, when after dinner he said to his servant, the old Lisa, who was waiting at table:

"My nephew, Jean, arrives to-night at Alsheim, and no doubt if I waited till to-morrow I should see him here, but I prefer to see him down there, and to-night. So I am starting. Leave the key under the door, and go to bed."

He had immediately whistled for Fidèle, taken his stick and gone down the path, which entered the wood at some fifty paces below Heidenbruch. M. Ulrich was clad, according to his custom, in a loose coat and trousers of dead-leaf colour and a velvet shooting-cap. He walked quickly, and in less than half an hour he found himself at a place where the path joined a wider alley, made for pedestrians and for the pilgrims of Sainte Odile. The place was mentioned in the guide-books, because for a hundred yards one could look down on the course of a swift stream which lower down the plain flowed through the village of Alsheim; and especially because in an opening of the ravine in the angle formed by two slopes of the mountains, one could see, in daylight, a corner of Alsace—villages, fields, meadows—and very far away a vague streak of silver, which was the Rhine, and beyond that the mountains of the Black Forest—blue as flax and rounded as the loops of a garland. In spite of the night, which limited his vision, M. Ulrich, on arriving in the alley, looked in front of him, through force of habit, but saw only a triangle of steel-coloured darkness in the upper part of which real stars shone, and lower down gleamed luminous points the same size as the stars, lightly veiled and surrounded with a halo—the lamps and candles of the village of Alsheim. The traveller thought of his nephew, whom he was presently to embrace, and asked himself: "Whom am I going to find? What has he become after three years' absence, and three years in Germany?"

It was only a momentary pause. M. Ulrich crossed the alley, and wishing to go the shortest way, passed under the branches of a forest of great beech-trees, which sloped steeply down towards a fir plantation, where he could regain the road. Some dead leaves still trembled at the ends of the lower branches, but the greater number had fallen on those of the preceding year. They had not left an inch of the soil uncovered, and as thin as silk themselves, and quite pale, they looked like a pavement of extremely smooth light-coloured flagstones: the trunks, marbled with moss, regular as columns, rose to a great height at the top, very high up, the tips leant towards each other, and their tenuous branches touched each other, outlined the arch, and let the light pass through. A few bushes broke the harmony of the lines. About a hundred yards lower down, the barrier of green trees seemed to form the solid wall of this ruined cathedral.

Suddenly M. Ulrich heard a slight noise, which another man would probably not have noticed: it was in front of him, among the green firs towards which he was advancing. It was the sound of a stone rolling down the slopes, faster and faster, striking against obstacles and rebounding. The noise grew fainter and fainter and ended with a detonation, sharply distinct, which proved that the stone had reached the pebbly bottom of the hollow and split. The forest had again become silent, when a second stone, much smaller still, to judge by the sound it called forth, also began to roll along in the shadow. At the same time the dog's hair stood up, and he came back growling to his master.

"Be quiet, Fidèle," he said. "They must not see me!"

M. Ulrich thrust himself behind the trunk of a tree, understanding that a living being was coming up across the wood, and guessing who was going to appear. Indeed, making a hole in the black curtain of pine-trees, he now saw the head, the two forelegs, and soon the whole body of a horse. A white, hurried breath escaped from its nostrils and smoked in the darkness. The animal was making immense efforts to climb the steep slope. With straining muscles its forefeet doubled up like hooks, its belly all but on the ground, it advanced by jerks, but almost noiselessly, sinking into the moss and the thick mass of vegetation heaped on the soil, and hardly displacing anything but the leaves, which slipped one over the other with a murmur as of dropping water. It carried a pale-blue horseman bending over the animal's neck and shoulders, and holding his lance almost horizontally, as if an enemy were near. The breath of the man mingled with the breath of the horse in the cold night air. They advanced, showing by their bearing the difficulty of the upward struggle. Soon the traveller distinguished the yellow cord on the rider's tunic, the black boots beneath the dark breeches, the straight sword hanging at the saddle-bow, and he recognised a horseman of the regiment of Rhenish Hussars garrisoned at Strasburg; then nearer still he was able to distinguish on the black-and-white flag of the lance a yellow eagle, indicating a non-commissioned officer; he saw under the flat cap a beardless face, ruddy and perspiring, with red-brown, fierce and restless eyes, a face buffeted by the horse's mane in motion, and frequently turning to the right, and he named under his breath Gottfried Hamm, quartermaster in the Rhenish Hussars, and son of Hamm the police-constable of Obernai. The man passed by, brushing against the tree behind which M. Ulrich was hiding; the shadow of his body and of his horse stretched across the feet of the Alsatian and on to the neighbouring moss: they left in their wake an odour of harness and of perspiration.

At the moment when he passed the tree he turned his head again towards the right. M. Ulrich looked in the same direction, which was where the greatest length of the beech-wood could be seen. Thirty yards farther on he discovered a second horseman coming up the same track, then a third, who had become no more than a grey silhouette between the columns of beech-trees and then, judging by the shadowy movements, farther on still, he divined that there were other soldiers and other horses climbing the mountain. Suddenly there was a flash in the depths of the wood, as if a glowworm were flying by. It was an order. All the men took one step to the right, and, forming in single file, silently, without uttering a word, continued their mysterious manœuvre. The shadows moved for an instant in the depths of the forest; the murmur of crushed and falling leaves became more and more indistinct, then ceased, and the night seemed once more to be empty of life.

"A formidable enemy," said M. Ulrich half aloud, "who is kept in training day and night! There was certainly an officer down there on the path. It was in his direction they were all looking. He raised his sword, bright in the moonlight, and those nearest saw it. They all turned. How little noise they made! All the same, I could have finished off two of them—if we had been at war."

Then, noticing that his dog was now quietly looking at him with nose in air and tail wagging, he added:

"Yes, yes, they are gone. You don't like them any more than I do."

Before continuing his way, he waited to make sure that the Hussars would not return in his direction. He did not like meeting German soldiers. These encountered hurt the sore and suspicious pride of the conquered man; they hurt him through his fidelity to France—through his love, which always dreaded a new war—a war, the date of which he saw with astonishment recede and recede. He would sometimes go a long way round in order to avoid a troop on the march on the high roads. Why had those Hussars come to disturb his descent to Alsheim? Always these manœuvres, always this thought of the West away down there, to which they clung with such tenacity; always this beast of prey who prowls supple and agile on the summit of the Vosges, and who watches the moment for descending.

M. Ulrich went down the beech-wood slopes, his head bent, his mind full of sad memories, which a word had been sufficient to call up—less than a word even—for alas! mingled with them, and ready to rise again out of the past, was all the youth of the man. He was careful to make no noise, keeping his dog behind him, and not caressing him when the poor beast rubbed his nose against his master's hand as if to say, "What is the matter then? Are they not gone?"

In a quarter of an hour, by the wider road which he re-entered at the end of the beech-wood, M. Ulrich gained the edge of the forest. A cooler, stronger breeze blew through the oak and hazel copses which bordered the plain. He stopped and listened towards the right, saying, with a displeased shrug of the shoulders:

"That is how they will come back! Not a soul will have heard them! For the moment let us forget them and go and say 'How do you do?' to Jean Oberlé."

M. Ulrich went down a last bit of short, steep path. A few more steps and the screens of undergrowth and brushwood which hid the view were passed. He saw the entire sky unveiled, and below him, in front, to the left and to the right, something of a softer, more misty blue, the land of Alsace. The smell of the fields and of plants wet with the dew, rose from the soil like a harvest of the night. The wind wafted it, the cold wind, the familiar passer-by on this plain, the vagabond companion of the Rhine. One could distinguish no detail in the shadow where Alsace slept, except at a distance of a few hundred yards, where lines of roofs clustered about a round grey belfry ending in a steeple. That was the village of Alsheim. M. Ulrich hastened on and soon found the course of the stream again, now more rapid than ever, the bank of which he had skirted in the mountain; walked along by it, and saw stand out, high and massive, in its park of trees despoiled by winter, the first house of Alsheim—the house of the Oberlés.

It was built on the right of the road, from which it was separated, first by a white wall, then by a brook which ran through the domain more than two hundred yards farther, providing the water necessary for the engines, and then flowing, enlarged and cunningly directed, among the trees, to its outlet. M. Ulrich went through the large gate of wrought iron which opened on to the road, and passing by the lodge-keeper's cottage, leaving to the right the timber-yard full of piled-up wood, of cris-crossed planks, of poles, and of sheds, he took the left avenue, which wound between clumps of trees and the lawn, and reached the flight of steps before a two-storied house, with dormer windows, built of the red stone of Saverne and dating from the middle of the century. It was half-past eight. He went eagerly up to the first floor and knocked at the door of a room.

A young voice answered:

"Come in!"

M. Ulrich had not time to take off his shooting-cap. He was seized round the neck, drawn forward, and embraced by his nephew, Jean Oberlé, who said:

"Good evening, Uncle Ulrich! Ah! How glad I am! What a good idea!"

"Come, let go of me! Good evening, my Jean! You have just arrived?"

"I got here at three o'clock this afternoon. I should have come to see you to-morrow, you know!"

"I was certain of it! But I could not wait so long. I simply had to come down and see you. It is three years since I saw you, Jean! Let me look at you!"

"At your leisure," said the young man, laughing. "Have I changed?"

He had just pushed a leathern arm-chair up to his uncle, and sat down facing him, on a sofa covered with a rug and placed against the wall.

Between them there was a table, on which burned a little oil lamp of chased metal. Near by through the window, whose curtains were drawn aside, the park could be seen all motionless and solitary in the moonlight. M. Ulrich scrutinised Jean with a curiosity at once affectionate and proud. He had grown—he was a little taller than his uncle. His solid Alsatian face had taken on a quiet firmness and more pleasing lines. His brown moustache was thicker, his easy gestures were now those of a man who has seen the world. He might have been mistaken for a Southerner because of the Italian paleness of his shaven cheeks, of his eyes encircled with shadow, because of his dark hair which he wore parted at the side, and because of his pale lips opening over fine healthy teeth, which he showed when he spoke or smiled. But several signs marked him a Child of Alsace. The width of his face across the cheek-bones, his eyes green as the forests of the Vosges, and the square chin of the peasants of the valley.

He had inherited some of their characteristics, for his great grandfather had guided the plough. He had their sturdy horseman's body. The uncle also guessed, by the youthfulness of the glance which met his, that Jean Oberlé, the man of twenty-four, whom he was now looking at once more, was not very different morally from him whom he had known formerly.

"No," he said, after a long pause, "you are the same!—only you are a man—I was afraid of greater changes."

"And why?"

"Because, my boy, at your age especially there are certain journeys which are crucial tests. But first, where do you come from, exactly?"

"From Berlin, where I passed my *Referendar* examination."

The uncle laughed a jerky laugh, which he repressed quickly, and which was lost in his grey beard.

"Let us call that the *Licence en droit* examination—if you kindly will."

"Most willingly, uncle."

"Then give me a fuller explanation and one more up-to-date, for you must have had your diploma in your pocket more than a year. What have you done with your time?"

"It's very simple. The year before last I passed my examination, as you know, in Berlin, so finishing my law studies. Last year I worked with a lawyer till August. Then I travelled through Bohemia, Hungary, Croatia, and the Caucasus—with father's permission. I took six months over it. I returned to Berlin to get my student's luggage and to pay some farewell visits—and here I am."

"Well, and your father? In my haste to see you again I have not asked after him. Is he well?"

"He is not here."

"What! Was he obliged to be absent on the very evening of your return?"

Jean answered with a little bitterness:

"He was obliged to be present at a great dinner at the Councillor von Boscher's. He has taken my sister. It is a very grand reception, it seems."

There was a short silence. The two men smiled no longer. They felt between them—quite near—the supreme question, imposing itself upon them after a three minutes' conversation, that exasperating and fatal question which cannot be avoided, which unites and divides, which lurks beneath all social intercourse, honours, mortifications, and institutions, the question which has kept Europe under arms for thirty years.

"I dined alone," said Jean, "that is to say, with my grandfather."

"Not much of a companion, poor man. Is he not always so depressed, and so very infirm?"

"But his mind is very much alive, I assure you!"

There was a second silence, after which M. Ulrich asked, hesitatingly:

"And my sister? Your mother? Is she with them?"

The young man nodded an affirmative.

The elder man's grief was so intense that he turned away his eyes so that Jean might not see all the suffering they expressed. He raised them by chance to a water-colour by that master of decorative art, Spindler, hanging on the wall, and which represented three beautiful Alsatian girls amusing themselves swinging. Quickly he looked his nephew straight in the face, and, his voice broken with emotion, said:

"And you? You, too, could have dined with the Councillor von Boscher, considering how intimate you are with these Germans. Did you not wish to follow your parents?"

"No."

The word was said decidedly, simply. But M. Ulrich had not got the information he sought. Yes, Jean Oberlé had certainly become a man. He refused to blame his family, to voice any opinion which would be an accusation of the others. His uncle continued with the same ironical accent:

"Nevertheless, my nephew, all the winter through your Berlin successes were dinned into my ears. They did not spare me. I knew you were dancing with our fair enemies. I knew their names."

"Oh, I beg you," said Jean seriously, "do not let us joke about these questions—like people who dare not face them and give their opinion. I have had a different education from yours, it is true, uncle—a German education. But that does not diminish my love for this country; on the contrary...."

M. Ulrich stretched his hand across the table and pressed that of Jean.

"So much the better," he said.

"Did you doubt it?"

"I did not doubt it, my child—I did not know. I see so many things that pain me—and so many convictions surrendered."

"The proof that I love our Alsace is shown by my intention to live in Alsheim."

"What!" said M. Ulrich, stupefied. "You give up the idea of entering the German Administration—as your father desires you should do? It is grave—a serious thing, my friend, to rob him of his ambition. You were the subject of the future. Does he know?"

"He suspects; but we have not yet had any explanations on the matter. I have not had time since my return."

"And what will you do?"

The youthful smile reappeared on the lips of Jean Oberlé.

"I shall cut wood, as he does, as my grandfather Phillipe does; I shall settle among you here. When I travelled in Germany and in Austria, after my examination, it was chiefly that I might study the forests, the saw-mills, and the factories like our own. You are weeping?"

"Not quite."

M. Ulrich was not weeping, but he was obliged to dry his wet eyelids with the tip of his finger.

"It would be for joy, in any case, my dear boy. Oh, for a true and great joy. To see you faithful to what I love best in the world. To keep you with us—to see you determined not to accept appointments and honours from those who have violated your country.... Yes, it was the dream I dared no longer dream.... Only, quite frankly, I cannot understand it. I am surprised. Why are you not like your father, or like Lucienne, who have so openly rallied to the enemy? You studied law in Munich, in Bonn, in Heidelberg, in Berlin; you have just passed four years in Germany, without speaking of your college years. How did you avoid becoming German?"

"I am less so than you."

"That is hardly possible."

"Less than you, because I know them better. I have judged them by comparison. Well, they are our inferiors."

"Well, I *am* pleased. We hear nothing but the opposite of this. In France, above all, the praise of the conquerors of 0 continues without intermission."

The young man, touched by M. Ulrich's emotion, leaned no longer on the sofa, but bending forwards, his face lit up by the lamp, which made his green eyes appear more brilliant, said:

"Do not mistake me, Uncle Ulrich. I do not hate the Germans, and in that I differ from you. I even admire them, for in some things they are admirable. Among them I have friends I esteem greatly. I shall have others. I belong to a generation which has not seen what you have seen, and which has lived differently—I have not been conquered!"

"Happily, not!"

"Only the more I know them, the more I feel myself different from them; I feel I am of another race, with another category of ideals into which they do not enter, which I find superior, and which, without knowing why, I call 'France.'"

"Bravo, Jean, bravo!"

The old dragoon officer bent forward—he also was quite pale—and the two men were only separated by the width of the table.

"What I call France, uncle, what I have in my heart, like a dream, is a country where there is a greater facility for thought."

"Yes——"

"For speech——"

"That's it!"

"For laughter."

"How right you are!"

"Where souls have infinite shades of colour! A country that has the charm of a woman one loves, as it were a still more beautiful Alsace."

Both had risen, and M. Ulrich drew his nephew towards him, and pressed that fervent head against his breast.

"Frenchman!" said he, "Frenchman to the marrow of your bones, and in every drop of blood in your veins! My poor boy!"

The young man continued, his head still resting on the older man's shoulder:

"That is why I cannot live over yonder—across the Rhine—and why I shall live here!"

"Well might I say 'poor boy'!" answered M. Ulrich. "All is changed—alas! Even here in your home. You will suffer, Jean, with a nature like yours. I understand everything now—everything."

Then letting his nephew go:

"How glad I am I came to-night. Sit down there quite close to me. We have so much to say to each other—Jean, my Jean!"

They sat down side by side, happy, on the sofa. M. Ulrich stroked his pointed beard into its habitual well-groomed neatness. He recovered from his emotion, and said:

"Do you know that by speaking of France as we have spoken this evening, we have committed misdemeanours such as I delight in? It is not allowed. If we had been out of doors and Hamm had heard us, we should have been speedily dealt with—there would have been an official report!"

"I met him this afternoon."

"And I saw the son pass by in the depths of the wood just now. He is a non-commissioned officer in the Rhenish Hussars—the regiment which will soon be yours. Is that the carriage I hear?"

"No."

"Listen, then!"

They listened, gazing out of the window at the park, which was lit up by the full high moon; at the lawn in the shape of a lyre with its two white avenues, at the clumps of trees, and farther on the tile roofs of the saw-mill. Not a sound could be heard save the fall of the brook at the factory sluice, a monotonous sound which seemed now near, now far, according to the direction and strength of the freshening wind which was now blowing from the north-east, "from the Cathedral platform," as Uncle Ulrich said, thinking of Strasburg.

"No; what you hear," said Jean Oberlé, after listening for a while, "is the noise of the sluice. Father told the coachman to go to Molsheim to wait for the eleven-thirty train. We have time to chat."

They had time, and they made good use of it. They began to speak softly, without haste or difficulty, like those who have recognised that they agree on essentials and who can now safely open up all other questions, even the smallest. They spoke of the year's voluntary service Jean had been allowed to postpone until he was twenty-four, and of that new life he was going to begin at Strasburg—of the ease with which he could come nearly every Sunday to Alsheim. Then, this dear name having been repeated, uncle and nephew took pleasure in their recollections of the country, first of Alsheim, then of Sainte Odile, of the forest-dwelling of Heidenbruch, of Obernai, of Saverne, where the uncle had forests, of Guebwiller, where he had relations. It was Alsace they evoked. They thoroughly understood one another. They smoked, their legs crossed, seated one in each corner of the sofa, letting their words flow freely, and laughing often. Their conversation was so prolonged that the Black Forest cuckoo clock hanging over the door struck midnight.

"Do you suppose we have disturbed your grandfather?" asked M. Ulrich, getting up, and pointing with his hand to the wall which separated the young man's room from that of the sick man.

"No," said Jean; "he hardly sleeps at all now—I am sure it has pleased him to hear me laugh. As my family left me at five o'clock I spent a good deal of my time with him, and I watched him closely. He hears and understands everything. He recognised your voice, I am sure, and perhaps he has caught a word here and there."

"That will have pleased him, my boy. He belongs to the very old Alsace, that country which seems almost fabulous to you, and to which I also belong, although I am much younger than M. Oberlé. It was wholly French, that Alsace, and not a man of that time has changed. Look at your grandfather—

look at old Bastian. We are the generation who suffered. We represent grief—we others. Your father embodies resignation."

"And I?"

Uncle Ulrich looked at the young man, with his far-seeing eyes, and said:

"You—oh, you are Romance."

They would have smiled, both of them, but they could not, as if that word had been too perfectly accurate, which is not always the case with human judgments—as if they felt that Fate was there in this room, invisible, who repeated to them at the bottom of their hearts at the same time: "Yes, it is true—"this one is Romance." The grief which was oppressing them was only to be explained by the imminence of life's mystery. It faded away. M. Ulrich reached out his hand to his nephew, more gravely than he would have done if that word had not escaped him, which he did not regret, but which remained present with him.

"Good-bye, dear Jean. I would rather not wait for my brother-in-law. I do not know what attitude I should take up towards him. All you have told me would embarrass me. You will wish him good night for me. I will go home through the woods by moonlight. What a pity I have not my gun with me and the good luck to come across a brace of grouse in the fir wood."

To reach the staircase he took some careful steps on the carpet in the passage.

"Uncle," said Jean, in a low tone, "if you would go to my grandfather I am sure he would be pleased—I am sure he is not sleeping."

Uncle Ulrich, who was walking in front, stopped and retraced his steps. Jean turned the handle of the door near which he was, and going first into the room, said, in a lowered voice:

"Grandfather, I bring you a visitor—Uncle Ulrich—who wishes to see you."

They were in the semi-darkness of a large room, the curtains of which had been drawn, and a nightlight, in transparent china, placed at the end of the room on the left between the closed window and a bed which occupied the corner, was the sole light. On the table beside the bed, in the little luminous halo which surrounded the nightlight, was a small crucifix of copper, and a gold watch, the only shining objects in the room. In the bed an old man was sitting rather than lying, his shoulders covered with a grey wool crossover, his back and head supported by pillows, his hands hidden under the sheets, which still kept the folds of the linen press. A tapestry riband, serving as bell-cord and finishing in a fringe, reached to the middle of the bed. The man who was sleeping or waking there was impotent. Life with him was withdrawing more and more within. He walked and moved with difficulty. He no longer spoke. Under his thick, pale cheeks his mouth moved only to eat and to say three words—three cries—always the same: "Hunger, Thirst. Go away!" A sort of senile laziness allowed his jaw to hang, the jaw that had commanded many men. M. Ulrich and Jean went to the middle of the room without his giving the least sign that he was conscious of their presence. This poor human ruin was, however, the same man who had founded the factory at Alsheim, who had raised himself from the condition of a little country proprietor, who had been elected *protesting* deputy, who had been seen and heard in the Reichstag, claiming the unrecognised rights of Alsace and demanding justice of Prince Bismarck. Intelligence was watching, imprisoned, like the flame which lit up the room that night; but it expressed itself no longer. In this uninterrupted dream what men and things must pass before the mental vision of him who knew the whole of Alsace, who had gone through it in every direction, who had drunk of its white wines at all the tables of the rich and the poor; traveller, merchant, forester, and patriot! And it was he—this wrinkled bald head, this lowering face, these heavy eyelids, between which a slow, sad eye slipped to and fro like a billiard ball in the immovable slit of a bell. However, the two visitors had the impression that his gaze rested on them with an unusual pleasure.

They kept silence so as to let the old man savour the sweetness of a thought they would never, never know. Then Uncle Ulrich went near the bed, and, placing his hand upon the arm of Philippe Oberlé, bending down slightly to be nearer his ear and to more easily meet his eyes, which were raised with difficulty:

"We have talked a good deal, M. Oberlé, your grandson and myself. He is a good fellow—your Jean!"

A movement of the whole upper part of the body slowly changed the position of the head of the old man, who was trying to see his grandson.

"A good fellow," continued the forester, "whose stay in Berlin has not spoiled him. He has remained worthy of you—an Alsatian, a patriot. He does you honour."

Though there was only the tiny floating light in the room, Uncle Ulrich and Jean thought they perceived a smile on the face of the old man, the answer from a soul still young.

They quietly withdrew, saying:

"Good night, M. Oberlé. Good night, grandfather."

The flame of the nightlight flickered, displacing lights and shadows; the door was shut, and the interrupted dream continued in the room, where hardly anything had entered since sunset save the hours struck in the belfry of the church of Alsheim. M. Ulrich and his nephew parted at the foot of the staircase. The night was cold, the grass all white with frost.

"Good time for walking!" said M. Ulrich; "I shall expect you at Heidenbruch."

He whistled for his dog, and stroking its red-brown head, said:

"Take me home, for I am going to dream all the time of what that boy told me!"

Scarcely had he gone some few hundreds of yards—the sound of his footstep could still be heard on the road going up towards the Wood of Urlosen—when in the calm of the night Jean caught the sound of the trotting horses coming from the Obernai district. The noise of their shoes striking the metalled road sounded like flails on a threshing-floor; it was a rural sound, and not disturbing; it broke no rest. Fidèle, who was barking furiously towards the edge of the forest, must have had other reasons to show her teeth and give tongue. Jean listened to the carriage coming nearer. Soon the noise grew less and less, then became deadened, and he knew that the carriage had passed between the walls of the village, or at least had entered the circle of orchards which made Alsheim in the summer a nest of apple-trees, cherries, and walnuts. Then it swelled and sounded clear like a train coming out of a tunnel. The gravel scrunched at the end of the avenue. Two lamps turned and passed rapidly across the park; the grass, the shrubs, the lower trunks of trees, arose abruptly out of the darkness and as abruptly sank back into it again, and the brougham stopped before the house. Jean, who had remained at the top of the staircase, went down and opened the door. A young girl got out at once; her face was rosy, and she was wrapped all in white—white mantilla, coat of white wool, and white shoes. In passing, almost in the air, she bent to the right, just touched Jean's forehead with a kiss, and half opened two lips heavy with sleep.

"Good night, little brother."

And picking up her skirt with a loose grasp, with wavering movements, her head already on the pillow as it were, she went up the stairs and disappeared into the vestibule.

"Good evening, my son," said the authoritative voice of a man. "You have waited for us; you were wrong. Come quickly, Monica, the horses are very hot. Auguste, you will give them twelve litres to-morrow. You would have done better to have gone with us, Jean. It was all very nice. M. von Boscher asked twice about you."

The person who spoke thus, now to one and now to the other, had had time to get out of the carriage, to shake hands with Jean, to turn towards Madame Oberlé, still seated in the back of the carriage, to go half-way up the flight of steps, to inspect with the eye of a connoisseur the two black horses, whose wet backs looked as if they had been rubbed with soap. His grey whiskers framed a full and solid face; his overcoat was unbuttoned, showing the open waistcoat and the shirt, where three Rhine stones shone; his oratorical hand only appeared a moment. After having given his opinion and his orders, Joseph Oberlé—vigilant master who forgot nothing—quickly raised his double chin and fixed his eyes on the end of the enclosure, where the pyramids of felled trees were resting, to see if there were any signs of fire visible, or if any shadow prowled round the saw-mill; then, nimbly mounting the second flight of steps two at a time, he entered the house. His son had answered nothing. He was helping Madame Oberlé out of the carriage, taking from her her gloves and fan, and asking:

"You are not so very tired, are you, mother darling?"

Her dear eyes smiled, her long mouth said:

"Not too tired; but it is not for me, now, my dear. You have an old mother!"

She leaned on the arm of her son—from a mother's pride more than from necessity. There was infinite sadness in her smile, and she seemed to ask Jean, at whom she looked while going up the steps, "You forgive me for having gone there? I have suffered."

She was wearing a black satin dress. She had diamonds in her hair, still black, and a collar of blue fox on her shoulders. Jean thought she looked like an unhappy queen, and he admired the elegance of her head, of her walk, and her fine carriage. She was of an old Alsatian family, and he felt himself the son of this woman with a pride he showed only to her.

He accompanied her, giving her his arm all the time so as to have the joy of being nearer to her, and to stop her on nearly every step of the staircase.

"Mamma, I have spent an excellent evening. It would have been delicious if only you had been there! Imagine, Uncle Ulrich came at half-past eight, and he only set out for home at midnight, just now."

Madame Oberlé smiled a melancholy smile and said:

"He never stops as long as that for us. He keeps away."

"You mean to say that he keeps away! I will bring him back to you."

She stopped in her turn, looked at this son, whom she had not seen since the afternoon, and smiled more gaily.

"You love my brother?"

"Better than I used to. I seem to have just discovered him."

"You were too young before."

"And how we have talked! We agree on all points."

The gentle maternal eyes sought those of her child in the twilight of the staircase.

"Oh, all?" she asked.

"Yes, mamma, on all!"

They had arrived at the top of the stairs. She placed her gloved finger on her mouth. She withdrew her arm which she had placed in that of her son. She was at the door of her room, facing M. Philippe Oberlé's room. Jean kissed her, withdrew a little, returned to her, and pressed her once again to his heart silently.

Then he took a few steps down the passage, looked again at this woman dressed in black, and whom mourning suited so well—so simple with her drooping white hands and her erect head, so firm of feature, so gentle in expression.

He murmured gaily:

"Saint Monica Oberlé, pray for us!"

She did not seem to hear him, but she remained, her hand on the door-handle without entering, as long as Jean could see her, Jean, who was going backwards step by step, farther away, into the shadows of the passage.

He entered his room, his heart joyful, his mind full of thoughts, all those thoughts of the past evening coming back now with swift flight in the solitude of the present. Feeling that he would not sleep at once, he opened the window. The cold air blew steadily from the north-east. The mist had fled. From his room Jean could see, beyond the wide strip of cultivated hilly ground, the forests where Shadow all night long wound and unwound her folds, away to the heights crowned here and there by a spiked cluster of ancient woods, which broke the line of hills and wreathed itself about in stars. He tried to find the house of M. Ulrich. And in thought he saw again him who ought to be arriving home, when voices began to sing on the edge of the forest. A shiver of pleasure seized the nerves of the young man, who was a passionate musician. The voices were beautiful, young, and in tune. There were more than twenty of them certainly, perhaps thirty or fifty. He missed the words because of the distance. It was like the sound of an organ in the night. They flung out to the wind of Alsace a song of a spirited rhythm. Then three distinct words reached Jean's ears. He shrugged his shoulders, irritated with himself for not having understood at once. It was a chorus of German soldiers coming back from the manœuvre of those Rhenish Hussars M. Ulrich had met coming down the mountain. According to custom, they sang to keep themselves awake, and because there was in their songs the power of the word Fatherland. The horses' hoofs accompanied the melody like muffled cymbals. The words escaped and vibrated:

Stimmt an mit hellem hohen Klang,
Stimmt an das Lied der Lieder.
Des Faterlandes Hochgesang,
Das Waldthal hall es wieder."

Jean would have been glad to stop the song. How many times, however, and in all the German Provinces, had he not heard the soldiers sing? Why should he feel sad at the song of these men? Why did the words enter into his soul so painfully, although he knew them and could repeat them from memory? When some two hundred yards from the village they became silent. Only the clatter of hoofs continued drawing nearer to Alsheim and echoing above it. Jean leaned forward to see the horsemen pass in the little market town. He could see them through a large opening in the wall surrounding the park, secured by an iron gate just in front of the house—a moving mass in a brown dust that the wind blew back, leaning like barley beards in the ear. The men were not to be distinguished from each other, nor the horses. Jean thought, with a secret and increasing pain, "How many there are!"

At Berlin, at Munich, at Heidelberg, they only aroused an idea of strength without any immediate aim or object. The enemy had not been specially singled out; it was everything opposed to the greatness of the German Empire. Jean Oberlé had more than once admired the march of regiments and the wonderful power of the man who commanded so many men. But here on the frontier, on the ground still bloody with the last war, there were memories which showed only too well who was aimed at and threatened. The sight—the noise—of the soldiers made him dream of butcheries, of death, and of the fearful mourning which remains. They were passing between the houses. The noise of the squadrons, of men and beasts shook the windows. The little town seemed asleep. Neither the soldiers nor their leaders noticed anything; but in many of the houses a mother woke and sat up in her bed, shivering; a man stretched out his fist and cursed these conquerors of past days. God alone knew the drama. They passed by. When the last squadron had finished throwing shadows across the road, between the two pillars of the gate, Jean thought he saw, in the dust that was settling, a horseman facing the house. Was the horse refusing to advance? No; he was at rest. The horseman must be an officer—something golden placed in several rows across his breast sparkled. He did not move, firm in his saddle, young certainly, he gazed in front of him. This lasted scarcely a minute. Then he lowered the sabre he held in his hand, and having saluted, put spurs to his horse, which rushed away. The scene had been so quick that Jean might have thought it an illusion, if the gallop of the beast had not sounded in the village street.

"Some Teutonic joke," he thought—"a way this officer has found of saying that the house pleases him! Thanks!"

The regiment had already left the village and ridden away to the wide plain. The houses had gone to sleep once more. The wind blew towards the green Vosges. In the opposite quarter, far away now, like a religious hymn, rose again the song of the German soldiers, who were celebrating the German Fatherland whilst marching towards Strasburg.

CHAPTER II
THE EXAMINATION

On the following day the morning was far advanced when Jean left his room and appeared on the flight of steps built of the red stone of Saverne like the house, which opened on to the park in two flights of long steps. He was dressed in shooting clothes—of which he was fond—gaiters of black leather, breeches and coat of blue wool, with a hat of soft felt, in the ribbon of which he stuck a grouse feather. From the steps he asked:

"Where is my father?"

The man whom he addressed, the gardener, busy raking the avenue, answered:

"Monsieur is in the office at the saw-mill."

The first thing that Jean Oberlé saw on raising his eyes was the Vosges mountains, clothed with forests of pines, with trails of snow in the hollows, and with low, rapid clouds hiding the peaks. He trembled with joy. Then having gazed at the lowest mountain slopes, at the vineyards, and then the meadows, as if to impress on his memory all the details of these places found again after a long absence, and above all with the added satisfaction of remaining among them, his eyes fastened on the red roofs of the saw-mill, which made a barrier at the end of the Oberlé property, on the chimneys, on the high building where the turbines were, to the right on the course of the mountain stream of Alsheim, and nearer on the timber-yard whence the factory got its supplies, on the heaps of wood from trees of all sorts—beams, planks, which rose in pyramids and enormous cubes, beyond the winding alleys and the clumps of trees, some two hundred yards from the house. Jets of white steam in many places escaped from the roof of the saw-mill, and rested on the north wind like the clouds up above.

The young man went to the left, crossed the park, formerly planted and designed by M. Philippe Oberlé, and which was now beginning to be a freer and more harmonious corner of nature, and turning towards the piles of oak trunks, elms, and pines, went to knock at the door of the long building.

He entered the glass pavilion which served the master for a workroom. He was engaged in reading the day's letters. Seeing his son appear, he put the papers on the table, made a sign with his hand which meant "I expected your visit—sit down"—and moving his arm-chair, he said:

"Well, my boy! What have you to say to me?"

M. Joseph Oberlé was a ruddy man, quick and authoritative. Because of his shaven lips, his short whiskers, the correctness of his clothes, the easiness of his words and manners, he had sometimes been taken for an old French magistrate. The mistake did not arise with those who thought thus. It had been made by circumstances which had taken M. Joseph Oberlé in spite of himself from the way wherein he had intended to go, and which should have led him to some public office in the magistrature or the administration. The father, the founder of the dynasty, Philippe Oberlé, son of a race of peasant proprietors, had founded at Alsheim in 0 this mechanical saw-mill, which had rapidly prospered. He had become in a few years rich and powerful, very much beloved, because he neglected no means to that end; increasingly influential, but without at all foreseeing the events which would one day induce him to put his influence at the service of Alsace.

The son of this industrial workman could hardly escape the ambition of being a public functionary. That is what happened—his education had prepared him for it. Taken early from Alsace, pupil for eight years at the Lycée Louis le Grand, then law student, he was at twenty-two years old attached to the office of the Prefect of Charente, when the war broke out. Retained for some months by his chief, who thought it would please his friend the great manufacturer of Alsace if he sheltered the young man behind the walls of the prefecture of Angoulême; then on his demand incorporated tardily in the Army of the Loire, Joseph Oberlé marched much, retired much, suffered much from cold, and fought well on rare occasions. When the war was finished he had to make his choice.

If he had consulted his personal preferences only, he would have remained French, and he would have continued to follow an administrative career, having a taste for authority and few personal opinions on the quality of an order to be transmitted. But his father recalled him to Alsace. He implored him not to leave the work begun and prospering. He said: "My industry is become German by conquest; I cannot leave the instrument of my fortune and your future to perish. I detest the Prussians, but I take the only means which I have of continuing my life usefully. I was a Frenchman, I become an Alsatian. Do the same. I hope it will not be for long."

Joseph Oberlé had obeyed with real repugnance—repugnance at submitting to the law of the conqueror, repugnance at living in the village of Alsheim, lost at the foot of the Vosges. He had even committed at this time imprudences of speech and attitude which he regretted now. For the conquest had lasted; the fortunes of Germany were strengthened, and the young man, associated with his father and become the master of a factory, had felt the meshes of an administration similar to the French administration, but more harassing, stricter, and better obeyed, knotting itself and drawing closer round him. He saw that on every occasion, without any exception, the

German authorities would put him in the wrong; the police, the magistrates, the functionaries established for public services which he used daily, the commission of public roads, the railways, the water supply, the forests, the customs. The malevolence which he met with on all sides and in all departments of German administration, although he had become a German subject, was aggravated and had become quite a danger to the prosperity of the house of Alsheim, when, in 4, M. Philippe Oberlé, giving to his son the direction of the saw-mill, had yielded to the insistences of that poor forsaken country, which wanted to make of him, and did make him, the representative of her interests at the Reichstag, and one of the protesting deputies of Alsace.

This experience, the weariness of waiting, the removal of M. Philippe Oberlé, who spent a part of the year at Berlin, modified sensibly the attitude of the young head of the industrial enterprise. His first fervour, and that of others, grew less. He saw the anti-German manifestations of Alsatian peasants becoming rarer and more prudent. He hardly did any business with France; he no longer received visits from French people, even those made from interested and commercial motives. France, so near by distance, became like a walled-in country, shut up, and whence nothing more came to Alsace, neither travellers nor merchandise. The newspapers he received left him in no doubt as to the slow abandonment which certain French politicians counselled under the name of wisdom and concentration.

In ten years M. Joseph Oberlé had used up, till he could no longer find a trace in himself, all that his temperament allowed him of resistance to oppose to an established power. He was rallied. His marriage with Monica Biehler, desired and arranged by the old and ardent patriot who voted in the Reichstag against Prince Bismarck, had had no influence on his new ideas and attitude, at first secret, soon suspected, then known, then affirmed, then scandalously published by M. Joseph Oberlé. He gave pledges to the Germans, then hostages. He overstepped the boundary. He went farther than obedience. The foremen of the factory, old soldiers of France, admirers of M. Philippe Oberlé, companions of his struggle against the Germanisation of Alsace, bore with difficulty the attitude of the new master and blamed him. One of them in a moment of impatience had said to him one day, "Do you think we are so particularly proud to work for a renegade like you?" He had been discharged. His comrades immediately had taken his part, interceded, talked, and threatened a strike. "Well, do it," the master had said; "I shall be delighted. You are all quarrelsome fellows; I shall replace you by Germans!" They did not believe in the threat, but when a fresh crisis arose M. Joseph Oberlé carried it into execution a little later, that he might not be accused of weakness, which he feared more than injustice, and because he thought he could gain some advantage by replacing the Alsatians, continual grumblers, by workmen from Baden and Wurtemburg who were better disciplined and more easily managed. A third of the employés at the saw-mill had thus been replaced. A little German colony had been established to the north of the village, in the houses built by the master, and the Alsatians who remained had to bend before the argument of daily bread. That happened in 2. Some years later, they learned that M. Oberlé had sent his son Jean to be educated in Bavaria at the Munich gymnasium. In the same way he sent off his daughter Lucienne, placing her in the charge of the mistress of the most German school in Baden-Baden, the Mündner boarding-school. This last measure roused public opinion most of all. They were furious at this repudiation of Alsatian education and influence. They pitied Madame Oberlé thus separated from her son and deprived, as if she had been unworthy, of the right of bringing up her own daughter. To all those who blamed him the father replied, "It is for their good. I have spoiled my life; I do not wish them to spoil theirs. They will choose their road later when they have been able to make comparisons. But I will not have them from their very youth catalogued, pointed at, and inscribed on the official list as Alsatian pariahs."

Sometimes he added: "You do not understand, then, all the sacrifice that I am making! I am sparing my children these sacrifices; I am devoting myself to them. But that does not mean that I am not suffering."

He did suffer in fact, and so much the more that the confidence of the German administration was hard to gain. The reward of so much effort did not seem enviable. True, those in office began to flatter, to draw nearer, to seek out M. Joseph Oberlé, a precious conquest, of which many district directors had boasted in high places. But they watched him, whilst loading him with invitations and kind attentions. He felt the hesitation, the mistrust, scarcely disguised, sometimes even emphasised by the new masters he wished to please. Was he safe? Had he taken the side of the Annexation without any mental reservation? Did he sufficiently admire the German genius, German civilisation, German commerce, the German future? One had to admire so much and so many things!

The answer, however, became more and more affirmative. There was the acknowledged desire to make his son, Jean, enter the German magistracy, and there was the systematic continuation of this kind of exile imposed on the young man. When his classical studies were finished and his final examination passed with success at the end of the scholastic year, 5, Jean spent his first year of law studies at the University of Munich; he divided the next year between Bonn and Heidelberg; then took his licentiate's degree at Berlin, where he went through the Referendar Examination. At last, after a fourth year, when as a licentiate in law he entered the office of a lawyer at Berlin, after long travel in foreign countries, the young man came back to his home to rest before joining a regiment.

Truly the plan had been thoroughly carried out. In the first years of his student life, in his holidays even, excepting some days given to his family, his time had been given to travelling. During the last years he had not even appeared in Alsheim.

The end of it was that the administration no longer suspected him. Besides, one of the great obstacles to a public reconciliation between the functionaries of Alsace and M. Joseph Oberlé had disappeared. The old protesting deputy, seized by the illness which became chronic, retired from political life in O. From that moment dated, for the son, the smiles, the promises, the favours so long solicited. M. Joseph Oberlé recognised in the development his affairs had taken—in the Rhenish country and even beyond it—in the diminution of the official reports directed against his employés, or against himself in cases of contravention, in the signs of deference which the small officials showed him—formerly the most arrogant of all, in the ease with which he had ruled disputable points, obtained authorisations, altered the rules in divers points—in all these signs, as well as in others, he recognised that the governmental mind, present everywhere, incarnate everywhere in a multitude of men of gold lace—was no longer against him.

More definite advances were made to him. The preceding winter, while Lucienne, who had returned from the Mündner school, pretty, witty, charming, was dancing in the German salons of Strasburg, the father was talking with the representatives of the Empire. One of them, the prefect of Strasburg, Count Kassewitz, acting probably in accordance with superior orders, had let drop that the Government would see, without displeasure, M. Joseph Oberlé present himself as candidate for the deputyship in one of the districts of Alsace, and that the official support of the administration would be given to the son of the old protesting deputy.

This prospect filled M. Oberlé with joy. It had revived the ambition of this man who found himself up to then repaid but badly for the sacrifices of self-respect, friendships, and memories, which he had had to make. It gave new energies and a definite object to this official temperament, depressed by circumstances. M. Oberlé saw his justification in it, without being able to reveal it. He said to himself that, thanks to his energy, to his contempt for Utopia, to his clear sight of what was possible and what was not, he could hope for a future for himself—a participation in public life—a part he had believed to be reserved for his son. And henceforward it would be the answer that he would make to himself; if ever a doubt entered his mind, it would be his revenge against the mute insults offered him by some backward peasants, who forgot to recognise him in the streets, and by certain citizens of Strasburg or Alsheim, who scarcely, or no longer, saluted him.

He was therefore now going to receive his son in a frame of mind very different from that of the past. To-day, when he knew himself in full personal favour with the Government of Alsace-Lorraine, he was less set on his son carrying out to the letter the plan that he had traced at first. Jean had already assisted his father, as Lucienne was assisting him. He had been an argument, and one of the causes of this long-expected change of the governmental attitude. His collaboration was still going to be useful, but not necessary; and the father, warned by certain allusions and a certain reticence in the last letters written from Berlin by his son, did not feel so irritated when he thought that perhaps he would not follow the career in the German magistracy so carefully prepared for him, and would give up his last three years of terms and his State examinations. Such were the reflections of this man, whose life had been guided by the most unadulterated egotism, at the moment when he was preparing to receive his son's visit. For he had seen Jean and had watched him coming across the park. M. Oberlé had built at the extreme end of the saw-mill a sort of cage or footbridge, from which he could survey everything at once. One window opened on to the timber yard, and allowed him to follow the movements of the men occupied in stowing away and transporting the wood. Another, composed of a double glazed framework, placed the book-keepers under the eye of their master, ranged along a wall in a room like the master's room; and by a third, that is to say by a glass partition, which separated him from the workshop, he took in at a glance the immense hall where machines of all kinds, great saws in leather bands, cogged wheels, drills, and planes, were cutting, boring, and polishing trunks of trees brought to them on sliding grooves. Round him the low woodwork painted water-green; electric lamps in the shape of violets, the call-buttons placed on a copper plaque which served as a pediment to his work bureau, a telephone, a typewriter, light chairs painted white, spoke of his taste for bright colours, for convenient innovations, and for fragile-looking objects.

Seeing his son enter, he had turned towards the window overlooking the park; he had crossed his legs, and placed his right elbow on the desk. He examined curiously this tall, thin, handsome man, his son, who sat down facing him, and he smiled. To see him thus, leaning back in his arm-chair, and smiling his own mechanical and irrelevant smile, by only judging from the full face framed by two grey whiskers, and the gesture of his raised right hand, touching his head and playing with the cord of his eyeglass, it would be easy to understand the mistake of those who took M. Oberlé for a magistrate. But the eyes, a little closed on account of the bright light, were too quick and too hard to belong to any but a man of action. They gave the lie to the mechanical smile of his lips. They had no scientific curiosity, worldly or paternal; they sought simply a way, like those of a ship's captain—in order to pass on. Scarcely had M. Oberlé asked, "What have you to tell me?" than he added, "Have you spoken with your mother this morning?"

"No!"

"With Lucienne?"

"Neither; I have just come from my room."

"It is better so. It is better for us to make our plans together, we two, without any one interfering. I have allowed you to return and to stay here precisely that we may arrange your future. Firstly, your military service in the month of October, with the fixed determination—am I right?"—and he dwelt on the following words—"to become an officer of the reserve?"

Jean, motionless, with head erect and straight look, and with the charming gravity of a young man who speaks of his future and who keeps a sort of quiet hold on himself which is not quite natural to him:

"Yes, father, that is my intention."

"The first point is then settled—and afterwards? You have seen the world. You know the people among whom you are called to live. You know that with regard to the German magistracy the chances of succeeding increased some time ago, because my own position has been considerably bettered in Alsace?"

"I know it."

"You know equally well that I have never wavered in my desire to see you follow the career which would have been mine if circumstances had not been stronger than my will."

As if this word had suddenly excited in him the strength to will, the eyes of M. Oberlé were fixed, imperious and masterful, on those of his son, like the claws of a bird of prey. He left off playing with his eyeglass, and said quickly:

"Your last letters indicated, however, a certain hesitation. Answer me. Will you become a magistrate?"

Jean became slightly pale, and answered:

"No!"

The father bent forward as if he were going to rise, and without taking his eyes off him whose moral energy he was weighing and judging at that moment:

"Administrator?"

"Neither. Nothing official."

"Then your law studies?"

"Useless."

"Because?"

"Because," said the young man, trying to steady his voice, "I have not the German spirit."

M. Oberlé had not expected this answer. It was a disavowal. He started, and instinctively looked into the workshop to make sure that no one had heard or even guessed at such words. He met the raised eyes of many workmen, who thought he was supervising the work, and who turned away at once.

M. Oberlé turned again to his son. A violent irritation had seized him. But he understood that it was best not to let it be seen. For fear that his hands should show his agitation, he had seized the two arms of the arm-chair in which he was seated, bent forward as before, but now considering this young man from head to foot, considering his attitude, his clothes, his manner, this young man who was voicing ideas which seemed like a judgment on the conduct of his father. After a moment of silence, his voice broken, he asked:

"Who has put you against me? Your mother?"

"No one," said Jean Oberlé quickly. "I have nothing against you. Why do you take it like that? I say simply that I have not the German spirit. It is the result of a long comparison, and nothing else."

M. Joseph Oberlé saw that he had shown his hand too much. He withdrew into himself, and putting on that expression of cold irony with which he was accustomed to disguise his true sentiments:

"Then, since you refuse to follow the career which I destined for you, have you chosen another?"

"Without doubt, with your consent."

"Which?"

"Yours. Do not be mistaken with regard to what I have just told you. I have lived without a quarrel for ten years in an exclusively German centre. I know what it has cost me. You ask me the result of my experience. Well, I do not believe that my character is supple enough, or easy-going enough if you like, to do more than that, or to become a German official. I am sure that I should not always understand, and that I should disobey sometimes. My decision is irrevocable. And, on the contrary, your work pleases me."

"You imagine that a manufacturer is independent?"

"No; but he is more independent than many are. I studied law so that I should not refuse to follow without reflection, without examination, the way you pointed out to me. But I have profited by the travels which you suggested, every year."

"You may say which I imposed upon you; that is the truth, and I am going to explain my reasons."

"I have profited by them to study the forest industry wherever I could—in Germany, in Austria, in the Caucasus. I have given more thought and consideration to those questions than you might suppose. And I wish to live in Alsheim. Will you allow me to?"

The father did not answer at first. He was trying on his son an experiment to which he deliberately submitted other men who came to treat with him about some important affair. He was silent at the moment when decisive words were to be expected from him. If the questioner, disturbed, turned away to escape the look which seemed to be oppressive, or if he renewed the explanation already made, M. Joseph Oberlé classed him among weak men, his inferiors. Jean bore his father's look, and did not open his mouth. M. Oberlé was secretly flattered. He understood that he found himself in the presence of a man completely formed, of a very resolute, and probably inflexible spirit. He knew others like him in the neighbourhood. He secretly appreciated their independence of temper, and feared it. With the quickness of combination and organisation habitual to him, he perceived very clearly the industry of Alsheim directed by Jean, and the father of Jean, Joseph Oberlé, sitting in the Reichstag, admitted among the financiers, the administrators, and the powerful men of Germany. He was one of those who know how to turn his mistakes to some advantage, just as he managed to get something from the factory waste. This new vision softened him. Far from being angry, he let the ironical expression relax which he had put on while speaking of his son's project. With a movement of his hand he pointed to the immense workshop, where, without ceasing, with a roar which slightly shook the double windows, the steel blades entered into the heart of the old trees of the Vosges, and said, in a tone of affectionate scolding:

"So be it, my son. It will give joy to my father, to your mother, and to Ulrich. I agree that you put me in the wrong on one point with regard to them, but in one point only. Some years ago I should not have allowed you to refuse the career which seemed to me the best for you, and which would have saved us all from difficulties which you could not take the measure of. At that moment you were not able to judge for yourself. And further, I found my work, my position, too precarious and too dangerous to pass it on to you. That has changed. My business has increased. Life has become possible for me and for you all, thanks to the efforts, and perhaps to the sacrifices, for which those about me are not sufficiently grateful. To-day I admit that the business has a future. You wish to succeed me? I open the door for you immediately! You will go through the practical part of your apprenticeship in the seven months which remain before you join your regiment. Yes, I consent, but on one condition."

"Which?"

"You will not mix yourself up with politics."

"I have no taste for politics."

"Ah, excuse me," continued M. Oberlé with animation; "we must understand one another, must we not? I do not think you have any political ambition for yourself; you are not old enough, and perhaps you are not of the right stuff. And that is not what I forbid—I forbid you to have anything to do with Alsatian chauvinism; to go about repeating, as others do, on every occasion—'France, France'; to wear under your waistcoat a tricolour belt; to imitate the Alsatian students of Strasburg, who, to recognise and encourage one another, and for the fun of it, whistle in the ears of the police the six notes of the Marseillaise 'Form your battalions.' I won't have any of those little proceedings, of those little bravadoes, and of those great risks, my dear fellow! They are forbidden manifestations for us business men who work in a German country. They go against our efforts and interests, for it is not France who buys. France is very far away, my dear fellow; she is more than two hundred leagues from here, at least one would think so, considering the little noise, movement, or money which come to us from there. Do not forget that! You are by your own wish a German manufacturer; if you turn your back on the Germans you are lost. Think what you please about the history of your country, of its past, and of its present. I am ignorant of your opinions on that subject. I will not try to guess what they will be in a neighbourhood so behind the times as ours at Alsheim; but whatever you think, either try to hold your tongue, or make a career for yourself elsewhere."

A smile stole round Jean's turned-up moustache, while the upper part of his face remained grave and firm.

"You are asking yourself, I am sure, what I think about France?"

"Let us hear."

"I love her."

"You do not know her!"

"I have read her history and her literature carefully, and I have compared: that is all. When one is oneself of the nation, that enables one to divine much. I do not know it otherwise, it is true. You have taken your precautions."

"What you say is true, though at the same time you intended to wound——"

"Not at all."

"Yes, I have taken my precautions, in order to free your sister and you from that deadly spirit of opposition which would have made your lives barren from the beginning, which would have made you discontented people, powerless, poor; there are too many people of that sort in Alsace, who render no service to France or to Alsace, or to themselves, by perpetually furnishing Germany with reasons for anger. I do not regret that you make me explain myself as to the system of education which I desired for you, and which I alone desired. I wished to spare you the trial I have borne, of which I have just spoken to you: to fail in life. There is still another reason. Ah, I know well that credit will not be given me for that! I am obliged to praise myself in my own family. My child, it is not possible to have been brought up in France, to belong to France through all one's ancestry, and not to love French culture."

He interrupted himself a moment to see the impression this phrase produced, and he could see nothing, not a movement on the impassible face of his son, who decidedly was a highly self-controlled man. The implacable desire for justification which governed M. Oberlé, made him go on:

"You know that the French language is not favourably looked upon here, my dear Jean. In Bavaria you had a literary and historical education, better from that point of view than you would have had in Strasburg. I was able to desire, without prejudicing your masters against you, that you should have many extra French lessons. In Alsace, you and I would both have suffered for that. Those are the motives which guided me. Experience will show whether I was mistaken. I did it in any case in good faith, and for your good."

"My dear father," said Jean, "I have no right to judge what you have done. What I can tell you is that, thanks to that education I have received, if I have not an unbounded taste or admiration for German civilisation, I have at least the habit of living with the Germans. And I am persuaded that I could live with them in Alsace."

The father raised his eyebrows as if he would say, "I am not so sure of that."

"My ideas, up to now, have made me no enemy in Germany; and it seems to me that one can direct a saw-mill in an annexed country with the opinions I have just shown you."

"I hope so," said M. Oberlé simply.

"Then you accept me? I come to you?"

For answer the master pressed his finger on an electric button.

A man came up the steps which led from the machine hall to the observatory that M. Oberlé had had built, and opened the port-hole, and in the opening one saw a square blond beard, long hair, and two eyes like two blue gems.

"Wilhelm," said the master in German, "you will make my son conversant with the works, and you will explain to him the purchases we have made for the past six months. From to-morrow he will accompany you in your round of visits to where the fellings and cuttings are being carried out in the interests of the firm."

The door was shut again.

That young enthusiast, the elegant Jean Oberlé, was standing in front of his father. He held out his hand to him and said, pale with joy:

"Now I am again some one in Alsace! How I thank you!"

The father took his son's hand with a somewhat studied effusion. He thought:

"He is the image of his mother! In him I find again the spirit, the words, and the enthusiasm of Monica." Aloud he said:

"You see, my son, that I have only one aim in view, to make you happy. I have always had it. I agree to your adopting a career quite different from the one I chose for you. Try now to understand our position as your sister understands it."

Jean went away, and his father, a few minutes later, went out also. But while M. Joseph Oberlé went towards the house, being in haste to see his daughter, the only confidante of his thoughts, and to report the conversation he had just had with Jean, the latter crossed the timber yard to the left, passed before the lodge, and took the road to the forest. But he did not go far, because the luncheon hour was approaching. By the road that wound upward he reached the region of the vineyards of Alsheim, beyond the hop-fields which were still bare, where the poles rose tied together, like a stack of arms. His soul was glad. When he came to the entrance of a vineyard which he had known since his earliest childhood, where he had gathered the grapes in the days of long ago, he climbed on to a hill which overlooked the road and the rows of vines at the bottom. In spite of the grey light, in spite of the clouds and the wind, he found his Alsace beautiful, divinely beautiful—Alsace, sloping down very gently in front of him, and becoming a smooth plain with strips of grass and strips of ploughed land, and whence the villages here and there lifted their tile roofs and the point of their belfries. Round, isolated trees—leafless because it was winter—resembled dry thistles; some crows were flying, helped by the north wind, and seeking a newly sown spot.

Jean raised his hands, and spread them as if to embrace the expanse of land stretching out from Obernai, which he saw in the farthest undulations to the left, as far as Barr, half buried under the avalanche of pines down the mountain-side. "I love thee, Alsace, and I have come back to thee!" he cried. He gazed at the village of Alsheim, at the house of red stone which rose a little below him, and which was his; then at the other extremity of the pile of houses, inhabited by the workmen and peasants, he marked a sort of forest promontory which pushed out into the smooth plain. It was an avenue ending in a great group of leafless trees, grey, between which one could see the slopes of a roof. Jean let his eyes rest a long time on this half-hidden dwelling, and said: "Good day, Alsatian woman! Perhaps I am going to find that I love you. It would be so good to live here with you!"

The bell rang for luncheon, rang out from the Oberlés' house, and recalled him to himself. It had a thin, miserable sound, which gave some idea of the immensity of free space in which the noise vanished away, and the strength of the tide of the wind which carried it away over the lands of Alsace.

CHAPTER III
THE FIRST FAMILY MEETING

Jean turned slowly towards this bell which was calling him. He was full of joy at this moment. He was taking possession of a world which, after some years, had just been opened to him and pointed out as his place of habitation, of work, and of happiness. These words played on his troubled mind deliciously. They pursued each other like a troop of porpoises, those travellers on the surface, and other words accompanied them. Family life, comfort, social authority, embellishments, enlargements. The house took to itself a name—"the paternal home." He looked at it with tenderness, following the alley near the stream; he went up the steps with a feeling of respect, remembering that they had been built by the grandfather to whom the house still belonged, as also all the grounds except the saw-mill and the timber yard.

After having gone across the entrance hall, which extended from the front to the back of the house, he opened the last door on the left. The dining-room was the only room which had been "done up" according to the directions and the taste of M. Joseph Oberlé. Whilst one found elsewhere—in the drawing-room, the billiard-room, and the other rooms—the furniture bought by the grandfather, of yellow or green Utrecht velvet and mahogany, "My Creation," according to the expression of M. Joseph Oberlé, showed a complete absence of line. Colour took the place of style. The walls were covered with wainscoting of veined maple, blue-grey, purple in places, ash-grey, and pink-grey, covering half the height of the room. Above this, and reaching to the small beams, were four panels of stretched cloth, decorated with designs of smooth felt representing irises, hollyhocks, verbena, and gladioli. Everywhere, as far as possible, the straight line had been modified. The door mouldings described curves which rambled madly like stalks of tropical bindweed without any apparent reason. The framework of the large window was curved. The chairs of bent beechwood came from Vienna. The whole had no character, but a charm of softened light, and a remote resemblance to the vegetable kingdom. One would have taken it for the dining-room of a newly married couple.

The four usual table companions Jean was going to meet there hardly corresponded to this joyous picture, and there was no harmony between them and the decorations of the room. They invariably sat in the same places, round the square table, according to the established order of deep affinities and antipathies.

The first to the left of the window, the nearest to the glass, which shed on her the reflection of its levelled edges, was Madame Monica Oberlé, tall and slender, with a face that had been rounded and fresh, but was now pale, lined, and thin. She gave the impression of a being accustomed only to hear around her the words "You are wrong." Her short-sighted eyes, very gentle, glanced at the guests who were introduced to her with a smile always ready to withdraw and fade away. They only paused after they had looked about for a little time, when nothing had repulsed or misunderstood them. Then they revealed a clear intelligence, a very kind heart, become a little shy and sad, but still capable of illusions and outbursts of youth. No one could have had a more careless youth, nor one that seemed a less fitting preparation for the part she had to play later. She was then called Monica Biehler, of the ancient family Biehler of Obernai. From the top of her father's house, whose fortified gable-end rises on the ramparts of the little town, she saw the immense plain all round her. The garden full of trimmed box and pear-trees, and hawthorn, where she played, was only separated by an iron railing from the public promenade built on the old wall, so that the vision of Alsace was printed each day on this child's soul, and at the same time love of her country, so happy then—love of its beauty, its peace, and its liberty, of its villages, whose names she knew, whose rosy bunches of grapes she could have pointed out among the harvest fields. Monica Biehler knew nothing else. She only left Obernai to go with all the family to spend two summer months in the lodge at Heidenbruch, in the Forest of Sainte Odile. Only once did she happen to cross the Vosges, the year before her wedding, to make a pilgrimage to Domrémy in Lorraine. Those had been three days full of enthusiasm. Madame Oberlé remembered those three days as the purest joy of her life. She would say: "My journey in France." She had remained simple; she had kept, in her very retired life at Alsheim, the easy fears, but also the sincerity—the secret boldness of her youthful affection for the country and for the country people. She had therefore suffered more than another would have done in her place, in seeing her husband draw near to the German party in Alsace, and finally join it. She had suffered in her Alsatian pride, and still more in her maternal love. For the same cause which separated her morally from her husband, her children were taken from her. The lines on her face, faded before its time, could each have borne a name, that of the grief which had scored them there: the line of despised goodness, the line of useless warnings, the line of her insulted country, of separation from Jean and Lucienne, of the uselessness of the treasure of love she had stored up for them during her single and married life.

Her bitterness had been the greater because Madame Oberlé had no illusions as to the true motives which guided her husband. And this he had divined. He was humiliated by this witness whom he could not deceive, and whom he could not help esteeming. She personified for him the cause which he had abandoned. It was to her he spoke when he felt the need of justifying himself, and he did so whenever he had the chance. It was against her that his anger rose, against her mute disapproval. Never once in twenty years had he been able to get her to agree—not by one word—that Alsace was German. This timid woman yielded to force but she did not approve of it. She followed her husband into German society; there she bore herself with such dignity that one could neither deceive oneself as to her attitude, nor bear a grudge against her for it. There she safeguarded more than appearances. A mother, separated from her children, she had not separated herself from her husband. They still used the twin-bedsteads in the same room. They had continual scenes, sometimes on one side, sometimes acrimonious and violent on both sides. Nevertheless Madame Oberlé understood that her husband only hated her clear-sightedness and judgment. She hoped she would not always be in the wrong. Now that the children were grown up she believed that some very important decisions would have to be made with regard to them, and that by her long patience and by her numerous concessions she had perhaps gained the right to speak then and be heard.

Near her, and at her right, the grandfather, M. Philippe Oberlé, had always sat. For some years, five minutes before the time of the meal the dining-room door would open, the old man would come in, leaning on the arm of his valet, trying to walk straight, clothed in an anomalous garment of dark wool, his red ribbon in his button-hole, his head weary and bent, his eyelids nearly closed, his face swollen and bloodless. They placed him in a large chair with arms upholstered in grey; they tied his table napkin round his neck, and he waited, his body leaning against the chair-back, his hands on the table—hands pale as wax, in which the knotted blue veins were distinctly visible. When the others arrived M. Joseph Oberlé shook him by the hand; Lucienne threw him a kiss and a number of words audibly spoken in her fresh young voice; Madame Oberlé bent down and pressed her faithful lips on the old man's forehead. He thanked her by watching her sit down. He did not look at the others. Then he made the sign of the cross, she and he alone, being a son of that old Alsace which still prayed. And served by this neighbour so silently charitable, who knew all his tastes, his shame of a certain clumsiness, and who forestalled his wishes, he began to eat, slowly, with difficulty moving his relaxed muscles. His dreamy head remained leaning against the chair. His head alone was watching in a body nearly destroyed. It was the theatre where, for the pleasure and pain of one alone, there passed before his mental vision the forebears of those whose names were mentioned before him. He did not speak, but he remembered. Sometimes he drew from his pocket a schoolboy's slate and pencil, and he wrote, with an uncertain writing, two or three words, which he made his neighbour read; some rectification, some forgotten date, his approval or disapproval to join in with the words just spoken on the other side of the table. Generally they knew when he was interested by the movement of his heavy eyelids. It was only for a moment. Life sank again to the depth of the prison whose bars she had tried to shake. Night closed in once more round those thoughts of his, unable to make themselves intelligible. And in spite of being accustomed to it, the sight of this suffering and of this ruin weighed on each of the members of the assembled family. It was less painful to strangers who sat for one evening at the Alsheim table, for the grandfather on those days did not try to break the circle of darkness and death which oppressed him. Until these last years M. Joseph Oberlé had always continued to present his guests to his father, up to the day when he wrote on his slate: "Do not present any one to me, above all, no Germans. Let them acknowledge my presence: that will be enough." The son had kept the habit—and it was a touching thought on the part of this selfish man—to give every evening an account of the business of the factory to the old chief. After dinner, smoking in the dining-room, while the two women went into the drawing-room, he told him all about the day's mail, the consignments, and the purchases of wood. Although M. Philippe Oberlé was now only the sleeping partner of the business he had founded, he was under the illusion that he was advising and directing still. He heard talk of the maples, pines and firs, oaks and beeches among which he had breathed for fifty years. He thought much of the "conference," as he called it, as the only moment in the day in which he appeared himself, to himself, and as some one of importance in the lives of others. Except for that he was only a shadow, a dumb soul present, who judged his house, but rarely gave voice to his decision.

His son on some important question disagreed with him. Seated at table just opposite his father, M. Joseph Oberlé could make a show of addressing himself to his wife and daughter only; during the whole of the meal he could avoid seeing the fingers which moved impatiently or which wrote to Madame Oberlé, but he was not the man to keep off painful subjects. Like all those who have had to make a great decision in their lives, and who have not taken it without a profound disturbance of their conscience, he was always reverting to the German Question. Everything gave him a pretext to begin it, praise or blame—various facts, political events announced in the morning's newspaper, a visiting card brought by the postman, an order for planks received from Hanover or Dresden, the wish expressed by Lucienne to accept an invitation to some ball. He felt the need of applauding himself for what he had done, like defeated generals who want to explain the battle, and to demonstrate how the force of circumstances had compelled them to act in such or such a manner. All the resources of his fertile mind were brought to bear on this case of conscience, on which he declared himself a long time resolute, and which aroused no more discussion, either on the part of the sick grandfather or on that of the depressed wife, who had decided to keep silence.

Lucienne alone approved and supported her father.

She did it with the decision of youth, which judges without consideration the grief of old people, the memories and all the charm of the past, without understanding, and as if they were dead things to be dealt with by reason only. She was only twenty, at once very proud and very sincere; she had an artless confidence in herself, an impetuous nature, and a reputation for beauty only partly justified. Tall, like her mother, and, like her, well made, she had her father's larger features more conformed to the usual Alsatian type—with a tendency to thicken. All the lines of her body were already formed and fully developed. To those who saw her for the first time, Lucienne Oberlé gave the impression of being a young woman rather than a young girl. Her face was extremely open and mobile. When she listened, her eyes—not so large as, and of a lighter green than, her brother's, her eyes and her mouth equally sharp when she smiled—followed the conversation and told her thoughts. She dreamed little. Another charm besides the vivacity of her mind explained her social success: the incomparable brightness of her complexion, of her red lips, the splendour of her fair hair, with its shining tresses of blonde and auburn intermingled, so abundant and so heavy that it broke tortoiseshell combs, escaped from hairpins, and hung down behind in a heavy mass and obliged her to raise her brow, which was enhaloed by the light from it, and gave to Lucienne Oberlé the carriage of a proud young goddess.

Her Uncle Ulrich said to her, laughing: "When I kiss you, I think I am kissing a peach growing in the open air." She walked well; she played tennis well; she swam to perfection, and more than once the papers of Baden-Baden had printed the initials of her name in articles in which they spoke of "our best skaters."

This physical education had already alienated her from her mother, who had never been more than a good walker, and was now only a fair one. But other causes had been at work and had separated them more deeply and more irrevocably from each other. Doubtless it was the entirely German education of the Mündner school, more scientific, more solemn, more pedantic, more varied, and much less pious than that which her mother had received, who had been educated partly at Obernai, and partly with the nuns of Notre-Dame, in the convent of the rue des Mineurs in Strasburg. But above all it was owing to the acquaintances she made, and her surroundings. Lucienne, ambitious like her father, like him bent on success, entirely removed from maternal influence, entrusted to German mistresses for seven years, received in German families, living among pupils chiefly German, flattered a little by everybody—here because of the charm of her nature, there for political motives and unconscious proselytism, Lucienne had formed habits of mind very different from those of old Alsace. Once more at home, she no longer understood the past of her people or her family. For her, those who stood up for the old state of things or regretted it—her mother, her grandfather, her uncle Ulrich—were the representatives of an epoch ended, of an unreasonable and childish attitude of mind. At once she placed herself on her father's side against the others. And she suffered from it. It depressed her to be brought into such close contact with persons of this sort, whom the Mündner school and all her worldly acquaintances of Baden-Baden and Strasburg would look upon as behind the times. For two years she had lived in an atmosphere of contradiction. For her family she felt conflicting sentiments; for her mother, for example, she felt a true tenderness and a great pity because she belonged to a condemned society and to another century. She had no confidants. Would her brother Jean be one? Restless at his arrival, almost a stranger to him, desiring affection, worn out with family quarrels, and hoping that Jean would place himself on the side she had chosen, that he would be a support and a new argument, she at once desired and feared this meeting. Her father came to tell her of the conversation he had had with Jean. She had said—cried out rather—"Thank you for giving me my brother!"

They were all four at table when the young man entered the dining-room. The two women who were facing each other and in the light of the window, turned their heads, one sweetly with a smile that said, "How proud I am of my child!"; the other leaning back on her chair, her lips half open, her eyes as tender as if he had been her betrothed who entered, desirous to please and sure of pleasing him, saying aloud: "Come and sit here near me, at the end of the table. I have made myself fine in your honour! Look!" and kissing him, she said in a low tone, "Oh, how good it is to have some one young to say good morning to!" She knew she was pleasant to look upon in her bodice of mauve surah silk trimmed with lace insertion. It also gave her real pleasure to meet this brother whom she had only seen for a moment last night, before catching the train to Strasburg. Jean thanked her with a friendly glance and seated himself at the end of the table between Lucienne and his mother. He unfolded his table napkin, and the servant Victor, son of an Alsatian farmer, with his full-moon face and eyes like a little girl's, always afraid of doing something wrong, approached him, carrying a dish of *hors-d'œuvre*, when M. Joseph Oberlé, who had just finished writing a note in his pocket-book, stroked his whiskers and said:

"You see Jean Oberlé here present, you my father, you Monica, and you Lucienne. Well, I have a piece of news to give you concerning him. I have agreed that he shall live definitely at Alsheim and become a manufacturer and a wood merchant."

Three faces coloured at once; even Victor, shaking like a leaf, withdrew his *hors-d'œuvre* dish.

"Is it possible?" said Lucienne, who did not wish to let her mother see that she had already been told of the arrangement. "Will he not finish his referendary course?"

"No."

"After his year's service he will come back here for always?"

"Yes; to stay with us always."

The second moment of emotion is sometimes more unnerving than the first. Lucienne's eyelids fluttered quickly and became moist. She laughed at the same time, tender words trembling on her red lips.

"Oh," said she, "so much the better. I don't know if it is in your own interest, Jean, but for us, so much the better."

She was really pretty at that moment, leaning towards her brother, vibrating with a joy which was not feigned.

"I thank you," said Madame Oberlé, looking gravely at her husband to try to guess what reason he had obeyed; "I thank you, Joseph; I should not have dared to ask it of you."

"But you see, my dear," answered the manufacturer, bending towards her, "you see, when proposals are reasonable I accept them. Besides, I am so little accustomed to be thanked that for once the word pleases me. Yes; we have just had a decisive conversation. Jean will accompany my buyer to-morrow and visit some of our cuttings in work. I never lose time—you know that."

Madame Oberlé saw the awkward hand of the grandfather stretch towards her. She took the slate which he held and read this line:

"That is the final joy of my life!"

There was no sign of happiness on this face, expressionless as a mask, none, if not perhaps the fixedness with which M. Philippe Oberlé looked at his son, who had given back a child to Alsace and a successor to the family. He was astonished, and he rejoiced. He forgot to eat, and all at the table were like him. The servant also forgot to serve; he was thinking of the importance he would have in announcing in the kitchen and in the village: "M. Jean has decided to take the factory! He will never leave the country again!" For some minutes in the dining-room of grey maple each of the four persons who met there every day had a different dream and passed a secret judgment; each had a vision, which was not divulged, of possible or probable consequences which the event would have relative to him or herself; each felt disturbed at the price.... Perhaps you did not give this a place in your calculations when you decided to return to Alsheim? I know I upset your ideas. You will have many such disturbances. What you must know, my dear Jean"—she laid stress on the word "dear"—"is that the home of the family is not an amusing one. We are irremediably divided."

Jean and Lucienne were silent for a moment, because the lodge was quite near; then they turned towards the lawn and took the second alley, which led to the house.

"Irremediably? You believe this?"

"It would be childish to doubt it. My father will not change and will not become French again, because that would be to give up his future for ever, and many commercial advantages. Mamma will not change, because she is a woman, and because to become a German would be to give up a sentiment which she thinks very noble. You surely do not aim at converting grandfather? Well then?"

She stopped and faced Jean.

"Well, my dear, as you cannot bring peace into the family by gentleness, bring it by being strong. Do not imagine you can remain neutral. Even if you would, circumstances will not permit it. I am sure of that. Join with me and father, even if you do not think as we do in everything.

"I have sought you out to implore you to be on our side. When mamma understands that her two children think her wrong she will defend her childhood's memories less energetically; she will advise grandfather to abstain from demonstrations like those of to-day, and our meals will be less like combats at close quarters. We shall command the situation. It is all that we can hope for. Will you? Papa told me, quickly this morning, that your tenderness for the Germans was not a lively one. But you do not hate them?"

"No."

"I only ask for tolerance and a certain amount of consideration for them—that is to say, for us who see them. You have lived ten years in Germany; you will continue to do here what you did there. You will not leave the drawing-room when one of them comes to see us?"

"Of course not. But you see, Lucienne, even if I act differently from mamma, because my education has made me put up with what is odious to her, I cannot blame her. I can find the most touching reasons why she should be what she is."

"Touching?"

"Yes."

"I find them unreasonable."

Jean's green eyes and Lucienne's lighter ones questioned one another for a moment. The two young people, both grave, with an expression of astonishment and defiance, measured each other and thought: "Is it she I saw just now so smiling and so tender?" "Is it really he who resists me, a brother brought up like me, and who ought to yield to me, if it were only because I am young and he is glad to see me again?" She was displeased. This first meeting had placed in opposition the paternal violence which Lucienne had inherited and the inflexible will which the mother had transmitted to her son. It was Lucienne who broke the silence. She turned to continue the walk, and shaking her head:

"I see," she said. "You imagine that you will have a confidante in mamma, a friend to whom you can open your heart fully? She is worthy of all respect, my dear. But there again you are mistaken. I have tried. She is, or thinks she is, too miserable. All you tell her will immediately serve her as an argument in her own quarrel. If you wished, for example, to marry a German——"

"No, no; but no."

"I am only supposing. Mamma would go at once to find my father, and would say to him: 'Look at this! It is horrible! It is your fault! Yours!' And if you wished to marry an Alsatian our mother would at once take advantage of it and say: 'He is on my side, against you, against you.' No, my dear, the real, true confidante at Alsheim is Lucienne."

She took Jean's hand, and without ceasing to walk she looked up at him, her face beaming with life and youthfulness.

"Believe me, let us be frank with each other. You do not know me well. You have travelled so much. I astonish you. You will see that I have great faults. I am proud and selfish, hardly capable of making sacrifices; something of a flirt, but I have no roundabout ways. Lately, when I was looking forward to your arrival, I promised myself a lasting joy, the joy of having your youth near mine to understand it. I will tell you all that is important in my life, all that I am resolved to do—I have no one here whom I can trust absolutely. You cannot know what I have suffered. Will you?"

"Oh yes."

"You will tell me your thoughts, but above all I shall have spoken to you. I shall not suffocate, as I have often done in this house. I shall have many things to tell you. It will be some way of regaining the intimacy we have almost lost, and will give us a little tardy fraternal companionship. What are you thinking about?"

"About this poor house."

Lucienne lifted her eyes above the slate roof which rose in front. She wished to say, "If you knew how sad it really is," then she embraced her brother, and said:

"I am not so bad as you think me, brother, nor so ungrateful to mamma. I am going to find her to talk about your return. She certainly wants to speak of her happiness to some one."

Lucienne left her brother, turning again to smile at him, and walking as a goddess might, with steps free and finely poised, with her hand replacing the pins which held up her hair so badly, disarranged as it was by the walk and blown about by the wind, she took the fifty steps which separated her from the staircase, and disappeared.

CHAPTER IV
THE GUARDIANS OF THE HEARTH

When Lucienne left Jean he had turned round the house, crossed a semicircular court formed by stables and coach-houses, then a large kitchen-garden surrounded by walls, and opening a private door at the end on the right he found himself in the country, behind the village of Alsheim. His first joy at his return had already lessened and faded. He heard again sentences which had sunk into the depths of his soul; their very accent came back to him with the appearance and the gesture of the one who had uttered them.

He thought of the "sad house" there quite close to the wall which enclosed the grounds, and it pained him to remember what an entirely different idea he had formed years ago of the welcome which awaited him at Alsheim, and the almost religious emotion he had felt far away, in the towns and on the roads of Europe and the East, when he thought, "My mother, my father, my sister! My first day at home after my father has said yes!" The first day had begun. It had not been, up to the present, worthy of this old-time dream.

Even the weather was bad. Before him the plain of Alsace, smooth, scarcely marked with some lines of trees, stretched out to the foot of the Vosges, covered with forests which made their height appear less than it was. The north wind, blowing from the sea, filling all the valley with its continuous wailing, chased the dark clouds from the sky, broken and heaped together like furrows in fields, clouds full of rain and hail, which would dissolve in compact masses to fall in the south, on the side of the Alps. It was cold.

Meanwhile Jean Oberlé, having looked to the left, from the side where the land declined a little, perceived the avenue ending in a little wood, which he had seen in the morning, and he felt again that his youth called to *her*. He made sure no one was watching him from the windows of his home, and he took the path which turned round the village.

It was really only a track traced by people going to, and coming from work. It followed very nearly the zigzag line made by the sheds, the pig-styes, the stables, the barns, the low boundaries commanded by the manure-heaps, fowl-houses, all the back buildings of the dwellings of Alsheim, which had on the other side, on the road, their principal façade, or at least a white wall, a cart-door, and a great mulberry-tree overflowing the edge of it. The young man walked quietly on the beaten track. He passed the church which, almost in the centre of Alsheim, raised its square tower, surmounted by a slate roof in the form of a steeple, with a metal point, and came to the centre of a group of four enormous walnut-trees, serving as landmarks, as ornament and shelter to the last farm in the village. There began the property of M. Xavier Bastian, the mayor of Alsheim, the old friend of M. Joseph Oberlé, a man of influence, rich and patriotic, and to whose house Jean was going. The sound of flails could be heard in the neighbouring yard. It must be the fine, big sons of the Ramspacher, the Bastians' tenants. One had served his time in the German army, the other was going to join his regiment in the month of November. They were threshing under the barn in the old style. Every autumn, every winter, when the miller's store of corn diminished, and when the weather was bad outside, they spread out some sheaves in the shelter, and their flails struck blithely and galloped like colts let loose in high grass. Nothing had stopped the tradition.

"Isn't my Alsheim old?" said Jean to himself. Although he was very anxious not to be recognised, he approached the latticed door which opened on to the fields on this side, and if he did not see the workers, hidden by an unharnessed cart, he saw again with a friendly smile the yard of the old farm, a kind of road bordered with buildings which were only apparently framework with a little earth between the wooden beams, a demonstration of the everlasting strength of the chestnut which had furnished the jambs, the raising pieces, the wooden balconies, and the framework of the windows. No one heard him, no one saw him. He went on his way and his heart began to beat violently. For immediately after the farm of the Ramspachers, the path fell, at right angles, to an avenue of cherry-trees leading from the village to the house of M. Bastian. It was not probable that in this bad weather the Mayor would be far from home. In a few moments Jean would speak with him; he would meet Odile; he would find some means of knowing if she were betrothed.

Odile. All Jean's early childhood was full of that name. The daughter of M. Bastian had formerly been the playfellow of Lucienne and of Jean when the evolution of M. Oberlé had not been affirmed and known in the country-side; a little later she had become the charming vision which Jean saw again at the Munich Gymnasium when he thought of Alsheim; the young, growing girl, whom one saw in the holidays, on Sundays in church, whom one saluted without approaching when Monsieur or Madame Oberlé were present, but also the passer-by of the grape harvest and of the woods, and the walker who had a smile for Lucienne or for Jean met at the turn of a road. What secret enchantment did this girl of Alsheim possess, brought up entirely in the country, except for two or three years passed with the nuns of Notre-Dame in Strasburg, not worldly—less brilliant than Lucienne, more silent and more grave? The same, no doubt, as the country where she was born. Jean had left her, as he had left Alsace, without being able to forget her. He had forbidden himself to see her during his last short stay in Alsheim, in order to prove himself and to find out if truly the memory of Odile would resist a long separation, studies, and travels. He had thought: "If she marries in the interval, it will be a proof that she has never thought of me, and I shall not weep for her." She had not married. Nothing showed that she was engaged. And certainly Jean was going to see her again.

He preferred not to go down the wild cherry avenue, celebrated for its beauty, which guarded the Bastians' property. The people of the little town, the few workers in the neighbouring country, although they were few, would have recognised the manufacturer's son going to the Mayor of Alsheim's. He followed the trimmed blackthorn hedge, which bounded the alley, walking on the red earth or on the narrow border of grass left by the plough at the edge of the ditch. Behind him the noise of the flails in the barn followed him, fading in the distance and scattered by the wind. Jean asked himself: "How shall I approach M. Bastian? How will he receive me? Bah! I arrive; I am supposed to be ignorant of much!"

Two hundred yards to the south of the farm the avenue of wild cherries ended, and the grove, which one saw from so far off, bordered the sown fields. The wood was composed of fine old trees, oaks, planes, and elms, at this time bare of leaves—under which evergreen trees had grown up: pines, spindletrees, and laurels. Jean continued to follow the hedge as it curved across a field of lucerne to a rustic gate, with worn paint and half rotten, which rose between two jambs. A piece of sandstone thrown across the ditch served as a bridge. The laurel-trees growing out over the fence of blackthorn on each side of the upright posts, closed in the view at two yards. When Jean came near, a blackbird flew off, uttering a warning note. Jean remembered that to enter one had only to pass one's hand through the hedge and to lift an iron hook. So he opened the door, and, a little uneasy at his audacity, grazed from his coat to his gaiters by the overgrown branches of an alley far too narrow and hardly ever entered, he came out on to a sanded space, passed several clumps of shrubs edged with box, and arrived at the house on the far side from Alsheim. Here there were plane-trees more than a hundred years old, planted in a semi-circle, which sheltered a tiny lawn and spread their branches over the tiles of an old, low, squat house, from which two balconies projected, topped with overhanging roofs. Store-rooms, presses, barns, and a bee-hive formed the continuation of the master's house, where abundance, good nature, and the simplicity of the old Alsatian homely spirit were in evidence. Jean, kept back for a moment by the irresistible attraction of these places, once so familiar to him, looked at the plane-trees, the roof, a window with a balcony on which ivy grew. He was going to take the few steps which separated him from the half-open door, when on the threshold a tall man appeared, and recognising the visitor made a sign of surprise. It was M. Xavier Bastian. No man of sixty years of age in the division of Erstein was more robust or of a more youthful turn of mind. He had wide shoulders, a massive head, as wide below as above, quite white hair, divided in short locks overlapping each other, his cheeks and the upper lip shaven, the nose large, the eyes fine and grey, the mouth thickset, and on his countenance the sort of prepossessing pride of those who have never known fear of anything. He wore the long frock-coat to which many notable Alsatians remained faithful, even in the villages such as Alsheim, where the inhabitants have no special costume or any memory of having had any.

Seeing Jean Oberlé, whom he had often dandled on his knees, he made a movement of surprise.

"Is it you, my boy?" he said, in the dialect of Alsace, which he mostly used, and with which he was more familiar than with French. "What has happened to bring you here?"

"Nothing, M. Bastian, if not that I have just come home."

He held out his hand to the old Alsatian, who took it, pressed it, and suddenly lost that gaiety which had been in his welcome, for he thought: "It is now ten years since your father last came here, ten years that your family and mine have been enemies." But he only said, in answer to himself, and as if doing away with an objection:

"Come in all the same, Jean; there is no harm for once."

But the gladness of the first meeting was gone, and did not return.

"How did you know that I was on your land?" asked Jean, who did not understand. "Did you hear me?"

"No; I heard the blackbird. I thought it was my servant, whom I have sent to Obernai to get the lamps of my victoria mended. Come into the hall."

He thought, with a feeling of regret and reprobation: "As your father used to come in when he was worthy."

In the corridor to the left he opened a door, and both went into the "big room," which was at the same time the dining-room and the reception-room of this rich citizen, heir of lands and of the traditions of a long series of ancestors, who had only left the house at Alsheim for the cemetery. Nearly all the picturesque furniture which one still meets with in the old houses of rural Alsace had disappeared from the dwelling of M. Bastian. No more carved cupboards; no more chairs of solid wood, with the backs cut in the shape of hearts; no clock in its painted case; no more little weights at the windows. The few chairs in the big, square, light hall, the table, the cupboard, and the big chest, on the top of which was the cast of a Pietà not known to fame, were all of polished walnut. The only thing that was old was the historical stove of faience, bearing the signature of Master Hugelin of Strasburg, and of which M. Bastian was as proud as if it had been a treasure. About two-thirds down the room, between the stove and the table, a woman of about fifty was sitting, dressed in black, rather stout, having regular, thick features, bands of grey hair, the forehead almost without lines, fine long eyebrows, and eyes as dark as if she had come from the south, calm and dignified, which she lifted first to Jean and then to her husband as if to ask, "How does he come here?"

She was sewing the hem of an unbleached linen sheet, which fell about her in big folds. Seeing Jean enter, she dropped it. She remained dumb with surprise, not understanding how her husband could bring to her the son, educated in Germany, of a renegade father, traitor to Alsace. During the war she had had three brothers killed in the service of France.

"I met him coming to see me," M. Bastian said, as if to excuse himself, "and I begged him to enter, Marie."

"Good day, madame," said the young man, who was hurt by the astonishment and coolness of Madame Bastian's first glance, and who had stopped in the middle of the hall. "Old memories brought me here."

"Good day, Jean."

The words died away before reaching the walls, papered with old peonies. One could hardly hear them. The silence which followed was so cruel that Jean grew pale, and M. Bastian, who had shut the door, and who, a little behind Jean, was scolding gently, with a shake of the head, those beautiful, severe eyes of the Alsatian woman, which did not lower themselves, intervened, saying:

"I have not told you, Marie, that I saw our friend Ulrich this morning in our vineyards of Sainte Odile. He spoke to me of this boy's return to Alsheim. He assured me that we ought to congratulate ourselves that we are going to see his nephew settle in the country. He told me that he was one of ours."

The silent lips of the Alsatian wore a vague smile of incredulity, which died as the words died. And Madame Bastian again began to sew.

Jean turned round, pale, as yet more miserable than irritated, and said in a low voice to M. Bastian:

"I knew that our two families were divided, but not to such an extent as they evidently are. I left Alsheim some time ago. You will excuse me for having come."

"Stay, stay! I will explain to you. Believe me that we have nothing against you, no animosity whatever, neither one nor the other."

The old man placed his hand on Jean's arm in a friendly manner:

"I do not want you to go like that. No; since you are here I will not let you say that I have sent you away without doing the honours. The thought would weigh heavy on me. I will not!"

"No, M. Bastian, I ought not to be here. I am in the way; I cannot stay one instant."

He moved to go away. The solid hand of the old Mayor of Alsheim fastened round the wrist he held. His voice rose and became harsh.

"Presently. But do not at least refuse the civility I am accustomed to show to all who come here. It is the custom of the country and of the house. Drink with me, Jean Oberlé, or I shall repudiate you, and we shall not even recognise each other."

Jean remembered that no house in the country round Barr or Obernai, not even the oldest and richest, possessed better recipes for making beam-tree-berry brandy or cherry brandy, or elderberry wine, or wine made with dried grapes, or spring drinks. He saw that the old Mayor of Alsheim would be deeply hurt by a refusal, and that the offer was a means of showing his cordiality without disavowing in words, or in thought, the mother, queen, and mistress of the big house, who continued to ignore the guest, because the guest was the son of Joseph Oberlé.

"So be it," he said.

Then M. Bastian called, "Odile!"

The hands that held the linen, near the stove, rested on the folds of her black dress, and for half a minute there were three human beings, each with very different thoughts, who awaited her who was going to enter at the end of the room, on the right, near the great walnut cupboard. She came out of the shadow of a neighbouring room and advanced into the light, while Jean controlled his feelings and was saying to himself, "I did well to remember her!"

"Give me the oldest brandy that we have," said the father.

Odile Bastian had at first smiled at her father, whom she saw near the door, then she had, with a movement of her brown eyebrows, shown her astonishment, without displeasure, when she recognised Jean Oberlé near him; then the smile had disappeared when she saw her mother, bending over her work-table, dumb and holding herself aloof from what was going on around her. Then her bosom heaved, the words she was going to say were arrested before reaching her lips; and Odile Bastian, too intelligent not to guess the affront, too much a woman to emphasise the secret trouble, had simply and silently obeyed. She had sought a key in the drawer of a chest, had gone to the big cupboard, and raising herself on the tips of her toes, one hand leaning on one of the doors at the top of the piece of furniture, her head thrown back, she ransacked the depths of the hiding-place.

She was just the same girl, but more developed, who had lived in Jean's memory for years, and who had followed him over the world. Her features were not regular. But in spite of that she was beautiful, with a strong, glowing beauty. She seemed like the statues of Alsace, which one sees on monuments and in French souvenir pictures, like those daughters of rich and warlike blood, wrathful and daring, while near them a more feminine Lorraine weeps sadly. She was tall; there were no hollows in her full cheeks, curving to a chin as firm and pink. It is true she did not wear the wide bows of black ribbon which make two wings on the head, but that only accentuated the unusual, the exceptional beauty of her hair, which was of the colour of ripe corn, of a perfectly dull, even tint, bound in bands round her temples and there twisted and raised on her head. Her eyebrows were of the same colour, long and finely marked, and the lashes, and even the eyes, slightly apart, where dwelt a soul at rest, were deep and passionate. In a moment M. Bastian had on a stand two glasses of cut crystal and a big-bellied black bottle. He took the bottle in one hand and with the other he drew out, without shaking it, a cork which swelled out as it left the neck, being damp as sapwood in spring time. At the same time a smell of ripe fruit was diffused under the beams of the room.

"It is fifty years old," said he, pouring a little of the liqueur into each of the glasses.

He added seriously, "I drink to your health, Jean Oberlé, and to your return to Alsheim!"

But Jean, without answering directly, and with every one silent, and looking at Odile, who had withdrawn to the cupboard, and who, standing erect against it, was also looking at and studying her old playfellow returned to his native country, said:

"I drink to the land of Alsace!"

By the tone of the words, by the gesture of the hand raising the little sparkling glass, by the look fixed on the end of the room, some one understood that the land of Alsace was here personified and present. The tall, beautiful daughter of the Bastians remained motionless, leaning against the cupboard, which framed her in its yellowish shadow. But her eyes had the brightness that wheat has when it waves at a breath of wind in the sunshine, and without turning her head, without ceasing to look straight in front of her, her eyelids slowly lowered and shut, saying thank you!

And that was all.

Madame Bastian had not even looked up. Odile had said not a word—Jean bowed and went out.

The old Mayor of Alsheim rejoined him outside.

"I will go with you to the other end of my garden," he said, "for it is better for us—for you—and for your father, that you should not be seen coming down the avenue. You will seem to be coming from the fields."

"What a strange country this has become!" said the young man in an angry tone. "Because you do not hold the same opinions as my father you cannot receive me, and when I leave you I must do so secretly, and after having had to submit to the insult of a silence which was hard to bear. I can tell you that!"

He spoke loudly enough to be heard from the house, from which he was only a few steps away. The usual paleness of his complexion was more noticeable, and emotion contracted the muscles of his neck and jaws, and all his face had a tragic expression.

M. Bastian led him on.

"I have another reason for taking you that way," he said, "it will be longer, and I have things to explain to you."

They took a path that was not gravelled, which went by the plane-trees, passed a kitchen garden and then crossed a little wood.

"You do not understand, dear boy," said M. Bastian, in a voice which was firm without being harsh, "because you have not yet really lived among us. It has not changed; what you see dates back for thirty years."

Through an opening in the trees they saw a little bit of the plain, with the belfry of Barr in the distance, and the blue Vosges mountains above and beyond.

"Formerly," continued M. Bastian, pointing vaguely to the country, "our Alsace was just one family. Big and little knew each other and lived happily together. You know that even now I make no difference between rich and poor, between a citizen of Strasburg and a wood-cutter from the mountain. But what is done is done—we have been torn away, against our will, from France, and treated brutally because we did not say 'Yes.' We cannot revolt—we cannot drive away our masters, who know nothing about our hearts or our lives. But we do not admit them to our friendship, neither them nor those amongst us who have taken the side of the stronger."

He stopped speaking for a moment, not wishing to say all that he thought on this subject, and went on, taking Jean's hand.

"You are very angry with my wife because of her reception of you; but you are not the cause of it, neither is she. Until the doubt which rests on you is lifted, you are he who was educated in Germany, and the woman you have just seen is this country. Reflect—you must not bear a grudge against her. We have not all been faithful to Alsace, we men; and the best of us have compromised and have more or less recognised the new master. Not so the women—Ah! Jean Oberlé, I have not the courage to disclaim them even when you whom I love so well are the subject. Our Alsatian women are not insulting you in any ordinary way when they do not receive you; they are defending their country, they are carrying on the war." The old man had tears in his red and wrinkled eyes.

"You will know me later," said Jean.

They were at the end of the little park before a wooden door as mouldy as the other. M. Bastian opened it, shook the young man's hand and stayed a long time at the end of the wood watching Jean go away and get smaller on the plain, his head bent against the wind, which was still blowing, and more violently.

Jean was troubled to the depth of his soul.

Between him and each family in this old country he felt he was going to find his father. He was suffering from having been born in the house towards which he was going. He saw the image of Odile as the only sweet thing of this first day, and her eyes were slowly, slowly closing.

CHAPTER V
COMPANIONS OF THE ROAD

The winter did not allow M. Oberlé's ideas about the professional education of Jean to be carried out exactly. The snow which remained on the summits of the Vosges, without being thick, made travelling very difficult. So Jean paid only two or three visits to the wood-cutting centres situated near Alsheim and in the Vosges valleys. The excursions to more distant places were put off for a warmer season. But he learned to cube a pine or a beech without making a mistake, to value it according to the place it occupied in the forest, according to the height of the trunk below the branches, the appearance of the bark, which indicated the health of the tree, and by other calculations into which a kind of divining quality enters, which cannot be taught anywhere, and which makes the expert. His father initiated him into the working of the factory and the management of the machines, the reading of agreements, and the traditions of fifty years kept up by the Oberlés regarding sale and carriage contracts. He put him into relationship with two officials of the administration of the forests of Strasburg, who showed themselves very ready to be of service, and proposed to Jean to explain to him personally the new forest legislation, of which he still knew but little. "Come," said the younger, "come to see me at my office, and I will tell you more things you will find it useful to know than you will learn in books. For the law is the law, but the administration is another thing."

Jean promised to profit when occasions offered themselves. But several weeks went by without his having the time to go to the town. Then March came in mildly and melted the snows. In a week, and much earlier than usual, the brooks swelled to overflowing, and the high peaks of the Vosges and Sainte Odile which one could see from Alsheim, which had had their slopes and paths white with snow, appeared in their summer robes of dark and pale green.

The walks round Alsheim were going to be exquisite and such as the young man had pictured to himself in his youthful memories. The home, without being a model of family unity, had witnessed no repetition of the painful scene which occurred the day after Jean's return. In each camp words were noted and deeds observed, which would one day become arguments and subjects of reproach and discussion, but just now there was a sort of truce brought about by different causes.

In M. Joseph Oberlé it was the desire not to be wrong in his son's eyes; for his son was going to be useful, and he did not wish to be accused of provocation. In Lucienne it was the diversion which the presence of her brother had brought into her life, and the interest, not yet exhausted, that she took in his tales of travel and student life. In Madame Oberlé it was fear of making her son suffer, and of alienating him by letting him see the family feuds. Nothing had really changed. There was only a superficial gaiety, an appearance of peace, a truce. But although Jean felt that the agreement of the hearts and minds around him was not real, he enjoyed it because he had spent long years in moral solitude.

The worries and clashing of interests came from elsewhere, and were not wanting. Nearly every day Jean had occasion to go through the village of Alsheim, which was built on each side of three roads forming a fork, the handle of which was the mountain side, and the two prongs towards the plain. At the bifurcation was the tavern, the Swan, which took up a corner of the church square. A little farther on, on the left road leading to Bernhardsweiler, dwelt the German workmen engaged by M. Joseph Oberlé, and lodged in little houses all alike, each with a little garden in front. So that in whatever part of Alsheim he showed himself, the young man could not help reading, in the faces and gestures of those he met, different opinions, and all equally distressing. The Germans and their wives—the workmen, better disciplined and more tame-spirited than the Alsatians, fearing all authority without respecting it, quartered in a corner of Alsheim by the hatred of the population on which they hoped to take vengeance some day, when they should be the more numerous, having with the other inhabitants no ties of origin, family, customs, or religion—could only have indifference or hostility for the master, which were badly disguised by the salutations of the men, and the furtive smiles of the women.

But many of the Alsatians were less under restraint. It was enough that Jean had entered the business and that he was seen constantly with his father, for their disapproval to extend to him. He saw himself covered with a prudent contempt, the kind that little people can always express towards powerful neighbours. The forest workmen, the labourers, the women, and even the children pretended not to see him when he passed, others withdrew into their houses; others, the old ones especially, watched the rich man come and go as if he had been from another country. Those who showed the most signs of respect were the tradesmen or the employés, or the relations of the employés of the house. And Jean found it difficult to bear the reopening of this wound each time he left the park.

On Sunday, at church, in the whitewashed nave, he waited for the coming of Odile. To reach the seat reserved for her family for years, which was the first on the Epistle side, she had to pass near Jean. She passed, with her father and her mother, without any of them appearing to know that Jean was there, and M. Oberlé, and Lucienne. She only smiled at the end of Mass, when she came down the aisle, but she smiled at whole rows of friendly faces, at women, old men, at big boys who would have died for her, and at the children of the choir, the chanters of the "Concordia," who scampered off by the sacristy door, to be able to salute, surround, and welcome at the door the daughter of M. Bastian, the Alsatian girl, the friend, the beloved of all this poor village; she did not give away more money than Madame Oberlé, but they knew that there was no division in her house, no treachery, and that the only difference between it and the other houses in the valleys and mountains of Alsace was its wealth. What did she think of Jean? She, whose eyes never spoke in vain, did not look at him. She who used to speak to him in the roads now said nothing.

The first month of Jean's new life passed away like this in Alsheim. Then spring was born. M. Joseph Oberlé waited two days and then, seeing the buds of his birch-trees burst in the sunshine, he said to his son on the third day:

"You are a good enough apprentice now to go alone and inspect our timber-yard in the Vosges. You will get ready to start. This year I have made exceptional purchases. I have cuttings as far as the Schlucht, and to visit them you will have to visit nearly all the Vosges. I give you no instructions, only observe, and bring me a report, in which you will note down your observations of each of our cuttings."

"When shall I start?"

"To-morrow, if you like—the winter is over." M. Oberlé said that with the assurance of a man who has had need to know the weather like a peasant, and who knows it. He had, before speaking, ordered a list to be prepared of the cuttings of wood bought by the house either from the German State or from the Communes, or from private people, with the detailed directions on the position they occupied in the mountains, and he gave this list to Jean.

There were a dozen cuttings distributed over the whole length of the Vosges, from the valley of the Bruche on the north to the mouth of the Schlucht.

The next day Jean put a little linen and a change of shoes in a bag, and without telling any one of his intention hurried to the mountain, and up to the lodge of Heidenbruch.

The square house, with green shutters, and the meadow, and the forest all round the clearing, were smoking as if a fire had devoured the heath and grass, and left the beech and pines intact. Long wreaths of mist seemed to emanate from the soil, and to grow tenuous, and uniting, lose themselves in the low clouds, which glided along, rising from the valleys and going up the slopes towards the invisible monastery of Sainte Odile. The humidity penetrated to the very depths of the forests. It was everywhere. Drops of water shone on the pine needles, streamed in threads down the bare trunks of the beeches, polished the pebbles, swelled the many mosses, and travelling over the land, and flowing on dead leaves, went to swell the brooks, whose cadenced song could be heard on all sides—the grasshopper of winter whose song never ceases.

Jean went up to the middle of the wooden palisade painted green, which surrounded Heidenbruch, passed through the gate, and in the front of the lodge called out gaily to the windows closed because of the fog, "Uncle Ulrich."

A cap appeared behind the window panes, the cap of an Alsatian woman who takes care of her big black ribbons—and under the cap there was the smile of an old friend.

"Lise, tell uncle!"

This time the last window to the left opened, and the refined face, the eyes of a watcher, the pointed beard of M. Ulrich Biehler were framed between two shutters thrown back against the white wall.

"Uncle, I have at least a dozen wood-cutting places to visit. I begin this morning, and I come to take you for a companion, to-day, to-morrow, and every day...."

"Twelve journeys in the forest," answered his uncle, who leaned, his arms crossed, on the window sill, "this is a fine ending to Lent! My compliments on your mission!" He looked at his nephew in walking-clothes, his strong, masculine face raised in the fog; he was thinking that one could have sworn that he was a French officer, and then, carried away by his imagination, he forgot to say whether or not he would accompany his morning visitor.

"Come, uncle," continued Jean. "Come! Don't refuse me! We will sleep in the inns; you will show me Alsace."

"I walked seven leagues yesterday, my friend!"

"We will only do six to-day."

"You really want me to come?"

"An absence of three years, Uncle Ulrich, think of that, and a whole education to go through!"

"Well! I won't refuse you, Jean; I am too delighted that you should have thought of me. I have even a second reason for agreeing to the journey and to thank you for it. I will tell you presently."

He shut the window. In the silence of the woods Jean heard him call the old valet, who was second in command in Heidenbruch.

"Pierre! Pierre! Ah! there you are! We are going for twelve days into the mountains. I take you with me. You will pack my bag; put it on your back with my nephew's bag. Take your shoes with the nails, your stick, and you will go in front to the halting-place, while Jean and I go to visit the cuttings. Do not forget my waterproof, nor my pocket medicine chest."

Going into the house, the young man saw Uncle Ulrich, full of business and radiant, pass him, open the drawing-room door, go to the wall, take down a long object in copper on two nails, and go quickly upstairs again.

"What are you taking away, uncle?"

"My telescope."

"Such an old one."

"I cling to it, my friend; it belonged to my great uncle, General Biehler. It saw the back of the Prussians at Jena!"

Half an hour later, in the meadow on the slope in front of the house was M. Ulrich, gaitered like Jean, with a soft hat, the telescope slung over his shoulder, his dog gambolling round him; old Pierre very dignified and solemn, carrying on his mountaineer's shoulders a great pack wrapped in linen and fastened by straps; then Jean Oberlé, bending over a staff-officer's map, which the others knew by heart, discussing the two ways to go—the way of the baggage and the way of the walkers. The discussion was short. The servant went on in front, bearing to the left to reach the village where they would sleep, while the uncle and nephew took a path to the middle of the mountain—in a north-easterly direction.

"So much the better that it is a long way," said M. Ulrich, when they gained the shade of the wood. "So much the better. I wish it were for a lifetime. Two people who understand one another and go through the forest—what a dream!"

He half shut his eyes, as painters do, and breathed in the mist with pleasure.

"Do you know," he added, in the way he would have confided to him something delightful, "Do you know that we have had spring here for three days? There it is—that's my second reason!"

The forester said with enthusiasm what the manufacturer had said without admiration. By the same signs he recognised that a new season had begun. With his stick he pointed out to Jean the pine buds, red like arbutus berries; the bursting bark on the beech trunks, the shoots of wild strawberries running along the stones. In the uncovered pathways the north wind still blew, but in the hollows, the combes, the sheltered spots, one felt, in spite of the fog, the first warmth of the sun, which goes to the heart and makes men tremble, that warmth which touches the germ of the plants.

That day, and during those which followed, uncle and nephew lived under wood. They understood one another perfectly, whether they spoke fully on any subject or were silent. M. Ulrich knew the forest and the mountains by heart. He enjoyed this opportunity which had been given him to explain the Vosges and to discover his nephew. Jean's ardent youthfulness often amused him and recalled bygone times. The instincts of the forester and hunter, slumbering in the young man's heart, were ripening and strengthening. But he had also his rage, his revolts, his juvenile threatening words, against which the uncle protested but feebly, because he really approved of them.

The plaint of Alsace rose to his ear for the first time, the complaining cry the stranger does not hear and the conqueror only half listens to, but can never understand. For Jean did not only observe the forest; he also observed the people of the forest, from the merchants and the officials, feudal lords on whom depend a multitude almost past numbering, down to woodcutters, jobbers, fellers, carters, charcoal burners, down even to wanderers, shepherds, and swineherds, pedlars of dead wood, freebooters, poachers, myrtle gatherers, who also gather mushrooms and wild strawberries and raspberries.

Introduced by Uncle Ulrich, or passing by in his shadow, he aroused no suspicions.

He talked freely with the people—in their words, their silence, and in the atmosphere in which he lived day and night, he absorbed unto himself the very soul of his race. Many did not know France, among the young ones, and could not have said if they loved her, but even those had France in their veins. They did not get on with the German. A gesture, a look, an allusion, showed the secret disdain of the Alsatian peasant for his conqueror. The idea of a yoke was everywhere, and everywhere there was antipathy against the master who only knew how to govern by fear. Other young men of the families with traditions, instructed by their parents in the history of the past, faithful without any precise hope, complained that the poor of the mountain and plain were denied justice and subjected to annoyances if they were suspected of the crime of regretting France. They spoke of the tricks played by way of revenge on the custom officers, on the police, on the forest guard—proud of their green uniform and of their Tyrolese hat—the stories of smuggling and desertion, of the Marseillaise sung in the taverns with closed doors, of fêtes on French land, of perquisitions, domiciliary visits and pursuits, of the comic or tragic duel, useless and exasperating, between the strength of a great country and the mind of a small one. When the latter suffered, its thoughts, inherited from ancestors, through habit and from affection, went over the mountains.

There were also the old folk, and it was M. Ulrich's delight to make them talk. When on the roads, and in the villages, he saw a man of fifty years or more, and he knew him to be an Alsatian, it was seldom that he himself was not recognised and that a mysterious smile did not prepare the question for the Master of Heidenbruch:

"Come, is this not another friend—a child of our family?"

If M. Ulrich, by the expression of the face, by the movement of the eyes, by a little fear sometimes, felt that his conclusion was justified, he added in a low voice:

"You—you have the face of a French soldier!"

Then there were smiles or tears, sudden shocks to the heart, which changed the expression of the face pallors, flushings, pipes taken from the corner of the lips, and often, very often, a hand raised, turned palm outwards, touching the brim of the felt hat, thus making the military salute, as long as the two travellers were in sight.

"Do you see him?" said Uncle Ulrich, quite softly; "if he had a bugle he would play 'La Casquette.'"

Jean Oberlé never ceased talking of France. He asked when he came to the top of a mountain ridge: "Are we far from the frontier?" He made the uncle tell him what Alsace was like under the "gentle rule"—what liberty was enjoyed by each and all, how the towns were administered? What difference was there between the French gendarmes—whom M. Ulrich mentioned with a friendly smile as good fellows, not too hard on the poor—and these German gendarmes, common informers, brutal, always officious and full of zeal, whom the whole of the Alsace of to-day hated? What was the name of that prefect of the First Empire who placed by the roadsides of Lower Alsace benches of stone of two tiers so that the women going to market could sit down, and place at the same time their load above them? "The marquis de Lezay Marnésia, my boy."

"Tell me the story of our artists, of our deputies in the old days, of our bishops. Tell me what Strasburg was like in your youth, and what a sight it was when the military band played at Contades?"

M. Ulrich, with the joy of living over again which mingles with all our memories, remembered and related. While climbing and descending the intersections of the Vosges he went through the history of French Alsace. He had only to let his ardent heart speak, and it made him weep. It also made him sing, with the gaiety of a child, the songs of Nadaud, of Béranger, La

Marseillaise, or the old Noels, which he sang to the pointed arches of the forest.

Jean took such a passionate interest in these evocations of old Alsace, and he so naturally entered into the hatreds and revolts of the present that his uncle, who was at first pleased at it as a sign of good family, ended by growing uneasy. One evening, when they had given alms to an old teacher, deprived of the right of teaching French, and reduced to misery because she was too old to get a German diploma, Jean's anger had carried him away.

"My dear Jean," said the uncle, "you must be careful not to go too far. You have to live with Germans."

Since then M. Ulrich had avoided returning so often to the question of the annexation. But alas! it was the whole of Alsace, it was the landscape, the descending road, the sign of some shop, the women's dress, the type of men, the sight of soldiers, the fortifications at the top of a hill, a finger-post, the different items in a newspaper bought in the Alsatian inn where they had dined in the evening—it was every hour of the day which called their minds back to the condition of Alsace, a nation conquered but not assimilated. In vain did M. Ulrich answer more carelessly and quickly—he could not hinder Jean's thought from travelling the road to the unknown. And when they climbed together a neck of the Vosges, the elder man saw with pleasure and apprehension Jean's eyes travel to seek the horizon on the west, and gaze there as at some loved face. Jean did not look so long at the east or the south.

A fortnight was employed in visiting the forest of the Vosges, and during this time M. Ulrich came back to Heidenbruch only twice for some hours. The separation took place only on Palm Sunday, in a village of the Valley of Münster.

It was evening—the hour when the valleys of the German side of the mountains were quite blue, and there was only a strip of light on the last pines which surrounded the shade. M. Ulrich Biehler had already said good-bye to this nephew, his dearest friend.

The servant had taken the train that same morning for Obernai, M. Ulrich, the collar of his cloak turned up because the cold was piercing, had just whistled to Fidèle and was leaving the inn, when Jean, in his blue hunting-costume, without a hat, came down the flight of steps.

"Again good-bye," he said.

And as the uncle, very upset, and not wishing to show it, made a sign with his hand to avoid words which might be tremulous—

"I will go with you to the last house of the village," continued Jean.

"Why, my boy, it is useless to prolong———"

His head turned towards his uncle, and his uncle, looking down the road, Jean began to walk. He commenced in his cajoling young voice:

"I am inexpressibly sorry to leave you, Uncle Ulrich, and I must tell you why. You understand before one says twenty words. You do not contradict aggressively: when you are not of my opinion, I know it by your mouth, which makes the point of your white beard rise—that is all. You are kind. You do not get angry, and I feel you are very decided. Other people's ideas all seem familiar to you—you are able to answer them so easily; you are respected by the weak. I was not accustomed to that on the other side of the Rhine."

"Bah! bah!"

"I even appreciate your fears about me."

"My fears?"

"Yes. Do you think that I did not see that there is another question which interests me intensely, and of which you have not spoken to me for six days?"

This time Jean did not see his uncle's profile; he saw his full face, and its expression was a little anxious.

"My boy, I did that purposely," said M. Ulrich. "When you questioned me, I told you what we were and what we are. And then I saw that I must not insist too much, because you would be full of grief. You see, grief is good for me; but for you, youth, it is better that you should start off like the horses which have not yet run a race, and only carry a very slight weight."

The last house was passed. They were in the country, between a stream strewn with many boulders, and a steep slope which joined the forest up above.

"Too late," said Jean Oberlé, holding out his hand and stopping, "too late; you have said too much, Uncle Ulrich. I feel I belong to the older times, as you do. And so much the worse, as to-morrow I go up to the Schlucht. I shall see her—I shall say good day to our country of France!"

He laughed as he uttered these words. M. Ulrich shook his head once or twice to scold him, but without answering, and he went away into the mist.

CHAPTER VI
THE FRONTIER

The next day Jean started in the morning on foot to go to the cutting bought by the House of Oberlé, which was situated on the crest of the mountains, enclosing the valley, to the left of the neck of the Schlucht, in the forest of Stosswihr. The way was long—the soil made slippery by a recent shower; besides, Jean lost several hours in going round a great rock he ought to have climbed. The afternoon was well advanced when he came to a wood cabin at the place where the road ended: just the time to talk to the German foreman who directed, under the supervision of the forest administration, the felling and transport of the firs; and the young man, continuing his climb, passed the workmen from the timber-yard coming down before the end of the day, to regain the valley. The sun, still splendid, was about to disappear on the other side of the Vosges. Jean was thinking with a beating heart of the frontier now quite near; however, he would not ask the way of the men who saluted him in passing, for he prided himself on hiding his emotions, and his words might have betrayed him before this gang of woodcutters released from work, and curious at the meeting. He entered the cutting they had just left. Around him the pine-trees, branchless and despoiled of their bark, were lying on the slopes, which they seemed to light up by the whiteness of their trunks. They had rolled—and stopped—one could not see why. At other times they had made a barrier and placed themselves pell-mell like spilikins on a game board. In the high forest there only remained one workman, an old man dressed in dark clothes who, kneeling, tied up in his handkerchief, a store of mushrooms he had gathered. When he had finished tying the ends of the red stuff with his clumsy fingers he got up, pushed his woollen cap well on to his head, and began to descend, with long strides over the moss, his mouth open to the odour of the forests.

"Ah," said Jean, "one minute, my man."

The man between two immense pine trunks, himself the colour of the bark, turned his head.

"Which is my nearest way to get to the neck of the Schlucht?"

"Go down by the waterfall, the way I go, and then turn up again. But do not go up there another two hundred yards, for then you go down into France; you will find paths which will lead you to the Schlucht. Good evening!"

"Good evening!"

The words rang out, soon lost in the vast silence. But one of them went on speaking to Jean Oberlé's heart: "You will go down into France." He was in a hurry to see her, this mysterious France, which held such a large place in his dreams, in his life—she, who had destroyed the unity of his family because the older members, some of them at least, remained faithful to her charms. France, for whom so many Alsatians had died and for whom so many others were waiting and whom they were loving with that silent love which makes hearts sad. So near him—she from whom he had been so jealously kept—she for whom Uncle Ulrich, M. Bastian, his mother, his grandfather Philippe, and thousands and thousands of others said a prayer every night!

In a few minutes he had reached the top and begun his descent on the other side. But the trees formed a thick curtain round him. And he began to run to find a road and a free space to see France. He took pleasure in sliding down and letting himself almost fall, head foremost, seeking the desired opening. On this side of the mountain the sun was touching the earth; here and there the air was still warm; but the pines always made a wall.

"Halt!" cried a man, showing himself suddenly, and coming out from behind the trunk of a tree. Jean went on running some steps—carried away by the impetus. Then he came back to the customs official who had called to him. Then the man, who was a brigadier, young and squat, with defective eyes, a little wild, two locks of yellow hair framing the thick-set face—the real type of a man of the Vosges, looked at the young man and said:

"Why the devil did you run? I thought you were a smuggler."

"I was trying to find a place to see a landscape in France...."

"Does that interest you? You are from the other side?"

"Yes."

"Not a Prussian all the same?"

"No; an Alsatian."

The man smiled slightly and said, "That is better!"

But Jean continued without taking up the conversation, and as if he had forgotten his question, to look at this poor officer of France, his face, his uniform, and to photograph them on his mind. The officer seemed amused at his curiosity and said, laughing:

"If it is a view you are after, you have only to follow me. I have one which the Government offers me to complete my treatment."

They both began to laugh, looking straight into each other's eyes quickly—less for what the customs officer had said than because of a certain sympathy which they felt for each other.

"We have no time to lose," said the brigadier, "the sun is dying down."

They went on under the vault of pines, turning round a cliff of bare rocks on which were planted at some distance two posts marking the spot where Germany ended and where France began, and at the end point, which was like a spur in the green, on a straight platform, which had its bed down in the forest, they found a watch-house of heavy planks of pines nailed on to the beams. From there one could see an immense landscape, which went on and on, sloping down—as far as human eye could see. In this moment and in the setting sun a pale golden light bathed the terraced lands, forests, villages, and rivers, the lakes of Retournemer and Longemer, softening the reliefs, and casting a colour like that of corn on uncultivated lands covered with heath. Jean remained standing, drinking in the picture to intoxication, and kept silence, while his emotion increased. He felt that the whole depth of his soul was full of joy.

"How beautiful it is!" he said.

The brigadier of customs, who was observing him from the corner of his eye, was flattered by the other's unstinted praise of his native district and answered:

"It is tiring, but in summer it is good to walk—for those who have the time. People come from Gérardmer, and from Saint Dié and Remiremont and from farther still. Many people come from over there——"

Over his shoulder, with his thumb reversed and turned backwards, he pointed to the country beyond the frontier.

Jean was shown in which direction lay the three towns of which the Custom House official had spoken. But he only followed his own thought with attention. What delighted him was the clearness of the air, and the idea of the illimitable, of the sweetness of life and of fertility which came to his mind at the sight of the French land. It was all he knew of France, what he had read, and what he had heard his mother, grandfather, and uncle Ulrich talk about, what he had pictured to himself, memories buried deep in his mind, which rose again suddenly like millions of grains of corn to the call of the sun.

The brigadier was seated on a bench, along the side of the hut; he had taken his short pipe from his pocket and was smoking.

When he saw the visitor turn towards him, his eyes full of tears, and seat himself on the bench, he guessed Jean's feelings; for Jean's admiration of the picturesque had escaped him, but the tears of regret at once made the brigadier grave. Those were from the heart, and a sublime equality united the two men. However, as he did not dare to question he stiffened his neck, until the muscles were visible, and began to study the horizon silently.

"What part of France do you come from?" asked Jean.

"About five leagues from here, in the mountain."

"Have you served your time in the army?"

The brigadier took his pipe from his mouth and his hand quickly touched the medal hanging on his breast.

"Six years," said he—"two furloughs. When I left I was a sergeant, with this medal, which I brought back from Tonquin. A fine time when it is finished." He spoke like travellers who prefer the remembrance of a journey but all the same have not disliked it. And he continued:

"With you, they say it is harder."

"Yes."

"I have always heard it said Germany is a great country, but the officer and the soldier are not relatives as in France."

The sun was going down; the great golden landscape became tawny in places and purple in shadow. This purple spread with the rapidity of racing clouds on shadowed slopes and veiled plains—how Jean Oberlé would have loved to see you again in strong light! He asked:

"Do you ever see any deserters?"

Those who pass the frontier before their service begins are naturally not known, only the soldiers serving in the Alsace-Lorraine regiments and who desert in uniform. "Yes; I have seen several poor fellows who had been too severely punished or whose tempers were too proud. You will say that some desert from our side too, and it is true; but then they are not so many——"

Shaking his head and looking tenderly at the sleeping forests:

"When one belongs to this side, you see, one can speak ill of it, but one is not satisfied elsewhere. You do not know the country, sir, and yet to look at you one would swear you belonged to it."

Jean felt himself getting red; his throat was dry; he could not answer. And the man, thinking that he had taken a liberty, said:

"Excuse me, sir; one never knows whom one meets; and it is better not to talk about these things. I must continue my rounds and go down again."

He was going to salute in military fashion; Jean took his hand and pressed it.

"You are not mistaken, my friend," he said.

Then, feeling in his pocket, he held out his cigar-case to him.

"Come, take a cigar!"

And then, with a kind of childish joy, he emptied his case into the hand which the Custom House official held out.

"Take them all; you will give me pleasure. Do not refuse me!"

It seemed as if he wanted to give something to France.

The brigadier hesitated for a moment, and closed his hand over them, saying:

"I will smoke them on Sunday. Thank you, sir! Good-bye!"

He saluted quickly, and was lost to sight almost immediately in the firs that clothe the mountains. Jean heard his footsteps growing fainter in the distance. Above all, he heard echoing in his soul, and with indescribable emotion, the words of this unknown man.

"You belong to us." "Yes, I belong here; I feel it, I see it; and that explains to me so many things in my life."

The shadow descended.

Jean saw the land darkening. He thought of those of his family who had fought there, round the villages submerged by the night, so that Alsace should remain united to that great country stretched out before him. "Sweet country—my country—every one has tender words for her; and I, why did I come? Why am I as moved as if she were living before me?"

In a little while, on the fringe of the sky just where the blue began, rose the evening star. Alone, faint but dominating as an idea.

Jean rose; the night was becoming quite dark, and he took the path which follows the crest of the hills; but he could not take his eyes from the star. Walking all alone in the deep silence, on the summit of the divided Vosges, he said to the star and to the shadow beneath:

"I belong to you; I am happy to have seen you. It frightens me to love you as I do!"

Soon he reached the frontier, and by the magnificent road crossing the Schlucht, went back again into the German-land.

The following day, the Tuesday of Holy Week, he was again at Alsheim, and handed to his father the report he had drawn up. Every one welcomed his return with such evident pleasure that he was very much touched by it. The evening after the "conference" between the old grandfather and the manufacturer, and at which Jean was present, since he had just returned from visiting the cuttings, Lucienne called her brother to the fire before which she was warming herself in the large yellow drawing-room. Madame Oberlé was reading near the window; her husband had gone out, the coachman having informed him that one of the horses had gone lame.

"Well!" asked Lucienne. "What is the most beautiful thing you saw?"

"You."

"No, do not joke; tell me, the most beautiful thing during your journey?"

"France!"

"Where?"

"At the Schlucht. You cannot imagine the emotion it made me feel. It was a shock—like a revelation. You do not seem to understand me."

She answered in an indifferent manner:

"Yes; I am delighted that you were pleased. It ought to be a very fine excursion at this time of the year. The first spring flowers, are there not? And the breeze in the woods? Ah, my dear boy, there is so much convention in all that!"

Jean did not go on. She it was who continued, and in a confidential voice, which she modulated, and made marvellously musical:

"Here we've had grand visits—oh, visits which nearly cost a scene. Imagine, two German officers came last Wednesday in a motor car to the lodge, and asked permission to see the saw-mills. Happily they were in mufti. The Alsheim people only saw two gentlemen like any others. Very fashionable; an old one—a commandant, and a young one with a grand air, and accustomed to society. If you had seen him bow to papa! I was in the park. They bowed to me too, and visited the whole of the works, personally conducted by our father. While this was going on that idiot Victor informed grandfather, who showed he was annoyed when we came in. I ought to have run away, it appears. As the gentlemen did not enter the house—'my house,' as grandfather says—his irritation did not last long. However, there was a sequel———"

Lucienne laughed a little stifled laugh.

"My dear, Madame Bastian did not approve of me."

"You were then present during their visit to the works, when these gentlemen——"

"Yes."

"All the time?"

"My father kept me. In any case, I do not see how that should affect the Mayor's wife. But I had such a cold bow from her, my dear, last Sunday at the church door. Do you care about the Bastians' bows?"

"Yes; in the same way that I care for the greetings of all good people."

"Good people—yes; but they do not know what life is! To be blamed by them is just the same to me as if I were to be blamed by an Egyptian mummy come to life for the purpose. I should answer: 'You do not understand anything about it; go and wrap yourself up again.' Is it not strange that you do not think as I do—you, my brother?"

Jean stroked the hand which was raised in front of him to make a screen.

"Even mummies can judge of certain things of our time, my darling—the things which are of all times."

"Oh! how serious you are. Come now, where was I wrong? Was it in going for a walk? In not looking away? In answering a greeting? In obeying my father, who told me to come and stay?"

"No; assuredly not!"

"What harm have I done?"

"None. I have danced with many German girls. You can acknowledge an officer's greeting."

"Then I did right?"

"As a fact, yes. But there are so many sorrows around us—real sorrows, and so noble. You must remember that they all come to life again at a word, or a gesture."

"I shall never consider that. Since what I do is not wrong, no one shall ever stop me. Do you hear?"

"That is where we differ, Lucienne. It is not so much in our ideas; it is in a whole range of feelings which your education prevents you from possessing."

He kissed her, and the conversation wandered to different topics.

CHAPTER VII
THE EASTER VIGIL

The weather had settled fine. Jean found the plain of Alsace in full spring glory.

However, he only felt a faint and mixed pleasure in the sight he had longed for. He came back from this excursion more upset than he cared to own to himself. It had revealed to him the opposition of the two nations—that is to say, of two minds, the persistent memory of many of the poor, and the difficulty they found to make a livelihood which their prudent and even hidden opinions created for them. He understood better now how difficult a part his would be to play in the family, at the works, in the village, in Alsace.

The pleasure he felt the morning after his return at his father's congratulations on the report of the forest cultivation by the House of Oberlé made only a short diversion in the midst of this worry. He tried in vain to appear quite happy, and he duly deceived those whose interest it was to be deceived.

"My Jean," said his mother, kissing him as he was going to sit down to breakfast, "I think you look splendid. The strong Alsheim air agrees with you, and also being near your poor mamma!"

"Fancy that!" said Lucienne, "and I thought him very gloomy!"

"Business," explained M. Joseph Oberlé, turning towards the window where his son was sitting, "cares of business. He has handed me a report, on which I must congratulate him publicly; it is very well drawn up, very clear, and the result of which will be that I shall economise, in four places at least, in the transport of my trees. You understand, father?"

The grandfather made a sign with his head. But he finished writing something on the slate, and showed it to his daughter-in-law.

"Has he already seen the country weep?"

Madame Monica rubbed the sentences out quickly with her fingers. The others looked at her, and all were uneasy, as if there had been some painful explanation between them.

Jean again experienced that intimate sorrow for which there is no remedy. All the afternoon he worked in the office at the saw-mills, but he was distracted and dreamy. He reflected that Lucienne would go away one day, and that nothing would be altered; that the grandfather might disappear also, and that the division would still go on. All the plans that he had had when far away, the hope of being himself a diversion, of bringing peace, of uniting them or of giving them an appearance of union: all that appeared childish to him now. He saw that Lucienne had spoken truly when she made fun of his illusions.

No, the evil was not in his family, it was in the whole of Alsace. Even if no one of his name lived at Alsheim, Jean Oberlé would meet at his door, in the village, among his workmen, his clients, and his friends the same annoyance at certain moments, always the same question. Neither his will nor any will like his could deliver his race, either now or later.

In this melancholy mood the idea of seeing Odile again, and making her love him, came back to him and took possession of his mind. Who else besides Odile could make life at Alsheim acceptable to him, and bring back his scattered and suspicious friends, and re-establish the name of Oberlé in the esteem of "Old Alsace"? He saw now that she was more than a pretty woman towards whom his youthful heart went out in song; he saw in her peace and dignity, and the only strength possible in the difficult future which awaited him.

She was the brave and faithful creature whom he needed here.

How to tell her? How to find an opportunity to speak freely to her, without the risk of being surprised, and troubling this orderly and jealous family? Evidently not at Alsheim. Then where should he arrange to meet her? And how could he forewarn her?

Jean thought of this all the evening.

The next day, Maundy Thursday, was the day on which in Catholic churches the Tomb would be decorated with flowers, branches of trees, materials, and torches placed in ledges, where the faithful hasten to adore the Host. It was beautiful weather, clear, even too clear for the time of year, when clearness calls up mist or rain.

After he had talked with his mother and Lucienne in M. Philippe Oberlé's room—it was the first time that he had felt that his home held a family—Jean went towards the orchards, which are behind the houses of Alsheim, and followed the road which he had taken a few weeks ago to call on the Bastians. But a little beyond the Ramspachers' farm he took the path which up to there ran at right angles to the avenue, and was now parallel with it, and with it joined the village road. He came out on to a piece of waste land, used for carts by many farmers on the plain. The neighbouring fields were deserted. The road was partially screened by a bank of earth planted with hazel-trees. Jean walked along the quick-set hedge which ran round the Bastians' property, approached the village, and came back again. He waited.

He hoped that Odile would soon come into the path on the other side of the hedge to go to the Alsheim church to pray at the Tomb.

The remembrance of former meetings, at the same place and on the same day, had come into his mind, and had decided him. As he began the walk for the third time he saw what he had not seen at first.

"How wonderful," he said to himself. "The road was made for her!"

At the end of the avenue, for more than two hundred yards in front, the fence, the clumps of trees, a small portion of the long roof appeared in a marvellous frame.

The old cherry-trees had flowered all together in the same week with the almond-trees and the pear-trees. The pear-trees blossom in clusters, the almond-trees in stars; as for the wild cherry-trees, from the forest transplanted to the plain—they blossom into white distaffs of bloom.

Round the substantial branches, swollen and coloured red with sap, thousands of white corollas like a drift of snowflakes, trembled on their fragile stalks, and so thick were they that in many places one could not see the branch itself. Every tree cast its flowery spindles in all directions. So many of the cherry-trees were old that from one side of the avenue to the other the points of the flowering branches touched and intermingled. A swarm of bees covered them with hovering wings. A subtle odour of honey floated in waves down the avenue, and was wafted on the wind far away to the plain, to the fields, to the scarcely covered ground surprised by this feeling of spring. There were no trees in the large open valley which could vie with these for splendour—only to the right—and quite close, the four walnut-trees of the Ramspachers had begun to show their leaves, and seemed with their heavy branches to be enamels encrusting the farm walls.

The minutes passed by—the petals of the cherry-blossoms fell in showers. And lo, here is a woman stooping to unlatch the gate—it is she! She stands erect, and walks onwards in the middle of the path, between its two borders of grass—quite slowly, for she is gazing upwards. She is looking at the white blossoms which are open. The idea of a bride's wedding wreath, an idea so familiar to young girls, passes through her mind. Odile does not smile, only her face beams with an uplifted look, and an involuntary stretching out of her hands gives the greeting and thanks of her youth to the joyous earth.

She goes down towards Alsheim. On her fur cap, on her rounded cheeks, on her blue cloth dress, the wild cherry-trees shed their blossoms. She is serious. In her left hand she carries a prayer book, half hidden in the folds of her skirt. She thinks she is alone.

The splendour of the day speaks to her. But there is nothing languid about her. She is a valiant creature; she is made to face life bravely. Her eyes, which seek the tree-tops, are alive and masters of her thoughts, and do not give themselves up to a tempting dream. She was drawing near, never suspecting that Jean was waiting for her. The meal-time ended, the usual noises were going on in the village of Alsheim, rumbling cart-wheels, barking dogs, voices of men, of children calling to each other, but all softened by the distance, scattered in the vast aerial space, drowned in the tide of the wind, as is the noise of a clod of earth which has become loose and falls into the sea.

As she came near, Jean took off his hat and stood up a little on the other side of the hedge. And she who walked between two walls of blossoms, although she was gazing upwards, turned her head, her glance still full of the spring which had excited her.

"Oh, is that you?" she said.

And she came at once across the strip of grass where the cherry-trees were planted, up to the place in the hedge where Jean was.

"I cannot come to you freely as I used to," he said, "so I came to wait for you. I have a favour to ask of you...."

"A favour? And you say that so seriously!" She tried to smile, but her lips refused. They had both become pale.

"I am going," said Jean, as if he was making a grave declaration; "I am going up to Sainte Odile the day after to-morrow—I shall go to hear the bells ring in Easter. If you also asked for permission to come———"

"You have made a vow?"

He answered:

"Something like it. I must speak to you—to you alone."

Odile withdrew slightly. With something of fear in her look she was trying to find out if Jean was speaking the truth—if she had guessed aright. He was watching her in an agony of anxiety. They were motionless, trembling, and so near and yet so far from each other that one would have said that they were threatening each other. And in fact both felt that the peace of their lives was at stake. They were not children, but a man and a woman of a strong and passionate race. All the powers of their being asserted themselves and broke through the hackneyed commonplaces of custom, because in these simple words, "I must speak to you," Odile had heard the breath of a soul which was giving itself, and which demanded a return.

In the deserted avenue the old cherry-trees lifted their white distaffs of blossom, and in the cup of each flower the spring sun was resting.

"The day after to-morrow?" she said, "at Sainte Odile—to hear the bells ring?"

She repeated what he had said. But that was to gain time, and to gaze deeper into those eyes fixed upon her, eyes which looked like the green depths of the forest.

There was a great calm in the plain and in the next village. The wind ceased for a moment—Odile turned away.

"I will go," she said.

Neither of them explained themselves further. A covered cart rolled along the road, not far off. A man shut the gate through which carts pass to the Bastians' farm. But the great thing was Jean had said what he had to say.

In the profound depths of their souls the words echoed and re-echoed. They were no longer alone. Both had the sacred moment of their meeting enclosed, as it were, in themselves, and they fell back on their own thoughts as the earth in the furrows does when the sowing is done, and the germinating seed is beginning to expand.

Odile went away. Jean admired the healthy and beautiful woman disappearing along the road. She walked well, without swinging her body. Above the white neck, Jean placed in imagination the big black bows of the Alsatian women who live beyond Strasburg. She no longer raised her eyes towards the cherry-trees. She let her skirt trail, and it swept the grass, making a little dust fly, and the petals of cherry blossoms, which flew about a little in the wind before dying.

The day after to-morrow was slow in coming. Jean had said to his father:

"Some pilgrims are going up to Sainte Odile on Saturday to hear the Easter bells. I have never been there at this time. If you do not mind, it is an excursion I should much like to make."

He did not mind.

Jean opened his window when he woke that morning. There was a thick fog. The fields near the house were invisible.

"You will not go in this weather?" asked Lucienne, when she saw her brother come into the dining-room, where she was drinking her chocolate.

"Yes, I shall go."

"You will see nothing."

"I shall hear."

"Is it then so extraordinary?"

"Yes."

"Then will you take me?"

She did not wish to go to Sainte Odile. Dressed in a light morning-gown trimmed with lace, and drinking her chocolate in little sips, she had no intention whatever of doing anything but stop her brother on his way and kiss him.

"Seriously, are you making a kind of pilgrimage up there?"

"Yes—a kind of———"

Bending at this moment over her cup, she did not see the quick smile which accompanied the words. She answered a little bitterly:

"You know I'm not devout. I fulfil my obligations as a Catholic but poorly, and the practices of devotion do not tempt me. But you, you have more faith than I have. I am going to tell you what you ought to ask for—it will be worth a pilgrimage, I can tell you." She changed her tone, and her voice became suddenly passionate; she raised her eyebrows, her eyes were at once self-willed and affectionate, and she said:

"You must ask for that miracle of perfection among women who will live with you here. When I am married and go away life will be terrible for you here. You will have to bear all alone the misery of the family quarrels, and the suspicions of the peasants. You will have no one to pity you. That is the part to play. Ask for some one strong enough, gay enough, and with a conscience fine enough to do it, since you would live at Alsheim. You see, my thought is that of a friend."

"Of a great friend."

They kissed each other.

"Good-bye, Pilgrim, good-bye—good luck!"

"Good-bye."

Jean got away. He was soon in the park, turned after passing through the gate, went through the hop-fields and the vineyards, and so into the forest.

The forest was also full of mist. The serried masses of pines, which took the hill as it were by storm, appeared grey from one bank of the stream to the other, and were almost immediately lost in a thick mist without sun and without shadow.

Jean did not go up the beaten track. He went gaily climbing up the woods when not too steep, and stopping sometimes to take breath and to listen if he could not catch above as below, somewhere in the mysterious and impenetrable mists of the mountain, either the voice of Odile or the chant of the pilgrims. But no; he only heard the rushing of water, or perhaps the voice of some one calling to his dog, or the timid call of some poor peasant of Obernai picking up dead sticks with his child, in spite of the regulation which allows wood-picking only on Thursdays. The saucepan must boil on Easter Sunday! And was not this fog which hid everything a divine protection against the forest guard?

Jean experienced great pleasure from this solitary, stiff climb. As he went up he thought of Odile more and more, and he was more and more glad that he had chosen this holy place of Alsace in which to meet her—and this day—doubly affecting. Everywhere around him the beautiful scalefern which carpets the rocky slopes unfolded its velvet fronds. On all last year's shoots of honeysuckle there were little leaves; the first strawberries were in flower, and the first lilies of the valley. The geraniums, which are so fine in Sainte Odile, lifted their hairy stalks, and the multitude of whortle berries and bilberries and raspberries, that is the entire undergrowth, whole fields of it, began to pour out on the breeze the perfume of their moving sap. The fog retained these few scents and kept them in like a net work on the sides of the Vosges.

Jean came close to Heidenbruch, looked at the green shutters and went on his way. "Uncle Ulrich," he murmured, "you would be glad if you saw me, and if you knew where I am going, and with whom, perhaps, I shall be presently!" Fidèle barked, half asleep, but did not come. The mountain was again deserted. A buzzard called above the mist. Jean, who had not been this way since his childhood, enjoyed the wildness and peacefulness of the place. He reached the higher part, which is the property of the bishopric of Strasburg, and followed the "pagan wall" which surrounds the summit for ten miles, that he might recall his school-boy impressions of long ago.

At midday he had passed the Männelstein rock and entered the convent courtyard, built on the mountain top, a crown of old stone placed above the summit of the pine forests; and there, although there was no crowd, he found groups of pilgrims, carriages with horses unharnessed, fastened to the trunks of ancient lime-trees, grown no one knew how at this altitude, and covering with their branches nearly the whole enclosure. Jean remembered the way; he went towards the chapels on the right. He merely passed through the first, which is painted, but stopped in the second, with elliptical arches leading to the shrine, where lies the wax figure of the patroness of Alsace, the Abbess Sainte Odile—so gentle, with her pink face, her veil, and her golden crozier, her purple mantle lined with ermine. Jean knelt down: with all the strength of his faith he prayed for his home, so sadly divided against itself, from which he felt glad to be away, and that Odile Bastian should not fail to keep this love tryst, the hour for which was so near at hand. As his was a sincere soul, he added: "Let our way be made clear to us! May we follow it together! Let us see all obstacles removed from our path!"

The whole of Alsace had knelt at the same spot for centuries.

Then he went out to the refectory, where the nuns had begun to help the first visitors. Odile was not there. After the lunch, which was very long, being continually lengthened by the arrival of fresh pilgrims, Jean went hastily to the foot of the great rock on which the convent is built, and finding once more the road which comes from Saint Nabor and passes by Sainte Odile's well, he posted himself in a thick part of the wood which overlooked a bend in the road. At his feet was the narrow strip of downtrodden earth, bare of grass and covered with pine needles, and which seemed hanging in the air. Far beyond that point the slope of the mountain became so steep that he could see no farther. In clear weather you could see to right and left two sunken wooden buttresses, but now the curtain of white mist hid everything—the abyss, the slopes, and the trees. But the wind blew and moved the mist, whose thickness, one could feel, varied from minute to minute.

It was two o'clock. In an hour the Easter bells would ring. The people who wanted to hear them could not now be far from the summit, and in the great silence Jean heard, rising upwards from below, voices blending round the bend of the wood. Then a phrase whistled: "*Formez vos bataillons!*" warned him that Alsatian students were near. Two young men—he who had whistled overtaken by another—came little by little out of the fog and went towards the abbey.

Then a young couple passed, the wife dressed in black, her square-cut bodice showing a white chemise, and wearing a lace cap like a helmet on her head; the man wore a flowered velvet waistcoat, a jacket with a row of copper buttons, and a fur cap.

Weissenburg peasants thought Jean.

Then he saw florid women from Alsheim and Heiligenstein pass, chattering, but not showing any trace of Alsatian dress.

Among them was a woman from the Münster valley, recognisable by her cap of dark stuff, bound round her head like the handkerchief of the southerners, and decorated in front with a red rosette. Two minutes slipped by. A step was heard through the fog, and a priest appeared—an old, heavy man, who wiped his face as he walked. Two children, very alert, doubtless the belated children of one of the women who had already gone by, overtook him, greeting him in Alsatian with the words, "Praised be Jesus Christ, M. le curé!"

"For ever and ever!" answered the priest.

He did not know them; he only spoke to them to answer the old and beautiful form of greeting. Jean, seated near a pine-tree and half hidden, heard an old man overtake the priest at the bend of the road and say, "Praised be Jesus Christ!"

How many times must that greeting have echoed through the vaults of the forest!

Jean looked before him as one in a dream, who sees only vague figures without attaching any meaning to them.

He stayed like that a short time. Then a murmur, almost imperceptible, so faint as to pass almost unheard, weaker than the twitter of a bird, was borne up on the fog: "Hail, Mary, full of grace; blessed art thou among women!" Another murmur followed, and finished with "Holy Mary, Mother of God, pray for us!" and an involuntary agitation, a mysterious certainty, preceded the appearance of two women.

They were both tall. The elder was an old spinster of Alsheim, whose face was the colour of the fog, and who lived in the shadow of the church, which she decorated on feast-days. She looked weary, but she smiled as she recited the rosary. The younger walked on the right, at the edge of the path, even with the slope, her proud head raised. Her fair hair was like a beautiful piece of pine bark, her body, robust and perfectly proportioned, stood out completely from the pale screen of cloudy mist which filled the bend of the road.

Jean did not move, nevertheless the younger woman saw him, and turned her head towards him. Odile smiled, and without interrupting her prayer, her eyes, turned towards the summit of the mountain, said:

"I will wait for you up there."

The two women did not slacken their steps. With even steps, upright, moving slightly the rosaries which they held in their hands by the swaying of their bodies, they mounted upwards, and were hidden in the shadow of the old wood. Jean let some moments pass by and followed the same road. At the turning, where the road becomes straight and crosses the crest of the mountain to reach the convent, he saw the two women again. They were walking more quickly, glad to have arrived, their sunshades open, for the mist, which had not dispersed, was now warm, and there were splashes of shadow at the foot of the trees. The sun was going down towards the peaks of the Vosges and towards the plains of France beyond.

The pilgrims who had arrived had already made their pilgrimage to the shrine of Sainte Odile, and were hastening to visit the places consecrated by pious or profane tradition: Sainte Odile's well, St. John's well, or by the pagan wall along the goat-path to the Rock of Männelstein, from where there is generally such a lovely view, to the tops of the Bloss and the Elsberg, to the ruined castles which lift their ancient towers among the pines—Andlau, Spesburg, Landsberg, and others. Jean saw the two women cross the courtyard and go towards the chapel. He retraced his steps to the beginning of the wind-swept avenue, along the old building, which reminds one of the advance works of old forts, and passes through a vaulted porch used as an entrance.

Ten minutes later Odile came out of the chapel alone, and guessing that Jean Oberlé was waiting for her elsewhere rather than in this courtyard too full of onlookers, took the road leading to the forest.

She was dressed in the clothes she had worn on Maundy Thursday, the same dark dress, but her hat was very simple, very youthful, and suited her to perfection: a straw, with a wide brim turned up on one side, and trimmed with a twist of tulle. She carried a summer jacket on her arm, and a sunshade. Odile walked quickly, with her head slightly bent, as those walk who are not interested in the road, or who are either praying or dreaming. When she came near Jean, who was on the right of the portico, she looked up, and said without stopping:

"The woman who came with me is resting. Here I am!"

"It is good of you to have trusted me!" said Jean. "Come, Odile!"

He followed, close to her, the avenue planted with sorry trees distorted by the winter winds. He was so much affected by the realisation of his dream that he could only think and speak of one thing: his gratitude to Odile, who was absolutely silent, only listening to what he did not say—and as full of emotion as he was.

They left the road at the place where it begins to slope downwards, and took a path through the forest of lofty pines in serried ranks which leads round the convent. There was no one there, and Jean saw that Odile's eyes of the colour of ripe corn, eyes deep and serious, were turned towards him. There was no sound in the wood save that from the drops of moisture falling from the leaves. They were quite close to each other.

"I asked you to come," said Jean, "so that you should decide what my life is to be. You were the love of my early youth. I want you to be my love always!"

Odile's look was far away, lost in the distance. She trembled slightly, and said:

"Have you thought?"

"Of everything!"

"Even of that which may separate us?"

"What do you mean by that? What are you afraid of? Of entering a disunited family?"

"No!"

"You would bring them together, I am sure of it. You would be its joy and peace. What do you fear—my father's or your father's opposition because they are now enemies?"

"That could be got over," said the young girl.

"Then it is because your mother detests me," said Jean hastily. "She does hate me, does she not? The other day she was so stiff to me, so offensive."

The fair head made a sign of denial.

"She will be slower in believing in you than my father was, slower than I was myself. But when she sees that your education has not changed your mind towards Alsace she will overcome her prejudices."

After a moment's silence Odile said:

"I do not think I am making any mistake. To-day's difficulties can be brushed on one side by you or by me, or by both of us. I am only afraid of what I do not know, the least thing which to-morrow might aggravate such a disturbed state———"

"I understand," said Jean, "you are afraid of my father's ambition?"

"Perhaps!"

"We have already suffered much from that. But he is my father. He is set on keeping me here; he says it every day. When he knows that I have chosen you, Odile, if he has personal projects which would prevent our marriage, he will at least put them off. Do not have any fear; we shall win!"

"We shall win!" she repeated.

"I am sure of it, Odile. You will make my life, Odile, which will be difficult, perhaps impossible, if you were not there. It was for you that I came back to the country. If I tell you that I have travelled much, and found no woman who had the charm for me that you have, or who made the same impression on me—how shall I tell you? The impression of a mountain stream so fresh and deep! Every time I think of my future marriage your image comes before my eyes. I love you, Odile!"

He took Odile's hand, and she answered, lifting her eyes to the light coming from above the trees.

"God is my witness that I love you, too!"

She thrilled with joy, and Jean felt her hand tremble.

"Yes," said Jean; and he tried to look into her eyes, which were still fixed on the distance.

"We shall overcome everything. We shall overcome the numerous obstacles arising from this terrible subject: that is all that is between us."

"Yes; it is the one and only question in this part of the world."

"It poisons everything!"

She stopped, and turned her radiant face full of love to him—of that beautiful and proud love which he had longed to know and to inspire.

"Say rather that it makes everything greater. Our quarrels here are not village quarrels—we are either for or against a country. We are obliged to have courage every day, to make enemies every day, every day to break with old friends who would willingly have remained faithful to us, but who are not faithful to Alsace. No action of our lives is indifferent; there is no action that is not an affirmation. I assure you, Jean, there is nobleness in that."

"That is true, Odile, my beloved."

They stopped to enjoy that delicious word to the full. Their souls were in their eyes, and they looked at each other tremblingly. In low tones, although there were no onlookers other than the pines swayed by the wind, they spoke of the future as of a battle already begun.

"Lucienne will be on my side," said Jean. "I shall entrust my secret to her when occasion occurs. She will help me, and I count on her."

"I count on my father," said Odile; "for he is already well disposed towards you. But take care not to do anything that would annoy him. Do not try to see me at Alsheim. Do not try to hurry on the time."

"That glorious time when you will be mine!"

They smiled at each other for the first time.

"I love you so dearly," continued Jean, "that I shall not ask you for the kiss that you would no doubt give me—I have no right to it. We do not entirely depend on ourselves, Odile. And then it pleases me to show you how sacred you are to me. Tell me at least that I shall take away with me a little of your soul?"

The lips so near his murmured "Yes!" And almost immediately:

"Do you hear down there? Is that the first Easter bell?"

They turned together towards the side where the wood sloped downwards.

"No; it must be the wind in the trees."

"Come," said she: "the bells are going to ring. And if I were not seen up there when they rang, old Rose would speak of it...."

Hardly saying a word, she led him to the base of the rock. There they separated to go back to the Abbey by two different paths.

"I shall find you again on the terrace," said Odile.

The daylight was growing blue in the hollows. That was the hour when waiting for the night does not seem long, and the morrow already dawns in the dreaming mind.

In a few minutes Jean had crossed the yard, followed the corridors of the convent, and opened a door leading to the garden in a sharp angle at the east of the buildings. There it was that all the pilgrims to Sainte Odile met to see Alsace when the weather was clear. A wall, high enough to lean on, runs along the top of an enormous block of rock, advancing like a spur above the forest. It overlooks the pines which cover the slopes everywhere. From the extreme point shut in, like the lantern of a lighthouse, one can see to the right quite a group of mountains, and in front and to the left the plain of Alsace. At this moment the fog was divided into two parts, for the sun was shining on the peaks of the Vosges. All the cloudy mist which did not reach that waving line of peaks, was grey and wan; but just above, almost horizontal rays pierced the mist and coloured it, giving to the second half of the landscape a look of brightness like luminous foam. And this separation showed with what quickness the mist came up from the valley towards the departing sun. The fleecy clouds intermingling, were wafted into the illumined space, were irradiated, showing thus their incessantly changing shapes, and the strength of the motion impelling them, as if the light had summoned their columns to greater heights.

There was at the entrance of this narrow place, arranged for pilgrims and visitors, an old man wearing the costume of the old Alsatians to the north of Strasburg; near him the priest with grey curly hair whom the children had greeted in the morning on the slope of Sainte Odile; a step or two farther on were the young Weissenburg peasants, and at the narrowest spot, squeezed close together on the wall, were the two students who might have been taken for brothers on account of their protruding lips and their beards divided in the middle, one fair, the other chestnut coloured. Both were Alsatians. They exchanged everyday remarks, as is usual among people who do not know each other. When they saw Jean Oberlé they turned round, and they felt themselves suddenly united by a common bond of race which becomes stronger in the face of a common danger.

"Is he a German—that one there?" asked a voice.

The old man who was near the priest cast a glance in the direction of the garden and answered:

"No; he wears his moustache in the French fashion and he looks like one of us."

"I saw him walking with Mademoiselle Odile Bastian, of Alsheim," said the young woman.

The group was reassured, and more so when Jean greeted the priest in Alsatian and asked:

"Are the bells of Alsace late?"

They all smiled, not because of what he had said, but because they felt at home among themselves without an inconvenient witness.

Odile came in her turn and leaned against a wall on the right of the first group. Jean took up a similar position on the other side of the group. They were suffering from loving so much, from having said it, and from only being sure of themselves.

The bells were not late. Their voices were encircled and enclosed by the rising mists. Suddenly they escaped from the cloudy masses, and it seemed as if each separate morsel of fog burst like a bubble on touching the wall and poured out on the summit of the sacred mountain all the harmony of the pealing bells. "Easter! Easter! The Lord is risen! He has changed the world and delivered men! The heavens are opened!" So sang the bells of Alsace. They were ringing from the foot of the mountain, and from the distance, and from far, far away, voices of the little bells, and voices of the great bells of cathedrals; voices which never ceased and from peal to peal were prolonged in re-echoing reverberations; voices that passed away lightly, intermittently, delicately, like a shuttle in a loom; a prodigious choir, whose singers were never visible to each other; cries of joy from a whole population of churches, songs of the spring eternal, which rose up from the depths of the misty plain and mounted to the summit of Sainte Odile to blend into one harmonious whole.

The grandeur of this concert of pealing bells silenced the few folk gathered together up there. The very air prayed. Souls thought of the risen Christ. Several thought of Alsace.

"There is some blue sky," said a voice.

"Some blue up there," repeated a woman's voice, as if in a dream.

They scarcely heard it, in the roar of sounds which rose from the valley. Yet all eyes were raised at once. They saw in the sky, amidst the masses of fog fleeing before the assailing sun, blue depths opening and opening with bewildering rapidity. And when they again looked downwards they perceived that the cloud of mist also was tearing itself to pieces on the slopes. It was the clearing up. Parts of the forest slipped, as it were, into the divisions made in the moving fog; then others; then black crevasses, the thickets, and rocks; then of a sudden the last rags of mist, drawn, thin, contorted, lamentable, went up in whirling masses, brushed against the terrace, and disappeared above. And the plain of Alsace appeared all blue and gold.

One of those who saw it cried out:

"How beautiful!"

All leaned forward to see in the opening of the mountain the plain growing lighter and lighter as far as eye could see.

All these Alsatian souls were touched. Three hundred villages of their own country lay below them scattered about amidst the young green of the cornfields. They were sleeping to the sound of the bells. Each was only a rose-red spot. The river, near the horizon, showed like a bar of dusky silver. And beyond rose stretches of country, whose shape was vanishing rapidly in the fogs which still hung above the Rhine. Quite near by, following the slope of the fir plantations, one saw, on the contrary, the smallest details of the forest of Sainte Odile. Several points of dark green jutted out into the valley and mixed with the pale green of the meadows. All was lit up by reflection from a sky full of rays of light. No bright spot attracted the eye. As the bells had united their voices, so the varying shades of the earth had melted into a harmonious unity. The old Alsatian, who kept his place at the side of the priest, stretched his arms, and said:

"I hear the cathedral bells."

He pointed, away in the distance over the flat country, to the celebrated spire of Strasburg, which looked like an amethyst the size of a thumbnail. Now that they could see the rose-red of villages, they imagined they could recognise the sound of the bells.

A voice said: "I recognise the sound of the bells of the Abbey of Marmoutier. How well they chime!"

"I," said another, "I hear the bells of Obernai!"

"And I the bells of Heiligenstein."

The peasant, who came from the neighbourhood of Weissenburg, also said:

"We are too far off to hear what the bells of Saint George of Haguenau are ringing. However, listen, listen; there—now."

The old Alsatian repeated seriously:

"I hear the cathedral!" and he added: "Look up there again!"

They could all see that the clouds had ascended to the regions of the sunbeams. The cloud, shapeless at the base of the mountain, had spread across the sky, and was like sheaves of gladioli thrown above the Vosges and the plain: some red, like blood, some quite pale, and some like molten gold. And all those witnesses looking up from between the two abysses, their gaze having followed the long light line, remarked that it lit up the earth with its reflection, and that the distant houses of the capital and the spire of the cathedral stood out in a tawny light from the thickening shadow.

"That is like what I saw on the night of August the 23rd, 0," said the old Alsatian. "I was just here——"

They, even the very young ones, had heard this date frequently spoken of. Their looks were fixed more steadily on the little spire, whence came still a little shining light and the sound of the resurrection bells.

"I was here with the women and girls from yonder villages, who had come up here because the noise of the cannons had redoubled. We heard the cannons as we now hear the bells. The bombs burst like rockets. Our women were weeping here where you stand. That was the night when the library caught fire, that the new church caught fire, and the picture gallery, and ten houses in Broglie. Then a yellow-and-red smoke rose, and the clouds looked like these we now see. Strasburg was burning. They had fired one hundred and ninety-three shells against the city.

One of the students, the younger one, shook his fist.

"Down with them!" muttered the other.

The peasant took his cap off and kept it under his arm, without saying a word.

The bells were still ringing, but not so many of them. They could no longer hear the bells of Obernai, nor of Saint Nabor, nor some of the others they thought they had heard. They were like lights going out. Night was coming.

Jean saw that the two women were almost weeping, and that every one was silent.

"Please say one prayer for Alsace," he said to the priest, "while the bells are still ringing for the resurrection."

"Right! that's right, my boy!" said the old peasant standing by the priest; "you belong to the country!"

The heavy, weary face of the priest brightened at the same time. His voice, which was slightly broken, was not steady. An old and enduring sorrow, yet always new, spoke through his lips, and while they were all looking, as he was himself, towards Strasburg, the city which night was hiding, he prayed:

"My God, here, now we can see from your Sainte Odile nearly all the beloved land, our towns, our villages, and our fields. But some of our land lies also on the other side of the mountains, and yet that is also our country. You permitted us to be separated. My heart breaks to think of it. For on the other side of the mountains is the nation we love, and which you still love. It is the oldest of the Christian nations; it is the nearest to Godlike things. It has more angels in its skies because it has more churches and chapels on earth, more holy tombs to defend, more sacred dust mixed with its fields, with its grass, with the waters which permeate the land and nourish it. Oh God, we have suffered in our bodies, in our goods; we still suffer in our memories. Nevertheless, make our memories last. Grant that France also will not forget. Make her more worthy to lead nations. Give her back her lost sister, who may also return. Amen!"

"As the Easter bells return."

"Amen!" said the voices of two men.

"Amen! Amen!"

The others wept in silence. There was only the hollow sound of one single bell in the cold air that came up from the depths. The ringers had left the towers, already lost in the shadow that covered the plain.

Above the high platform in the garden the darkened clouds, flying to the west, left a border of purple on the crest of the mountains. Stars came out, in the black depths of the night, as the first primroses were coming out, at the same time under the pines. Only three persons were left on the terrace. The others had gone when the secret of their Alsatian souls had been revealed.

The old priest, seeing before him two young people close to each other, and Odile's head near Jean's shoulder, asked:

"Betrothed?"

"Alas!" answered Jean. "Wish that it may become true."

"I do wish it. What you just said is right. I wish that you, who are young, may see Alsace once more French."

He went away.

"Good-bye," said Odile quickly, "Good-bye, Jean!"

She held out her hand, and went away without turning to look back. Jean remained near the terrace wall.

The night birds—owls, sea-eagles, eagle-owls, and horned owls—mingling their cries, flew from wood to wood. For a quarter of an hour, the time of their passage, which they made in sweeping flights, their calls resounded over the mountain sides. Then complete silence settled down. Peace arose with the perfumes of the sleeping forests.

CHAPTER VIII
AT CAROLIS

At the beginning of the rue de Zurich, facing the Quay des Bateliers, one of the relics of old Strasburg, there is a narrow house, much lower than its neighbours, with a roof of two stories like a Chinese pagoda. The front, formerly adorned with the pattern of its painted beams, is now covered with whitewash, on which is this inscription:

"JEAN, CALLED CAROLIS, *WEINSTUBE*."

This wine-shop, whose exterior has nothing about it to arouse the curiosity of the passer-by, is not a nondescript place, nor is it an ordinary public-house. The place is historical. The inhabitants of Zurich came here in 6, or, at least, the best shots among them, to take part in the grand shooting competition to which Strasburg had summoned the Empire and the confederated States. They had brought with them a pot of boiled millet, and scarcely were they out of the boat than they made the Strasburg people understand that the pudding was still warm.

"We could easily come to your aid, neighbours," they said; "by the Rhine and the Ill, the distance between our cities is very short." The word given in 6 was kept in 0, as is testified to by an engraved inscription just near by on the Zurich Fountain. At the moment when besieged Strasburg was in the most distressed condition the people of Zurich intervened, and obtained from General Werder permission to allow the old men and children to leave the city. This house was noted for something else—thanks to the Southerner who in 0 established a shop there for wines of the South.

Jean, called Carolis, bore a remarkable resemblance to Gambetta. He knew him, and copied his gestures and his clothes, the cut of his beard, and the sound of his voice. His trade was fairly flourishing before the war, but he became prosperous in the years that followed. And a certain number of German officers got into the habit of coming there to drink the black wines of Narbonne, Cette, and Montpellier.

One morning towards the end of April, Jean Oberlé, who was going to see the Chief of the Administration of Forests, whom he had long promised to visit, was passing along the quay, when a woman of about forty, clothed in black, evidently an Alsatian, came out of the café, crossed the road, and, apologising, said:

"Pardon me, monsieur, but will you kindly come in? One of your friends is asking for you."

"Who is it?" asked Jean, astonished.

"The youngest officer there."

She pointed with her finger to the confused mass of shadow moving under the lowered linen blind, and which he saw to be the inside of the room with its groups of customers.

Jean, after hesitating for a moment, followed her, and was surprised—for not belonging to Strasburg, he was ignorant of the reputation and also of the customers of this wine-shop—at finding there six officers, three of whom were Hussars, seated at tables covered with red and blue check cloths, talking loudly, smoking, and drinking Carolis wine.

The first glance he gave, on coming from the light into the semi-darkness, showed him that the room was small—there were only four tables—and decorated with allegorical pictures in the German style; he saw a monkey, a cat, a pack of cards, a packet of cigarettes, but above all there was a semi-circular mirror filling a recess in the left wall and round which hung framed photographs of the present or past habitués of the house. Jean looked again to see who could have sent for him, when a very young cavalryman got up. This simple movement displayed the beauty of his slender form in its sky-blue tunic with gold lace. He rose from the back of the room to the left. Near him, and round the same table, a captain and a commandant remained seated.

The three officers must have returned from a long march; they were covered with dust, their foreheads were wet with perspiration, their features were drawn, and the veins stood out on their temples. The youngest had even brought back from this country ride a branch of hawthorn, which he had slipped under his flat epaulet, on the side near the heart.

The Alsatian recognised Lieutenant Wilhelm von Farnow, a Prussian, three years older than himself, whom he had met before during his first year's law course in Munich, where Farnow was then sub-lieutenant in a regiment of Bavarian Uhlans. Since then he had not seen him. He only knew that in consequence of an altercation between Bavarian and Prussian officers in the regimental casino, some of the officers implicated had been removed, and that his old comrade was among their number.

No; doubt was not possible. It was Farnow, with the same elegant, haughty way of offering his hand, the same fair, beardless face, too thick-set and too flat, with thick lips, an impertinent little nose, slightly turned up, and fine eyes of steel-blue—a hard blue where dwelt the pride of youth, of command, of a bold and disputatious temper. His body gave promise of developing into that of a solid and massive cuirassier later on. But at present he was still thin, and so well-proportioned, so agile, so evidently inured to warlike exercises, so vigorous, there was such disciplined precision in all his movements, that de Farnow, although he had not a handsome face, had gained a reputation for good looks, so much so that in Munich one would call him sometimes "Beauty" Farnow, and sometimes "Death's Head" Farnow. With reddish moustaches, bushy brows, and a helmet accentuating the shadow over his eyes, he would have been terrifying. But, though scarcely twenty-seven, he gave the impression of a warlike being, violent, conqueror of himself, disciplined even to his acquired and perfectly polished manners.

Jean Oberlé remarked that when he rose Farnow spoke to the commandant, his immediate neighbour, a robust soldier with slow, sure eyes. He was explaining something, and the other approved, with an inclination of his head, at the moment when the lieutenant made the introduction.

"Will the commandant permit me to present to him my comrade, Jean Oberlé, son of the factory owner of Alsheim?"

"Certainly, sir. An intelligent Alsatian—very well known."

Jean's introduction to the captain, a man still young, with straight features, evidently cultured, and no less evidently of a haughty temper, led to the same flattering expressions regarding the factory owner at Alsheim: "Yes, truly Monsieur Oberlé is well known—an enlightened mind. I have had the pleasure of seeing him—kindly remember me to him."

Jean felt humiliated by the marked attentions of these two officers. He had the impression that he was the object of exceptional attention, he, a civilian, a citizen; he, an Alsatian; he, who from every point of view should have been looked upon by these lofty personages as their inferior. "What my father has done then is of great importance," he thought, "that they should requite him in this fashion. Neither his fortune, nor his style of living, nor his conversation, can justify this. He does not live at Strasburg, nor has he filled any office."

A sign from the commandant almost at once put an end to the awkward situation, and gave the young men liberty to go and sit at the table farthest away from the window at the back of the room.

"It is quite by chance that you meet me here," said Farnow, in a slightly sarcastic tone, which revealed the pride of the Prussian lieutenant.

"My regiment is hardly ever here—it is mostly infantry officers who come here.... I generally go to the 'Germania'—but we have just been reconnoitring, as you see, and my commandant was very hot.... You will pardon me, my dear Oberlé, for having sent for you."

"On the contrary, it was very friendly. You could hardly leave your chiefs."

"And I wanted to renew my acquaintance with you. I have not seen you for so long, not since Munich days. You had just gone past the corner of the house over there, when I said to the servant, 'That is one of my friends! Run and fetch M. Oberlé here!'"

"And truly, you see me very happy, Farnow."

The two young men looked at each other with the curiosity of two beings who try to fill in the unknown years. "What sort of a life has he led? What does he think of me? How far can I trust him?"

"I fancy," said Farnow, "that you have arrived quite recently?"

"Just so; I came at the end of February."

"They told me that you were going to commence your military service in October in the Hussars."

"That is true."

"Do you know, Oberlé, that I had the honour of meeting your father in society last winter? I asked to be introduced."

"Excuse me, I am still such a new-comer...."

Conversation languished at this moment at Carolis, and Jean noticed that the two blue tunics had turned towards him, and that the commandant and the captain were both examining the face of the future volunteer.

They finished drinking the wine like Bordeaux they had ordered in a sealed bottle.

"I should much like to see more of you," said Farnow, lowering his voice. "I hope we shall be able to meet."

"Do you know Alsheim?"

"Yes; I've been through it several times during manœuvres."

The lieutenant was visibly trying to find out how far he could go.

He was in an annexed country; many incidents of daily life had taught him that. He did not care about renewing the experience. He was feeling his way. Should he promise a call? He did not know yet. And this uncertainty, so contrary to his energetic nature; this caution, so wounding to his pride—made him hold up his head as if he were going to pick up a challenge.

Jean, on his side, was disturbed. This simple thing, the receiving a former comrade, seemed to him now a delicate problem to solve. Personally he should have inclined towards the affirmative. But neither Madame Oberlé nor the grandfather would admit any exception to the rule so strictly kept up to now—that no Germans, except quick and commonplace business men, should be admitted to the house of the old protesting deputy. They would never consent. But it was hard for Jean to show himself less tolerant in Strasburg than he had been in Munich, and at the the first meeting on Alsatian ground to offend the young officer who had come to him with hand outstretched. He tried at least to put a note of cordiality into his answer:

"I will come and see you, dear Farnow, with pleasure."

The German understood, frowned, and was silent. Evidently others had refused even to visit him. He did not meet in Oberlé that systematic and complete hostility. His anger did not last, or he did not show it. He reached out his slender hand, the wrist of which looked like a bundle of steel threads covered with skin, and with the tips of his fingers he touched the hilt of his sword, which had not left his side.

"I shall be charmed," he said at last.

He ordered a bottle of Burgundy, and having filled Jean's glass and his own, drank.

"To your return to Alsheim!" he said.

Then, drinking it in a draught, he placed the glass upon the table.

"I am really very pleased to see you again. I live pretty well alone, and you know my tastes outside my profession, which I adore, above which I place nothing whatever, nothing if it be not God, who is the great judge of it. I love hunting best—I think man is made to move in large spaces, to strengthen his power and his dominion over the beasts, when he has not the occasion to do it over his kind. For me there is no pleasure to equal it. Apropos of this, it seems that M. Oberlé has been ousted from his hunting rights?"

"Yes," said Jean; "he has given them up almost entirely———"

"Would you like to have a turn at my place? I have rented some shooting near Haguenau, half wood and half plain; I have roebuck which come from the forest—the ancient Sacred Forest; I have hares and pheasants, and snipe at the time of passage; and if you like glowworms, I have some who fly under the pine-trees and shine like the lances of my Hussars."

The conversation ran on for a while on this subject. Then Farnow finished the bottle of Carolis wine with Jean, and lifting the hawthorn which beflowered his epaulet and letting it drop to the ground, said:

"If you will allow me, Oberlé, I will go some way with you. What direction do you take?"

"Towards the University!"

"That is my way."

The two young men got up together. They were nearly of the same height and figure; both were of an energetic type, although different in expression—Oberlé, careful to relax all that was too serious in his face when at rest; Farnow exaggerating the harshness of his whole personality. The young lieutenant drew down his tunic to take out the creases, took from a chair his flat cap decorated in front with a cockade of the Prussian colours, and walking first with a studied stiffness, half turned towards the table where the commandant and the captain were sitting, saluted them with an almost invisible and several times repeated inclination of the body. The respectful good-fellowship of a short time ago was not now in place. The two chiefs from habit inspected this lieutenant leaving Carolis. Gentlemen themselves, very jealous of the honour of their corps, having learned by heart all the articles of the code of the perfect officer, they interested themselves in all that had to do with the conduct, the attitude, the dress, and the speech of a subordinate, who is the object of public criticism. The examination must have been favourable to Farnow. With a friendly and protective movement of his hand, the commandant dismissed him.

As soon as they were in the street Farnow asked:

"Well, they were perfect, were they not?"

"Yes."

"How you say that? Did you not find them kindly? You ought to see them in the service."

"On the contrary," interrupted Jean, "they were too amiable. I see every day more and more that my father must have humiliated himself very much to be so honoured in high places. And that wounds me, Farnow."

The other looked serious, and said:

"*Franzosenkopf!* What a strange character this nation has—who cannot accept their position as the conquered, and think themselves dishonoured if Germans make advances to them!"

"It is because they do nothing gratuitously," said Oberlé.

Farnow was not displeased at the word. It seemed to him a kind of homage to the hard, utilitarian temperamant of his race. Besides, the young lieutenant would not enter into a discussion where he knew that friendships ran the risk of being spoilt. He greeted a young woman, who came towards him, and followed her with his eyes.

"That is the wife of Captain von Holtzberg. Pretty, isn't she?"

Then pointing to the left, beyond the bridge to the quarters of the old city, illumined by the vaporous light of this spring morning, he added, as if the two thoughts were united naturally in his mind:

"I like this old-world Strasburg. How feudal it is!"

Above the river, whose waters were soiled by works and sewers, rose the long sloping roofs, with their high dormer windows, the tiles of all shades of red—the mediæval purple of Strasburg, mended, patched, and spotted, and washed, violet in places, nearly yellow in others adjoining, rose-colour on certain slopes, orange-coloured in some lights, royally beautiful everywhere and stretched out like a marvellous Eastern carpet of soft faded silks round the cathedral. The cathedral itself, built in red stone, viewed from this point, seemed to have been, and still to be, the pattern which had decided the colour of all the rest; it was the ornament, the glory, and the centre of all. A stork, with open wings, cleaving the air with wide strokes, as an oarsman cleaves water, his feet horizontally prolonging his body and acting as rudder, his bill a little raised like a prow, an heraldic bird, was flying through the blue, faithful to Strasburg, like all its ancient race, protected, sacred like the place, and always returning to the same nests above the same chimney stacks.

Jean and Farnow saw it inclining towards the cathedral spire, and seen from behind, foreshortened, it looked like some bird beating the air with its bow of feathers, and then it disappeared.

"These are the inhabitants," said Farnow, "whom neither the smoke of our factories, nor the tramways, nor the railways, nor the new palaces, nor the new order of things can astonish."

"They have always been German," said Jean with a smile. "The storks have always worn your colours—white belly, red bill, black wings."

"So they have," said the officer, laughing.

He went on his way along the quays, and almost immediately stopped laughing. Before him, coming from the direction of the new part of the town, an artillery soldier was leading two horses, or rather he was being led by them. He was drunk. Walking between the two brown horses, holding the reins in his raised hands, he went on stumbling, knocking against the shoulder of one or the other of the beasts, and to save himself from falling, dragged from time to time at one of them, which resisted and moved away.

"What is this?" growled Farnow—"a drunken soldier at this time of day!"

"A little too much malt spirit," said Oberlé. "He is not merry in drink."

Farnow did not answer. Frowning, he watched the man who was approaching, and who was only about ten yards away.

At this distance, according to regimental rules, the man ought to have walked in step and turned his head in the direction of his superior officer. Not only had he forgotten all his instruction and continued to roll painfully between the horses; but at the moment when he had to pass Farnow he murmured something, no doubt an insult.

That was too much. The lieutenant's shoulders shook with anger for a moment, and then he marched straight to the soldier, whose frightened horses backed. The officer felt humiliated for Germany.

"Halt!" he cried. "Stand straight!"

The soldier looked at him, stupefied, made an effort, and succeeded in standing still and nearly erect.

"Your name?"

The soldier told his name.

"You will have your punishment at the barracks, you brute! But in expectation of better things, take this on account, for dishonouring the uniform as you have!"

Saying this, he stretched his right arm out at full length, and with his gloved hand, hard as steel, he hit the man on the face. The blood ran out at the corner of his mouth; he squared his shoulders; he drew up his arms as if about to box. The soldier must have been terribly tempted to retaliate. Jean saw the wandering eyes of the drunkard when he was thus thrust backwards, turn right round in their sockets with pain and rage. Then they looked down on the pavement, overcome by a confused and terrifying remembrance of the power of the officer.

"Now march!" cried Farnow. "And do not stumble!"

He was in the middle of the quay—erect, booted, a head higher than his victim, as it were surrounded by sunlight, with flashing eyes, the lower lids and the corners of his lips wrinkled by anger; and those who called him "Death's Head" must have caught a glimpse of him like that.

The loafers who had hurried up to witness the scene and formed a circle, stood aside at the order of the lieutenant, and let the soldier pass through, who was trying not to pull the reins too hard. Then, as a certain number of them remained gathered together, either silent or merely muttering their opinion, Farnow, turning on his heels and crossing his arms, looked at them one after the other. The little bank clerk went by first, adjusting his eyeglasses; then the milk-woman with her copper pot on her hip passed on by herself, shrugged her shoulders, ogling Farnow; then the butcher who had come from the neighbouring shop; then two boatmen who tried to look as if they did not care, although both had flushed faces; then the urchins who at first wanted to cry, and who now nudged each other and went off laughing. The officer drew near to his companion, who had remained on the left near the canal.

"I think you went a little too far," said Oberlé. "What you have just done is forbidden by the Emperor's express orders. You risk a reprimand."

"That is the only way to treat those brutes!" said Farnow, his eyes still blazing. "Besides, believe me, he has already passed on my blow to his horses, and to-morrow he will have forgotten all about it."

The two young men walked side by side to the University gardens, without speaking to each other, thinking over what had just happened. Farnow put on a new pair of gloves to replace the others, probably soiled by the soldier's cheek. He bent towards Jean, saying gravely and with evident conviction:

"You were very young when I met you, my dear fellow. We shall have to tell each other a few things before we shall know exactly our respective opinions on many points.

"But I am astonished that you have not yet perceived, you who have stayed so long in all the German provinces, that we were born to conquer the world, and that conquerors are never gentle men, nor ever perfectly just."

He added, after a few steps:

"I should be vexed if I have hurt your feelings, Oberlé; but I cannot hide from you that I do not regret what I did. Only understand that behind my anger there is discipline, the inviolable prestige and dignity of the army of which I am a unit. Do not report the incident to your people, dear fellow, without also adding the excuse *for* it. That would mean to betray a friend. Well, good-bye."

He held out his hand. His blue eyes lost for the moment something of their haughty indifference.

"Good-bye, Oberlé! Here is the door of your Clerk of the Forests."

CHAPTER IX
THE MEETING

Jean came back in fairly good time to the Strasburg station and took the train to Obernai, where he had left his bicycle. While going from Obernai to Alsheim he saw in the meadows through which the Dachs ran, near Bernhardsweiler, a second stork—motionless on one leg.

This was the first thing he told Lucienne, whom he met under the trees in the park. She was reading, and wore a grey linen dress with lace on the bodice. When she heard the noise of the bicycle on the gravel she lifted her intelligent eyes, smiling.

"My dear, how I have missed you. What in the world makes you go away so constantly?"

"I make discoveries, dear sister. First, I have seen two storks, arriving on the sacred day—April 23—punctual as lawyers."

A slight pout of her red lips showed that the news did not interest her much.

"Then?"

"I spent three hours in the offices of the Forest Conservators, where I learned that——"

"You can tell all that to father," she interrupted. "I see so much wood here, living and dead, that I have no wish to occupy my mind with it unnecessarily. Tell me some Strasburg news, or about some costumes, or some conversation you had with some one in society."

"That is true," said the young man, laughing. "I did meet some one."

"Interesting?"

"Yes; an old acquaintance of Munich, a lieutenant in the Hussars."

"Lieutenant von Farnow?"

"Yes, the very man—Lieutenant Wilhelm von Farnow, lieutenant in the 9th Rhenish Hussars. What is the matter?"

They were halfway down the avenue, hidden by a clump of shrubs. Lucienne, bold and provoking as ever, crossed her arms and said, in a quieter tone of voice:

"Only this—he loves me."

"*He?*"

"And I love him!"

Jean stepped away from his sister in order to see her better.

"It is not possible!"

"And why not?"

"Why, Lucienne, because he is a German, an officer—a Prussian!"

There was silence; the blow had struck home. Jean, quite pale, went on:

"You must also know that he is a Protestant."

She flung her book on the seat and, holding up her head, quivering all over at the protest:

"Do you imagine I have not thought it all over? I know all you can possibly say. I know that the people in the midst of whom we live in Alsace here, intolerant and narrow-minded as they are, will not hesitate to say what they think on the subject. Yes; they will make a fuss, they will blame me and pity me and try to make me give way. And you; are you not beginning the game? But I warn you that arguments are quite useless—all your arguments. I love him. It is not to be done, it *is* done. I have only one wish, and that is to know if you are on my side or against me. For I shall not alter my mind."

"Oh, my God! my God!" cried Jean, hiding his face in his hands.

"I never thought it could hurt you so much. I do not understand. Do you share their stupid hatred? Tell me. I am putting a strong control on my feelings that I may talk to you. Tell me then. Speak. You are paler than I am—I, whom this alone concerns."

She caught hold of his hands and uncovered his face. And Jean gazed at her strangely for a moment as do those whose look does not as yet correspond with their thoughts.

Then he said:

"You are mistaken; we are both concerned, Lucienne!"

"Why?"

"We are one against the other, because I, too, must tell you that I love—I love Odile Bastian!"

She was terrified at what she foresaw in connection with this name; she was touched at the same time because the argument had reference to love, and was a confidence. Her irritation passed at once. She put her head on her brother's shoulder. The curls of her fair hair intermixed with auburn lay ruffled and disordered against Jean's neck.

"Poor, dear Jean," she murmured. "Fate pursues us. Odile Bastian and the other. Two love affairs which exclude each other! Oh! my poor dear, it is the drama of our family perpetuating itself through us!" She straightened herself, thinking she heard a step, and taking her brother's arm went on nervously: "We cannot talk here, but we must talk about other than merely surface things. If father suddenly came across us, or mamma, who is working in the drawing-room at heaven knows what everlasting piece of embroidery. Ah, my dear, when I think that only a few steps away from her we are exchanging such secrets as these, which she little suspects! But first we must think of ourselves, must we not? Ourselves...!" For a moment she thought of returning to the house, and of going up to her room with Jean. Then she decided on a better place of refuge. "Come into the fields, there no one will disturb us."

Arm-in-arm, hastening their steps, speaking to each other in low tones and short sentences, they went through the gate, passed the end of the enclosure, and to the right of the road, which was higher than the surrounding land; they went down a sloping path, which could be seen like a grey ribbon winding its seemingly endless way through the young corn. Already each of them, after the first moment of surprise, of dejection, and of real pain caused by the thought of what the other would suffer, had come back to thoughts of self.

"Perhaps we are wrong to worry ourselves," said Lucienne, entering the path. "Is it certain that our plans are irreconcilable?"

"Yes. Odile Bastian's mother will never agree to her daughter becoming the sister-in-law of a German officer."

"And how do you know that this officer would not perhaps prefer marrying into a family a little less behind the times than ours?" said Lucienne, hurt. "Your plan may also injure mine."

"Pardon me; I know Farnow—nothing will stop him."

"To tell the truth, I think so too!" said the young girl, looking up, and blushing with pride.

"He is one of those who are never in the wrong."

"Exactly so."

"You share his ambitions."

"I flatter myself that I do."

"You can rest assured then: he will have no hesitation. The scruples will come from the Bastian side, who are the souls of honour...."

"Ah! if he heard you," said Lucienne, letting go her brother's arm, "he would fight you."

"What would that prove?"

"That he felt your insult as I felt it myself, Jean. For Lieutenant von Farnow is a man of honour!"

"Yes, in *his* way—which is not our way."

"Very good! Very noble!"

"Rather feudal, this nobility of theirs. They have not had the time to have that of a later date. But after all it does not matter. I am not in a mood for discussion. I suffer too much. All I wish to say is that when I ask for Odile's hand I shall be refused. I foresee it, I am sure of it; and that von Farnow will not understand why, and if he did understand he would not withdraw, he would never think of sacrificing himself. In speaking like this, I am not slandering him. I simply understand him."

They walked on, enveloped in an atmosphere of light and warmth, which they did not enjoy, between long strips of young corn, smiling unnoticed around them. In the plain, some labourers seeing them pass side by side, walking together, envied them. Lucienne could not deny that her brother's forebodings were reasonable. Yes, it must be so, judging from what she herself knew of Lieutenant von Farnow and the Bastians. In any other circumstance she would have pitied her brother, but personal interest spoke louder than pity. She felt a kind of disturbed joy when she heard Jean acknowledge his fears. She felt encouraged *not* to be generous, because she felt he was anxious. Not being able to pity him, she at any rate drew near to him, and talked to him about herself.

"If we had lived together longer, Jean," she said, "you would have known my ideas on marriage, and I should astonish you less to-day. I had made up my mind to marry only a very rich man. I dislike the fear of what to-morrow may bring; I want certainty and to lead...."

"The conditions are fulfilled," said Jean, with bitterness. "Farnow has a vast property in Silesia. But at the same time he is also lieutenant in the 9th regiment of Rhenish Hussars!"

"Well!"

"Officer in an army against which your father has fought, your uncle has fought, and all your relations, every one old enough to carry arms."

"Quite right. And I would not have asked anything better than to marry an Alsatian. Perhaps I even wished to do so without saying anything about it. But I did not find what I wished. Nearly all who had name, fortune, or influence have chosen France; that is to say, they all left Alsace after the war. They called it patriotism. Truly, words can serve every use. Who remain? You can easily count the young people of Alsatian origin belonging to wealthy families, and who could have aspired to the hand of Lucienne Oberlé."

She went on more excitedly:

"But they did not ask for me; and they will not ask for me, my dear! That is what you have never understood. They kept away, they and their parents, because father...."

"They have put us and our family under an interdict. I am, in consequence, one of those they do not marry. Owing to their intolerance, the narrowness of their conception of life, I am condemned by them. They call me the 'beautiful Lucienne Oberlé,' but none of those who like to look at me, and greet me with affected respect would dare to defy his people and make me his wife. I have not had to choose; you cannot reproach me on that score. The situation is such that, willing or not, I shall not be asked in marriage by an Alsatian. It is not my fault. I knew what I was doing when I accepted Lieutenant von Farnow!"

"Accepted?"

"In the sense that I am bound—certainly. During last autumn, but especially for the last four months, Lieutenant von Farnow has paid me a great deal of attention."

"Then it was he on horseback, there on the road, the night I returned?"

"Yes."

"Was it he who recently came to visit the saw-mills with another officer?"

"Yes; but I have met him mostly in society at Strasburg, when father took me to balls and dinners.—You know that mamma, because of her poor health—but above all because of her hatred of everything German—generally avoids accompanying me. I met Lieutenant von Farnow constantly. He had every chance of talking to me.

"At last, when he came here, just lately, he asked father if I would allow him to pay me definite attentions. And this very morning, after lunch, I answered 'Yes.'"

"Then father consents?"

"Yes."

"The others?"

"Know nothing about it. And it will be terrible. Think of it. My mother, my grandfather, Uncle Ulrich! I hoped for your support, Jean, to help me overcome all these difficulties, and to help me also to heal all the wounds I am going to inflict. First of all, von Farnow must be introduced to mamma, who does not know him. Alsheim is quite impossible. We have been thinking of a meeting at some mutual friend's house in Strasburg. But if I have to consider you as one more enemy, what good is there in my telling you my plans?"

They stood still, Jean reflecting for a moment, as he faced the plain, which unrolled its strips of barley, and young corn, intermingling at the edges like the flow and counterflow of running water. Then, gathering his thoughts together and looking at Lucienne, who was waiting for his words, with raised face, suppliant, restless, and ardent.

"You cannot imagine how much I am suffering. You have destroyed all my joy!"

"My dear, I did not know about your love!"

"And I—I have not the courage to destroy yours...."

Lucienne threw her arms round his neck.

"How generous you are, Jean! How good you are!"

He put her away from him, and said sadly:

"Not so generous as you imagine, Lucienne, for that would be to show myself very weak. No; I do not approve of your decision. I have no confidence in your happiness...."

"But at least you will leave me free? You will not go against me? You will help me against mamma?"

"Yes, since you have gone so far, and since our father has given his consent, and since our mother's opposition might only cause still greater unhappiness...."

"You are right, Jean. Greater unhappiness, for father told me that——"

"Yes, I guess. He told you that he would crush all opposition, that he would leave our mother rather than give in. That is all very likely. He would do it. I shall not enter into any struggle with him. Only, I keep my liberty of action with regard to von Farnow."

"What do you mean by that?" she asked quickly.

"I wish," Jean replied, in a tone of authority, in which Lucienne felt her brother's invincible determination, "I wish to let him know exactly what I think. I shall find some means of having an explanation with him. If he persists, after that, in his desire to marry you, he will make no mistake, at least as to the difference of feeling and ideas which separate us."

"I do not mind that," answered Lucienne, reassured, and she smiled, being certain that von Farnow would stand the trial.

She turned towards Alsheim. A cry of victory was on her lips, but she restrained it. For some time she stood silent, breathing quickly, and seeking with her eyes and mind what she could say so that her happiness should not appear an insult to her brother.

Then she shook her head.

"Poor house," she said. "Now that I am going to leave it, it is becoming dear to me. I am persuaded that later on, when life in the garrison takes me away from Alsace, I shall have visions of Alsheim. I shall see it in imagination, just as it stands there."

In the midst of its girdle of orchards were massed together the red roofs of the village. And both village and trees formed an island among the corn and April clover. Little birds, gilded by the sunshine, were flying over Alsheim. The house of the Oberlés at this distance seemed only to be one of many. There was so much sweetness in all things that one might have imagined life itself sweet.

Lucienne gave herself up to this appreciation of beauty, which only came to her as a consequence of her thoughts of love. Again she heard her own words, "I shall have visions of Alsheim just as it stands there." Then the undulating line of the Bastians' wood, which rose like a little blue cloud beyond the farthest gardens, reminded her of Jean's trouble. She only then realised that he had not answered her. She was moved, not enough to ask herself if she should renounce her happiness to make Jean happy, but up to the point of regretting, with a sort of tender violence, this conflict between their loves. She would have liked to soothe the pain she had caused, to comfort it with words, to put it to rest, and not to feel it so close to her and so alive.

"Jean, my brother Jean," she said, "I will requite you for all you are doing for me by helping you, by doing my very best for you. Who knows but by working together we may not be able to solve the problem?"

"No; it is beyond your power and mine."

"Odile loves you? Yes, of course she loves you. Then you will be very strong."

Jean made a movement of weariness.

"Do not try, Lucienne. Let us go back."

"I beseech you. Tell me at least how you came to love her? I can understand that. We said we would tell each other more than the names. You have only me to whom you can speak your mind without danger."

She was making herself out to be humble. She was even humiliated by her secret happiness. She renewed her request, was affectionate, and found the right words to describe Odile's stately beauty, and Jean spoke.

He did it because his need to confide to some one the hope which had been his—a hope which was still struggling not to die. He told of the Easter vigil at Sainte Odile and how he had met the young girl on Maundy Thursday in the cherry avenue. From that, each helping the other to recall happenings, to fix dates, to find words, they went back into the past, up to long-ago times when their parents were not at variance, or at least when the children were ignorant of their dissensions or did not perceive them, when in the holidays Lucienne, Odile, and Jean might believe that the two families, united in intimate friendship, would continue to live as important land-owners, respected and beloved by the village of Alsheim.

Lucienne did not realise that in calling up these pictures of the happy past she was not calming her brother's mind. He may have found pleasure in them for a moment, hoping to get away from the present, but a comparison was immediately drawn, and his revolt was only the more profound, arousing all the powers of his being, against his father, against his sister, against that false pity behind which Lucienne's incapability of sacrifice was hidden. Soon the young man gave up answering his sister. Alsheim was getting nearer, and was now a long outline broken here and there. In the calm evening the Oberlés' house raised its protecting roof amid the tops of the trees, still bare. When the park gates, closed each day when the workmen left, were opened for the two pedestrians, Jean slipped behind Lucienne, and, making her go on, said, in very low, ironical tones:

"Come, Baroness von Farnow, enter the house of the old protesting deputy, Philippe Oberlé."

She was going to make a retort, but an energetic footstep scrunched the gravel, a man turned into the avenue round a gigantic clump of beeches, and a resonant, imperious voice, which was singing in order to appear the voice of a happy man without any regrets, cried:

"There you are, my children! What a nice walk you must have had! From the waterfall by the works I saw you in the corn leaning towards each other like lovers."

M. Joseph Oberlé questioned the faces of his children, and saw that Lucienne at least was smiling.

"Did we have things to tell each other?" he went on. "Great secrets, perhaps?"

Lucienne, embarrassed by the nearness of the lodge, and still more so by the exasperation of her brother, answered quickly:

"Yes; I have spoken to Jean. He has understood. He will not oppose my wishes."

The father seized his son's hand. "I expected nothing else from him. I thank you, Jean. I shall not forget that."

In his left hand he took Lucienne's, and, like a happy father between his two children, he crossed the park by the long, winding carriage drive.

A woman behind the drawing-room window saw them come, and her pleasure in looking at this scene was not undiluted. She asked herself if the father and children had united against her.

"You know, dear Jean," said the father, holding up his head and, as it were, questioning the front of the château. "You know that I wish to spare susceptibilities and to prepare solutions, and not to insist on them until I am forced to do so. We are invited to the Brausigs'——"

"Ah! is it already settled?"

"Yes, to a dinner, to a fairly large evening party—not too many people. I think that would be a very good opportunity to present Lieutenant von Farnow to your mother. I shall only speak of this to your mother later on. And in order not to bias any of her impressions—you know how timid she is—so that she does not meet my look when she talks to this young man, I shall refuse for myself—I shall confide Lucienne's future to you. All my dream is to make this dear one happy. Not a word to my father. He will be the last to learn what does not really concern him but secondarily."

The great empty space by the flight of steps had not seen for a long time such a united group walk on the well-rolled gravel.

In the drawing-room, keeping herself a little back, trying to make her mind easy and not succeeding, Madame Oberlé had left off working. The embroidery was on the floor.

Jean was thinking.

"I shall thus assist at the interview, and I shall take mamma there, who will suspect nothing. What a part to play to avoid greater evils! Happily, she will forgive me one day when she knows everything."

Late that night, kissing her son, Madame Oberlé said:

"Your father insists upon my accepting the Brausigs' invitation. Are you going, my darling?"

"Yes, mamma."

"Then I shall also go."

CHAPTER X
THE DINNER AT THE BRAUSIGS'

At seven o'clock the guests of the Geheimrath Brausig were gathered together in the blue drawing-room—with its plush and gilded wood—which that official had taken with him to the different towns he had lived in. The Geheimrath was a Saxon of excellent education, and of amiable though somewhat fawning manners. He seemed always to bend in any direction in which he was touched. But the frame-work was solid; and, on the contrary, he was a man whose ideas were unchangeable. He was tall, ruddy, nearly blind, and wore his hair long, and his red beard streaked with white, he wore short. He did not wear spectacles, because his eyes, of a pale agate colour, were neither shortsighted nor longsighted, but were worn out and almost dead. He was a great talker. His speciality was to reconcile the most opposite opinions. In his offices, in his relations with his inferiors one saw the real basis of his character. Herr Brausig had an Imperial spirit. He never allowed private people to be in the right. The words "Public interest" seemed to him to answer all arguments. In the official world they talked about raising him to the nobility. He repeated this. His wife was fifty years old, had the remains of beauty and an imposing figure; she had received the officials of eight German towns before coming to live in Strasburg. At her entertainments she gave all her attention to supervising the servants, and her impatience at the countless annoyances connected with their service, which she tried to hide, did not allow her to reply to her neighbours except in sentences absolutely devoid of interest.

The guests formed a mixture of races and professions which one would not so easily come across in any other German town. There are so many imported elements in the Strasburg of to-day! They were fourteen in number, the dining-room could seat sixteen with a little over two feet of table for each person, such space being an essential in the eyes of the Geheimrath. He had in his house, around him—and he dominated them with his sad, insipid head—some protégés, people recommended to him, or friends gathered together from various parts of the empire: two Prussian students from the University of Strasburg, then two young Alsatian artists, two painters who had been working for a year at the decoration of a church; these were the unimportant guests, to which we must add the two Oberlés, brother and sister, and even the mother, who was looked upon in the official world as a person of limited intellect. The guests of note were Professor Knäpple, from Mecklenburg, cultured and studious, whose erudition consisted chiefly of minutiæ, and the author of an excellent work on the socialism of Plato. He was the husband of a pretty wife, round and pink, who seemed fairer and pinker by the side of her dark husband, with his black beard curling like an Assyrian's. The Professor of Æsthetics, Baron von Fincken from Baden—who shaved his cheeks and chin, so that the scars gained in the duels of his student days might be better seen, was of a slender, nervous build; his head was of the energetic type, his nose was turned up and showing the cartilage very plainly; ardent, passionate, and very anti-French, and yet he looked more like a Frenchman than any one present, except Jean Oberlé. There was no Madame von Fincken. But there was beautiful Madame Rosenblatt, the woman who was more envied, sought after, looked up to, than any other woman in the German society of Strasburg, even in the military world, because of her beauty and intelligence. She came from Rhenish Prussia, as did also her husband, the great iron-master, Karl Rosenblatt, multi-millionaire, a man of sanguine temperament, and at the same time methodical and silent, and one said that he was bold and cold and calculating in business.

This party was like all the parties that the Geheimrath gave; there was no homogeneity. The official himself called that conciliating the different elements of the country. He also spoke of the "neutral ground" of his house and of the "open tribunal," for each and every opinion. But many Alsatians did not trust this eclecticism and this liberty. Some maintained that Herr Brausig was simply playing a part, and that whatever was said in his house was always known in higher spheres.

Madame Oberlé and her children were the last to arrive at the Geheimrath. The German guests welcomed Lucienne, who was intimate with them already. They were polite to the mother, because they knew she only went into Government society under constraint. Wilhelm von Farnow, introduced by Madame Brausig, who alone knew about the officer's plans, bowed ceremoniously to the mother and the young girl, drew himself up erect, stood stiffly, then returned at once to the group of men standing near the mirror.

A servant announced that dinner was served. There was a movement among the black coats, and the guests entered the large room, decorated as at the Oberlés' house with evident predilection. But the taste was not the same. The vaulted bays with two mullions, decorated with rose windows in the pointed arch, and filled with stained-glass, of which at this time only the lead-work was to be seen; the sideboards with torso pillars with sculptured panels; the wainscoting rising to the ceiling and ending in little spires; the ceiling itself divided into numerous sunk panels, and in the carving of which electric lamps shone like fire blossoms: the whole decoration recalled to mind Gothic art.

Jean, who came in one of the last in the procession of diners, gave his arm to pretty Madame Knäpple, who had eyes only for the wonderfully made and equally wonderfully worn dress of Madame Rosenblatt. Professor Knäpple's little wife thought she saw that Jean Oberlé was noticing the same thing. So she said:

"The low neck is indecent. Don't you think so?"

"I find it irreproachable. I think that Madame Rosenblatt must go to Paris for her dresses."

"Yes; you have guessed rightly," answered the homely little woman. "When one has such a fortune one has often odd fancies, and but little patriotism."

The beginning of the meal was rather silent. Little by little the noise of different conversations rose. They began to drink. M. Rosenblatt had large bumpers of Rhine wine poured out for him. The two students in spectacles came back to Wolxheim wine, with as serious a mien as if it were some difficult passage in the classics. The voices grew louder. The servants' footsteps could no longer be heard on the parquet floor. General conversation began as the froth of intellects had been moved by the light and the wine. Professor Knäpple, who had a quiet voice, but a manner of pronouncing very clearly and distinctly, was heard above the hum of conversation, when he answered his neighbour, Madame Brausig:

"No; I do not understand that one should join the strong because one is strong. I have always been a liberal."

"You are alluding to the Transvaal perhaps," said the Geheimrath opposite, with a loud laugh, pleased at having guessed.

"Precisely, Herr Geheimrath. It is not political greatness to crush small nations."

"You find that extraordinary?"

"No; very ordinary. But I do say there is nothing to boast about in that."

"Have other nations acted differently?" asked Baron von Fincken.

He turned up his insolent nose. No one carried on the discussion, as if the argument were unanswerable. And the wave of general talk rolled on, intermingling and drowning the private conversations of which it consisted.

Madame Rosenblatt's musical voice broke the hum of talk. She was saying to little Madame Knäpple, placed on the other side of the table:

"Yes, madame, I assure you that the question has been discussed. Everything is possible, madame; however, I should not have thought that the Municipality of a German town could even discuss such an idea."

"Not so devoid of sense; don't you think so, Professor, you who lecture on æsthetics?"

Professor von Fincken, seated at the right hand of the beautiful Madame Rosenblatt, turned towards her, looked into the depths of her eyes, which remained like an unrippled lake, and said:

"What is it about, madame?"

"I told Madame Knäpple that in the Municipal Council the question had been raised of sending the Gobelin Tapestries which the town possesses, to Paris to be mended."

"That is right, madame, the noes have it."

"Why not to Berlin?" asked Madame Knäpple's pretty red mouth. "Do they happen to work so badly in Berlin?"

The Geheimrath found it time to "conciliate." "To make Gobelin tapestry, without doubt, Madame Rosenblatt, is right, and Paris is necessary; but to mend them! I think—it seems to me—that can be done in Germany."

"Send our tapestry to Paris!" expostulated Madame Knäpple. "How do they know if they would ever come back?"

"Oh!" one of the young painters at the end of the table answered gravely. "Oh, madame!"

"How! Oh! You are an Alsatian, sir," said the homely little woman, pricked by the interjection as if it had been the point of a needle. "But we—we have the right to be mistrustful."

She had gone too far. No one stood up for her verdict—general conversation stopped, and was replaced by flattering appreciations made by each guest on some quails in aspic which had just been served. Madame Knäpple herself came back to subjects with which she was more familiar, for she but rarely took any part in discussions when men were present. She turned towards her neighbour, von Farnow, which prevented her from seeing the elegant Madame Rosenblatt, and Madame Rosenblatt's beautiful dress, and the periwinkle-blue eyes of Madame Rosenblatt, and she undertook to explain to the young man how to do quails in aspic, and how to make "Cup" according to her recipe. However, for the second time their thoughts had been turned to the vanquished nation—and this thought continued to disturb their minds in a vague way, while champagne, German-labelled, was sparkling in the glasses.

Madame Brausig had only exchanged very unmeaning words with M. Rosenblatt, her neighbour on the right, and with Professor Knäpple, her neighbour on the left, who preferred talking to Madame Rosenblatt, and

Baron von Fincken, her *vis-à-vis*, and sometimes with Jean Oberlé. It was she, however, who started a fresh discussion, without wishing to. And the conversation rose at once to a height it had not yet reached. The councillor's wife was speaking to M. Rosenblatt—looking all the time angrily at a servant who had just knocked against the chair of her most important guest, Madame Rosenblatt; she was speaking of a marriage between an Alsatian and a German from Hanover, the commandant of the regiment of Foot Artillery No. 10. The iron-master answered quite loudly, without knowing that he was sitting beside the mother of a young girl sought after by an officer:

"The children will be good Germans. Such marriages are very rare, and I regret it, because they add immensely to the Germanisation of this obstinate country."

Baron von Fincken emptied his champagne glass at a draught and, placing it on the table, said:

"All means are good, because the end is good."

"Certainly," said M. Rosenblatt.

Jean Oberlé was the best known of the three Alsatians present, and the best qualified to make a reply, and yet the most disqualified, it seemed to him, to give his opinion, because of the discussions which this question had caused in his own house. He saw that Baron von Fincken had looked at him as he spoke, that Herr Rosenblatt was staring at him, that Professor Knäpple cast a glance at his left-hand neighbour, that Rosenblatt smiled with the air of one who would say "Is this little fellow capable of defending his nation? Will he answer to the spur? Let us see!"

The young man answered, choosing his adversary, and, turning towards the Baron, "On the contrary, I think that the Germanisation of Alsace is a bad and clumsy action."

At the same time his face grew harder and the green in his eyes vibrated, like the green of the forests when the wind blows the leaves of the trees the wrong way.

The Professor of Æsthetics looked like a man of the sword.

"Why bad, if you please? Do you look upon the conquest as unpleasant? This is the sequel of that? Do you think so, really? But say so, then!"

In the silence of all present the answer of Jean Oberlé fell clear and distinct.

"Yes."

"You dare, sir!"

"Allow me," said the Geheimrath Brausig, stretching out his hand as if to bless them. "Here we are all good Germans, my dear baron! You have no right to suspect the patriotism of our young friend, who is only speaking from a historical point of view!"

Madame Oberlé and Lucienne signed to Jean.

"Be quiet! be quiet!"

But Baron von Fincken saw nothing and heard nothing. The bitter passion of which his face was the symbol was let loose. He half rose, and leaning forward, with his head over the table, he said:

"France is pretty! united! powerful and moral!"

Little Madame Knäpple went on:

"Above all, moral!"

Voices high, low, ironical, and irritated rang out confusedly.

"Deceivers, the French! Look at their novels and plays! France is decadent! A worn-out nation! What will she do against fifty-five millions of Germans?"

Jean let the avalanche pass; he looked now at Fincken, who was gesticulating, now at von Farnow, who was silent, with head held high and frowning brows.

"I believe France is very much calumniated," he said at last. "She may be governed badly. She may be weakened by dissensions; but since you attack her, I am delighted to tell you that I look upon her as a very great nation. Even you yourselves have no other opinion."

Veritable clamours arose. Ah! Oh! Indeed.

"Your very fury against her proves this. You have conquered her, but you have not left off envying her!"

"Do you read the commercial statistics, young man?" asked the resolute voice of Herr Rosenblatt.

"Her merchant navy is in the sixth rank!" whispered one of the students.

Professor Knäpple fixed his spectacles on his nose and very clearly articulated the following proposition:

"What you say, my dear Oberlé, is true as regards the past. Even to-day I think I can add, that if we had France to ourselves she would rapidly become a great country. We should know how to improve her."

"I beg you," added von Fincken insolently, "not to discuss an opinion which is not tenable."

"I beg you, in my turn," said Jean, "not to use in discussion arguments which are not conclusive, and do not really touch the question. One cannot judge a country simply and solely by its commerce, its navy, or its army."

"On what would you form your judgment then, sir?"

"On the soul of the country, sir. France has hers; that I know from history and from I know not what filial instinct I feel within me; and I firmly believe that there are many superior virtues, eminent qualities, generosity, disinterestedness, love of justice, taste, delicacy, and a certain flower of heroism, which are to be found more often than elsewhere in the past and in the present of this nation. I could give many proofs of it. Even if she were as weak as you assert, she holds treasures which are the honour of the world, which must be torn from her before she merits death, and by the side of these things the remainder seems very small. Your Germanisation, sir, is only destruction or diminution of those virtues or French qualities in the Alsatian soul. And that is why I maintain that it is bad!"

"Come now," said Fincken, "Alsace belongs naturally to Germany; she has made her come back. We make our repossession sure. Who would not do as much?"

"France!" answered Oberlé; "and that is why we love her. She might have taken the territory, but she would not have done violence to the soul. We belong to her by right of love."

The baron shrugged his shoulders.

"Go back then to her!"

Jean almost shouted, "Yes." The servants stopped to listen, in passing round the sweets. He went on:

"I find your attempt bad in itself, because it is a repression of consciences; but I also find that it is clumsy, even from a German point of view."

"Charming," said the little falsetto of Madame Knäpple. "You should have the interest to keep what originality and independence remains to us. It would be a useful example to Germany."

"Thanks," said a voice.

"And more and more useful," insisted the young man. "I was educated in Germany and I am sure of my contention. What struck me most, and shocked me, is the want of personality in Germans, their increasing forgetfulness of liberty, their effacement before the power of——"

"Take care, young man!" interrupted the Geheimrath quickly.

"I shall say before the power of Prussia, Geheimrath, which devours consciences, and which allows only three types of men to live, and these she has moulded from childhood—taxpayers, officials, and soldiers."

From the end of the table one of the students rose from his chair:

"The Roman Empire did the same, and it was the Roman Empire!"

A vibrating voice near him cried:

"Bravo!"

All the guests looked up. It was Wilhelm von Farnow, who had said only this one word since the beginning of the discussion. The violence of the debate had irritated him like a personal provocation. It had excited others. Herr Rosenblatt clenched his fists. Professor Knäpple muttered stormy sentences as he wiped his spectacles. His wife laughed nervously.

Then the beautiful Madame Rosenblatt, letting her pearl necklace run through her fingers, smiled, and looking pleasantly at the Alsatian, said:

"M. Oberlé has at least the courage of his opinions. No one could be more openly against us."

Jean felt far too irritated to answer pleasantly. He looked intently at the faces of Fincken, Rosenblatt, and Knäpple, at the student who was moving restlessly near Lucienne, and then leaning slightly towards Madame Rosenblatt, said:

"It is only through the women that the German nation can acquire the refinement which is wanting, madame. Germany has some accomplished women."

"Thank you for us!" answered three men's voices.

Madame Knäpple, furious at the compliment paid to Madame Rosenblatt, said:

"What is your scheme then, sir, for shaking off the yoke of Germany?"

"I have none."

"Then what do you ask for?"

"Nothing, madame; I suffer."

It was one of the Alsatian artists, the painter with the yellow beard, who looked like one of Giotto's pupils, who continued the conversation, and all the table turned towards him.

"I am not like M. Oberlé, who asks for nothing. He has only just come into the country after a long absence. If he had lived here some time, he would come to a different conclusion. We Alsatians of the new generation through our contact with three hundred thousand Germans have had the difference of our French culture from that of Germany conclusively demonstrated. We prefer our own; that is permitted? In exchange for the loyalty that we have shown to Germany, the taxes we pay, the military service we perform—we desire to remain Alsatians. And you determinedly refuse to understand. Our demand is that we should not be compelled to submit to exceptional laws, to this sort of state of siege which we have endured for thirty years. We demand that we should not be treated and governed as a country of the Empire—after the fashion of the Cameroons, Togoland, and New Guinea, the Bismarck Archipelago, or the Isles of Providence, but like a European province of the German Empire. We shall not be satisfied until that day comes when we can feel we are in our own home here—Alsatians in Alsace, as the Bavarians are Bavarians in Bavaria. Whilst as things are, we are the conquered ones waiting on the good pleasure of a master. That is my demand!"

He spoke clearly, with apparent coldness, and his golden beard looked like the point of an arrow. His measured words succeeded in exciting their minds—and one could foresee the angry answer when Geheimrathin Brausig rose.

Her guests followed suit, and went into the blue drawing-room.

"You were absurd! What were you thinking about?" Lucienne asked in an undertone as she passed Jean.

"Perhaps what you said was imprudent," added Madame Oberlé, a moment after; "but you defended Alsace well—and I approve of you."

The Geheimrath was already turning to all sides, making use of the usual formula, which he murmured into the ears of Fincken, von Farnow, of Rosenblatt and Professor Knäpple, the two students, Jean, and the two Alsatian artists:

"Do me the pleasure of following me to the smoking-room!"

The smoking-room was a second drawing-room, separated from the first by plate-glass.

M. Brausig's guests were soon reunited there. Cigars and beer were brought. Smoke spirals went up, mingled together, and rose to the ceiling. M. Rosenblatt became a centre of conversation. The Professor Knäpple became another. The loud voices seemed to be wrangling, but were only explaining simple ideas with difficulty.

Alone, two men were talking of a serious subject and making but little noise. They were Jean Oberlé and von Farnow. Scarcely had the former lit his cigar when von Farnow touched Jean's arm and said:

"I want to have a little conversation with you apart."

To be more free, the young men seated themselves near the monumental mantelpiece, facing the bay which opened into the drawing-room, while the other smokers grouped round M. Rosenblatt and Baron von Fincken occupied the embrasure of the windows.

"You were violent to-night, my dear fellow," said von Farnow, with the haughty politeness which he often adopted; "I was tempted twenty times to answer you, but I preferred waiting. Were you not aiming at me a little?"

"Much of what I said was meant for you. I wanted to tell you very clearly what I was and to teach it to you before witnesses, so that it should be clearly understood that if you persevere in your projects, I have made no concessions to you, no advances; that I have nothing whatever to do with the marriage you are contemplating. I am not going to oppose my father's wishes, but I will not have my ideas confused with his."

"That is how I understood it. You have evidently learned that I have met your sister in society and that I love her?"

"Yes."

"Is that all you have to answer?"

A rush of blood suffused the German's cheeks.

"Explain yourself quickly!" he went on. "My family is of the nobility; do you recognise that?"

"Yes."

"Do you recognise that it is an honour for a woman to be sought by a German officer?"

"For any except an Alsatian woman. But although you do not understand that feeling, we are not like other people—we are the people of Alsace. I esteem you very much, Farnow, but your marriage with my sister will cruelly affect three persons among us—myself first of all."

"How? I ask you!"

They were obliged to speak in an undertone and to avoid any gestures, because of the presence of the Geheimrath's guests at the farther end of the room, who were observing the young men, and were trying to interpret their attitudes. All their emotion and their irritation was in their eyes and in the whispering of words which must only be heard by one person.

Through the sheet of plate-glass, Lucienne could see von Farnow, and getting up and crossing the drawing-room, or pretending to admire the basket of flowers which stood out from the frame-work, she looked inquiringly at the faces of the officer and of her brother.

"You are a man of heart, von Farnow. Think what our home in Alsheim will be when this fresh cause of dissension is added to the others?"

"I shall go away," said the officer; "I can exchange and leave Strasburg."

"The memory will remain with us. But that is not all. And from now on there is my mother, who will never consent...."

With a movement of his hand von Farnow showed that he brushed aside that objection.

"There is my grandfather, whom Alsace once elected to protest, and who cannot to-day give the lie to all his past life."

"I owe nothing to M. Philippe Oberlé," interrupted Farnow.

His voice became more imperious.

"I warn you that I never give up a resolution once taken. When M. von Kassewitz, the prefect of Strasburg, and the only near relation remaining to me, returns from the holiday he is going to take in a few days' time, he will go to Alsheim, to your house; he will ask for the hand of Mlle. Lucienne Oberlé for his nephew, and his request will be granted, because Mlle. Lucienne Oberlé wishes to accept me, because her father has already consented, and because I will have it so—I, Wilhelm von Farnow!"

"It remains to be seen whether you have done well...."

"According to my will: that is sufficient for me."

"How much pride there is in your love, Farnow!"

"It is in everything I do, Oberlé!"

"Do you think I am mistaken? My sister pleases you because she is pretty?"

"Yes."

"Intelligent?"

"Yes."

"But also because she is an Alsatian girl! Your pride has seen in her a victory to be gained. You are not ignorant of the fact that the women of Alsace are in the habit of refusing Germans. They are queens not easily accessible to your amorous ambitions, from the country girls, who at their gatherings refuse to dance with the emigrants, up to our sisters, who are not often seen in your drawing-rooms or on your arms. In the various regiments you will belong to you will boast that you have won Lucienne Oberlé. It will even be a good mark for you in high quarters? Will it not?"

"Perhaps," said Farnow with a sneer.

"Go on then, break, or finish breaking, three of us!"

They were getting more and more irritated, each trying to control himself.

The officer rose, threw away his cigar, and said haughtily:

"We are civilised barbarians—that is understood, less burdened than you with prejudices and pretensions to justice. That is why we shall conquer the world. But in the meantime, Oberlé, I am going to join your mother and talk to her, as amiably as an enemy possibly can. Will you accompany me?"

Jean Oberlé shook his head in the negative.

Farnow crossed the smoking-room, leaving Oberlé there.

Lucienne was anxiously awaiting him in the drawing-room. She saw him direct his steps towards Madame Oberlé, and, forcing himself to smile, place a chair near the arm-chair in which the fragile Alsatian lady in black was sitting. At the same time the Geheimrath called out, "Oberlé! You have smoked a cigar without even drinking one glass of beer. But that is a crime! Come. Professor Knäpple is explaining the measures the Government is taking to prevent the Russianising of the eastern provinces of Germany."

Late that night, a landau bore away to Alsheim three travellers; it had fetched them from the station at Molsheim.

The way there was a long one, and Lucienne soon went to sleep in the carriage. Her mother, who had hardly said anything up to then, bent towards her son, and, pointing to the beautiful creature sound asleep, asked him:

"You knew?"

"Yes."

"I guessed it. There was no need to tell me much. I have seen her look at him. Oh, Jean, this trial that I hoped to escape!—the fear of which has made me accept so many, many things! I have only you left, my Jean! But you remain to me!"

She kissed him fervently.

CHAPTER XI
IN SUSPENSE

As things do not usually happen as we foresee, the visit of Herr von Kassewitz to Alsheim did not take place on the date Farnow said it would. Towards the end of June—at the moment when the prefect, returned from taking the waters, was getting ready to go to ask for Lucienne's hand, a telegram had asked him to put off the visit. The condition of M. Philippe Oberlé had suddenly become worse.

The old man, whom it was necessary to inform of what was going on in the house, had just learned the truth. His son had gone up one morning to the sick man's room. "With circumlocution and in ways that he took out of respect and consideration for him, he let it be seen that Lucienne was not indifferent to the advances of a cavalry officer belonging to a high German family; he had said that the liking was spontaneous; that he, Joseph Oberlé, in spite of certain regrets, did not believe that he had the right to thwart the freedom of his children, and that he hoped that his father, in the interests of peace, would be resigned.

"My father," he said, "you are not ignorant of the fact that your opposition would be useless and purely vexatious. You have a chance to give Lucienne a great proof of your affection, as we ourselves have given; do not repulse her."

The old man had asked in signs:

"And Monica; has she consented?"

M. Joseph Oberlé had been able to answer yes, without telling a lie, for the poor woman, threatened with a separation, had yielded once more. Then the sick man put an end to his son's long monologue by writing two words, which were his answer:

"Not I!"

The same evening, fever declared itself. It continued the following day, and soon became so persistent and weakening that the condition of the sick man troubled the Oberlés.

From this day on, the health of M. Philippe Oberlé became the topic of anxious inquiries, evening and morning. They questioned Madame Monica or Jean, whom he received whilst excluding the others.

"How is he? Is his strength returning? Has he still all his wits about him—the full use of his mental faculties?"

Each one was wondering what was happening up above in the room where the old fighter, who had half disappeared from the world of the living, still governed his divided family, holding them all dependent on him. They spoke of their uneasiness, and under this name, which they rightly used, what projects were hid, what different thoughts!

Jean himself awaited the issue of this crisis with an impatience in which his affection for his grandfather was not the only interest involved. Since the explanation he had had with Lucienne, especially since the party at the Geheimrath's, all intimacy between brother and sister had ceased. Lucienne was as amiable and just as officiously kind as she could be, but Jean no longer responded to her advances. When work kept him no longer at the factories he fled from the house: sometimes to the country, where the first hay harvest attracted all the life from the Alsatian farms. Sometimes he would go and talk to his neighbours the Ramspachers, already his friends, when at nightfall they came back from the plain; and there he was led on by the hope that he should see the daughter of M. Bastian walking along the path. But more often still he went up to Heidenbruch. M. Ulrich had received his nephew's confidences and a mission at the same time. Jean had said to him:

"I have now no hope of winning Odile. My sister's marriage will prevent mine. But in spite of that I am bound to ask for the hand of her to whom I have confessed my love. I wish to be certain of what is already breaking my heart, although I am only afraid of it. When M. Bastian has heard that Lucienne is betrothed to Lieutenant von Farnow or that she is going to be—and that will not be delayed if grandfather gets better—you will go to M. Bastian. You will speak to him on my behalf. He will answer you, knowing fully all the facts; you will tell me if he refuses, once for all, his daughter to the brother-in-law of von Farnow; or if he insists on some time of probation—I will accept it, no matter how long it may be; or if he has the courage—in which I do not believe—to pay no attention to the scandal which my sister's marriage will cause."

M. Ulrich had promised.

Towards the middle of August the fever which was wearing out M. Philippe Oberlé disappeared. Contrary to the expectation of the doctor, his strength returned very quickly. It was soon certain that the robust constitution of the invalid had got the better of the crisis. And the truce accorded by M. Joseph Oberlé to his father had come to an end. The old man, having recovered to that sad condition of a sick man whom death does not desire, was going to be treated like the others, and would not be spared. There was no fresh scene between the sick man and his son. All went on quietly. On the 22nd of August, after dinner in the drawing-room, where Victor had just brought the coffee, the factory owner said to Madame Oberlé:

"My father is now convalescent. There is no longer any reason to put off the visit of Herr von Kassewitz. I give you notice, Monica, that it will take place during the next few days. You would do well to tell my father, since you alone go to him. And it is necessary that everything should be done in order, without anything like surprise or deception. Is that your opinion?"

"You do not wish to put off this visit any longer?"

"No."

"Then I will tell him!"

Jean wrote the same evening to Heidenbruch, where he was not able to go.

"My uncle, the visit is settled. My father makes no mystery about it; not even before the servants. He evidently wishes that the report of the marriage should be spread abroad. As soon as you hear some one from Alsheim get indignant or sad about us, go and see, I implore you, if the dream that I dreamed can still live on. You will tell M. Bastian that it is the grandson of M. Philippe Oberlé who loves Odile."

CHAPTER XII
THE HOP-PICKING

At the foot of Sainte Odile, a little below the vineyards in the deep earth formed by gravel and leaves fallen from the mountain, M. Bastian and other land-owners or farmers of Alsheim had planted hop-fields. Now the time was come when the flower produces its maximum of odorous pollen—a quickly passing hour difficult to seize.

The hop-planters appeared frequently in the hopfields. The brokers went through the villages. One heard buyers and sellers discussing the various merits of Wurtemburg hops and the Grand Duchy of Baden hops, and of Bohemian and Alsatian hops. The newspapers began to publish the first prices of the most famous home-grown: Hallertan, Spalt, and Wolnzach.

A Munich Jew had come to see M. Bastian on Sunday August 26, and had said to him:

"Wurtemburg is promising: Baden will have fine harvests: our own country of Spalt, in Bavaria, has hops which are paying us one hundred and sixty francs the fifty kilos, because they are rich hops—they are as full of the yellow aromatic powder as a grape of juice. Here you have been injured by the drought. But I can offer you one hundred and twenty francs on condition that you pick them at once. They are ripe."

M. Bastian had given in, and had called together his daily hop-pickers for August 28. That was also the day when the Count von Kassewitz was to pay his visit to M. Joseph Oberlé.

From dawn of a day already warmed by wafts of hot air, women had set themselves to walk up what is called "the heights of Alsheim," the region where the cultivated land, hollowed like a bow, will bear hops. Some hundreds of yards from the border of the forest high poles in battle array bore up the green tendrils. They looked like very pointed tents of foliage, or belfries—for the millions of little cones, formed of green scales sprinkled with pollen, swung themselves from the extreme top to the ground like bells whose ringer is the wind. All the inhabitants know the event of the day— one picks hops for M. Bastian. The master, up before dawn, was already in the hop-field, examining each foot, calculating the value of his crop, pressing and crushing in his fingers one of the little muslin-like pine cones whose perfume attracts the bees. At the back on the stubble furrows are two narrow wagons, harnessed to a horse, waiting for the harvest, and near them was Ramspacher the farmer, his two sons Augustin and François, and a farm servant. The women, on the direct road leading up there, came up in irregular bands, three in file, then five abreast, then one following the others, the only one who was old. Each one had put on a working dress of some thin stuff, discoloured and the worse for wear, except, however, the grocer's daughter, Ida, who wore a nearly new dress, blue with white spots, and another elegant girl from Alsheim, Juliette, a brunette, the daughter of the sacristan, and she had a fashionable bodice and a checked apron, pink and white. The greater number were without hats, and had only the shade of their hair, of every tint of fairness, to preserve their complexions. They walked along quietly and heavily. They were young and fresh. They laughed. The farm boy mounted on a farm horse, going to the fields, the reapers, encamped in a corner, and the motionless man with the scythe in the soft lucerne turned their heads, and their eyes followed these women workers, whom one did not generally see in the country: needlewomen, dressmakers, apprentices, all going as if to a fête towards the hop-field of M. Bastian. The vibration of words they could not hear flew to them on the wind that dried the dew. The weather was fair. Some old people, the pickers of fallen fruit beneath the scattered apple- and walnut-trees, rose from their stooping posture, and blinked their eyes to see the happy band of girls coming up the forest road. These girls without baskets such as the bilberry and whortleberry pickers, and raspberry gatherers had to carry.

They went into the hop-field, which contained eight rows of hops and disappeared as if in a gigantic vineyard. M. Bastian directed the work, and pointed out that they must begin with the part touching the road. Then the old farmer, his two sons and farm servant, seized each of them one of the poles, heavy with the weight of harvest, the tendrils, the little scaly bells, the leaves all trembled; and after the women had knelt down and had cut the stalks even with the ground, the loosened poles came out of the earth and were lowered and despoiled of the climbing plants they had carried.

Stalks, leaves, and flowers were thrown down and placed in heaps—to be carried away by the wagons. The workers did not wait to pick the hops which they would gather at Alsheim in the farmyard in the afternoon. But, already covered with yellow powder and pieces of leaves, the men and women were hurrying to strip the lowered poles. The hops exhaled their bitter, healthy odour, and the humming of the band of workers, like the noise of early vintage, spread out over the immense stretch of country, striped with meadows, stubble, and lucerne, and the open and fertile Alsatian land which the sun was beginning to warm.

This light, the repose of the night still neighbouring the day, the full liberty which they did not enjoy every day of the week, the instinctive coquetry evoked by the presence of the men, even the desire of being pleasant to M. Bastian, whom they knew to be of a gay disposition, made these girls and children who picked the hops joyful with a boisterous joy. And one of the farm servants having called out while his horses stopped to take breath: "Is no one singing then?" the daughter of the sacristan, Juliette, with the regular features and the beautiful deep eyes under her well combed and nicely dressed hair, answered:

"I know a lovely song."

As she answered she looked at the owner of the property, who was smoking, seated on the first row of stubble above the hop-field, and who was contemplating with tenderness now his hops and now his Alsace, where his mind always dwelt.

"If it is pretty; sing it," said the master. "Is it a song that the police may hear?"

"Part of it."

"Then turn round to the forest side: the police do not often go that way because they find nothing to drink there."

The workers who were stooping and those who were standing upright laughed silently because of the detestation in which they held the gendarmes. And the beautiful Juliette began to sing—of course in Alsatian—one of those songs which poets compose who do not care to sign their works, and who rhyme in contraband.

The full, pure voice sang:

"I have cut the hops of Alsace—they have grown on the soil we tilled—the green hops are certainly ours—the red earth is also ours."

"Bravo!" said gravely M. Bastian's farmer. He took his pipe from his mouth in order to hear better.

"They have grown in the valley—in the valley where every one has passed along, many sorts of people, and the wind, and also anguish—we have chosen our own friends.

"We will drink beer to the health of those who please us. We will have no words on our lips—but we will have words in our hearts—where no one can efface them."

The heavy, solid heads, young and old, remained motionless for a moment when Juliette had finished. They waited for the remainder. The young girls smiled because of the voice and because of life. The eyes of M. Bastian and the Ramspachers shone because of bygone days. The two sons had grown grave. Juliette did not begin to sing again: there was no more to follow.

"I think I know the miller who composed that song," said M. Bastian. "Come, my friends, hurry yourselves; there is the first cart starting for Alsheim. All must be gathered and put in the drying-house before night."

Everybody except that big young François, who had to do his military service in November, and who was driving the wagon, bent again over the hop roots. But at the same moment, from the copse on the border of the great forest, from among the shrubs and the clematis, which made a silky fringe to the mountain forests, a man's voice answered.

What was happening? Who had heard them? They thought they knew the voice, which was strong and unequal, worn, but with touches of a youthful quality; and whisperings arose.

"It is he. He is not afraid!"

The voice answered, in the same rugged tongue:

"The black bow of the daughters of Alsace—has bound my heart with sorrow—has bound my heart with joy. It is a knot of love.

"The black bow of the daughters of Alsace—is a bird with great wings. It can fly across the mountains—and look over them.

"The black bow of the daughters of Alsace is a cross of mourning which we carry in memory of all those—whose soul was like our own soul."

The voice had been recognised. When it had finished singing, the hop-pickers, men and women, began to talk to M. Ulrich, who, barely tolerated in Alsace, had nevertheless more freedom of language than the Alsatians who were German subjects. The noise of laughter and words exchanged grew louder and louder in the hop-field, so the master withdrew.

M. Bastian, with his heavy, sure step, mounted to the edge of the forest whence came the voice, and plunged under the beeches. Some one had seen him coming and waited for him. M. Ulrich Biehler, seated on a rock starred with moss—bare headed, weary with having walked in the sun—had hoped, by singing, to make his old friend Xavier Bastian climb up to him. He was not mistaken.

"I have a place for you here, hop-picker!" he cried from afar, pointing to a large block of stone which had rolled to the foot of the mountain, between two trees, and on which he was seated.

Although they were friends, M. Ulrich and the Mayor of Alsheim saw each other but seldom. There was between them less intimacy than a community of opinions and of aspirations and of memories. They were chosen friends, and old Alsace counted them among her faithful ones. That was enough to make them feel the meeting was a happy one, and to make the signal understood. M. Ulrich had said to himself that M. Bastian having set the workers to work would not be sorry to have a diversion. He had sung in answer to Juliette's song, and M. Bastian had come. Now the pale, fine face of the hermit of Heidenbruch reflected a mixture of pleasure in welcoming his friend and an anxiety difficult to conceal.

"You still sing?" said M. Bastian, pressing M. Ulrich's hand. "You hunt, you run about the hills!"

He sat down breathless on a stone, his feet in the ferns, and looking towards the descending slopes wooded with oaks and beeches and bushes.

"That only in appearance. I am a walker, a forester, a wanderer. You, on the contrary, are the least travelled of men. I visit—you cultivate: these are at bottom two kinds of fidelities. Tell me, Xavier, may I speak to you of something which I have very much at heart?"

The heavy face trembled, the thick lips moved, and one could see by the great change which took place in M. Bastian's face how sensitive he was. As he was of just as reticent a nature, he did not make any reply. He waited.

"I am going to tell you about something which touches me as nearly as if it were a personal matter. He who begged me to see you is my dearest relative. I take the direct method with you, Xavier. Have you guessed that my nephew loves your daughter Odile?"

"Yes."

"Well?"

Suddenly these two, who had been gazing into the distance for a while, looked at each other eye to eye, and they were afraid, one because of the refusal he read there—and the other because of the pain he was going to give.

"No!" said the voice, grown harsh in order to dominate its emotion, which would have made it tremble. "I will not!"

"I expected that; but if I tell you that they love each other?"

"That may be. I cannot!"

"You have some very serious reason then?"

"Yes."

"What is it?"

M. Bastian pointed through the trees to the house of the Oberlés.

"To-day, in that house, they are expecting the visit of the Prefect of Strasburg."

"I could not tell you, and I had to wait before speaking about it till every one knew it."

"It is public property now. All the town of Alsheim has been told by the servants. They even say that M. von Kassewitz is coming to ask for the hand of Lucienne for his nephew, Lieutenant von Farnow."

"I know it!"

"And you would have it so?"

"Yes!"

"That I should give my daughter to Jean Oberlé so that she should have a father-in-law who will be a governmental candidate in the coming elections and a brother-in-law who is a Prussian officer?"

M. Ulrich kept calm under the indignant gaze of M. Bastian and answered:

"Yes; these are terrible things for him, but it is not Jean's fault. Where will you find a man more worthy of you and of your daughter?"

"What is he doing to oppose this marriage? He is here—his silence gives consent. He is weak."

M. Ulrich stopped him with a movement.

"No; he is strong!"

"Not like you—you who knew how to close your house."

"My house belongs to me."

"And I have the right to say 'Not like me!' All these young people accept things too easily, my friend. I do not mix myself up with politics. I keep silent. I plough my land. I am looked on with suspicion by the peasants, who no doubt like me, but who begin to find me 'compromising.' I am hated by Germans of every kind and colour. But, as God hears me, that only makes me drive my roots deeper in, and I do not change. I will die with all my old hatreds intact—do you understand—intact?"

His eyes had a gleam in them such as a sharpshooter has when, with gun in hand, and sure that his hand will not tremble, he covers his enemy.

"You stand for something in this generation, Xavier; but you must not be unjust. This man you refuse, because he is not like us, is not the less valiant for that."

"That has to be seen."

"Has he not declared that he will not enter the Government employ?"

"Because the country pleases him better—and my daughter pleases him also!"

"No; firstly because he is Alsatian."

"Not like us, I will answer for that!"

"In a new way. They are obliged to live in the midst of Germans. Their education is carried out in German schools, and their way of loving France leaves room for more honour and more strength of mind than was necessary in our time. Think, it is thirty years ago!"

"Alas!"

"They saw nothing of those times, they have only a traditional love, or a love which is of the imagination, or of family, and examples of forgetfulness are frequent around them!"

"Jean has had, in truth, examples of that sort."

"That is why you ought to be more just to him. Think that your daughter in marrying him will found here an Alsatian family—very powerful, very wealthy. The officer will not live in Alsheim, nor even long in Alsace. He will soon be only a name."

M. Bastian placed his heavy hand on M. Ulrich's shoulder, and spoke in a tone which did not allow the discussion to be continued.

"Listen, my friend, I have only one word. It cannot be, because I will not have that marriage: because all those of my generation, dead and living, would reproach me. And then, even if I yielded, Ulrich, there is a will near me stronger than mine, who will never say yes, do you understand, never!"

M. Bastian slipped down among the ferns, and shrugging his shoulders, and shaking his head—like some one who will hear no more—went downwards to his day workers. When he had passed between the rows of the cut hops and reprimanded each of the workers, there was no more laughing, and the girls of Alsheim, and the farmer's sons, and the farmer himself, stooping under the burning sun, went on in silence with their work, which had been so joyously begun.

Already M. Ulrich was going up to his hermitage on Sainte Odile, distressed, asking himself what serious effect the refusal of M. Bastian was going to have on Jean's destiny, and anxious to tell his nephew the news. Without hoping, without believing that there was any chance of it, he would try to make Odile's father give way, and plans hummed round him, like the gadflies in the pine woods, drunk with the sun, and following the traveller in his lonely climb. The streams were singing. There were flocks of thrushes, harbingers crossing the ravines, darting through the blue air to get to the vines and fruits of the plain. It was in vain—he was utterly downcast. He could think of nothing but of his nephew, so badly rewarded for his return to Alsheim. Between the trees and round the branches he gazed at the house of the Oberlés.

Any one going into that house just then would have found it extraordinarily quiet. Every one there was suffering. M. Philippe Oberlé, as usual had lunched in his room. Madame Oberlé, at the express wish of her husband, had consented to come out of her room when M. von Kassewitz should be announced.

"All the same, I repeat," she said, "that I shall not go out of my way to entertain him. I will be there because by your orders I am bound to receive this person. But I shall not go beyond what is strictly necessary."

"Right," said M. Oberlé, "Lucienne, Jean, and I will talk to him. That will suffice."

And after his meal he had gone at once to his workroom, at the end of the park. Jean, who had shown no enthusiasm, had gone out, for his part, promising to return before three o'clock. Lucienne was alone in the big yellow drawing-room. Very well dressed in a grey princess dress, which had for its only ornament a belt buckle of two shades of gold, like the decorations in the dining-room; she was placing roses in crystal glasses and slender vases of transparent porcelain, which contrasted well with the hard, definite colour of the velvet furniture. Lucienne had the collectedness of a gambler who sees a game coming to an end, and knows she has won. She had herself, in two recent soirées at Strasburg carried the business through, which now wanted only the signatures of the contracting parties; the official candidature promised to M. Joseph Oberlé in the first vacant district.

The visit of M. von Kassewitz was equivalent to the signing of the treaty. The opposing parties held their tongues, as Madame Oberlé held hers, or stood aside in silent sulkiness, like the grandfather. The young girl went from the mantelpiece to the gilt console, surmounted by a mirror, in which she saw herself reflected, and she thought the movement of her lips very pretty when she made them say "Monsieur the Prefect!" One thing irritated her, and checked the pride she felt in her victory: the absolute emptiness which was making itself felt around her.

Even the servants seemed to have made up their minds not to be there when they were wanted. They did not answer the bell. After lunch M. Joseph Oberlé had been obliged to go into the servants' hall to find his father's valet, that good-tempered big Alsatian who looked upon himself as being at the beck and call of every one.

"Victor, you will put on your livery to receive the gentleman who will come about three o'clock!"

Victor had grown red and answered with difficulty:

"Yes, sir!"

"You must be careful to watch for the carriage, and to be at the bottom of the steps——"

"Yes, sir."

Since this promise had been given, which no doubt went very much against Victor's feelings—he had hid himself, and only came at the third or fourth call, quite flustered and pretending that he had not heard.

The Prefect of Strasburg is coming. These words which Lucienne had spoken, Madame Oberlé thought over shut up in her room. They weighed, like a storm cloud, on the mind of the old protesting representative of Alsace—that old forester, Philippe Oberlé, who had given orders that he was to be left alone; they agitated the nervous fingers of M. Joseph Oberlé, who was writing in his room at the saw mills, and he left off writing in order to listen; they rang sadly, like the passing bell of something noble in Jean's heart taking refuge with the Bastians' farmer. They were the theme—the *leitmotiv* which recurred in twenty different ways, in the animated and sarcastic conversation of the hop-pickers.

For these women and girls of the farm, and the day labourers who had worked in the morning in the hop-field, had assembled, since the mid-day meal in the narrow, long yard of the Ramspachers' farm. Seated on chairs or stools, each one having on their right a hamper or a basket and on their left a heap of hops, they picked off the flowers and threw away the stripped stalks. They formed two lines—one along the stable walls and the other the length of the house. This made an avenue of fair heads and bodies in movement among the piles of leaves, which stretched from one woman to another and bound them together as it were with a garland. At the end, the cart door opened wide on to the square of the town of Alsheim, and allowed the gables of several houses situated opposite to be seen—with their wooden balconies and the flat tiles of their roofings. By this road every half hour fresh loads of hops arrived drawn by one of the farm horses. Old Ramspacher, the farmer, was at his post, in the enormous barn in front of the dwelling-house, and before which sat the first pickers, at work on the little hop cones.

In this building, whose vast roof was supported by a wall on one side, on the other by Vosges pines, the greater part of the work of the farm was done, and much wealth was stored here. Here they trod the grapes; in the autumn and winter months they threshed corn. They kept all the implements of labour in the corner—the covered carts, planks and building materials, empty barrels, and a little hay. There were also many great wooden cases piled up, tiers of screens, on which they put the hops to dry every year. The farmer never allowed others to do this delicate work. So he was at his place, in front of the drying-room, where the first shelves were already full, and standing on a ladder he spread equal layers of the gathered hops, which his sons brought him in hampers.

The heat of the afternoon, at the end of August, the odour of crushed leaves and flowers, which clung to their hands intoxicated the women slightly. The laughter rose louder than in the hop-fields in the morning, and questions were asked and remarks made which called forth twenty answers. Sometimes it was the work which furnished a pretext for this fusillade of words. Sometimes it was a neighbour passing across the square all white with dust and sunshine; but mostly the talk was about two things: the visit of the Prefect and the probable marriage of Lucienne.

The beautiful Juliette, the sacristan's daughter, had begun the conversation saying:

"I tell you Victor told it to the mason's son: the Prefect is to arrive in half an hour. Do you think I shall move when he comes?"

"He would see a very pretty girl," said Augustine Ramspacher, lifting up two hampers of hops. "It is only the ugly ones who will let themselves be seen."

Ida, who had lifted up her blue-and-white-spotted dress, and then Octavie the cow-woman, who wore her hair plaited and rolled like a golden halo round her head, and Reine the daughter of the poor tailor, and others answered together laughing:

"I shall not be seen then. Nor I, nor I!"

And an old woman's voice, the only old woman among them, muttered:

"I know I am as poor as Peter and Paul, but I would rather that he went to other folk's houses than to mine—the Prefect!"

"Certainly."

They were all speaking freely. Words re-echoed from the walls and were lost amid bursts of laughter and the rustling of the broken and crushed leaves. In the barn in the half light, seated on a pile of beams, his chin in his hands, there was a witness who heard, and that witness was Jean Oberlé. But the inhabitants of Alsheim began to know the young man, who had lived among them for five months. They knew he was a good Alsatian. On the present occasion they guessed that Jean had taken refuge there with the Bastians' tenant farmer because he disapproved the ambition to which his father was sacrificing so many things and so many persons. He had come in, under the pretext of resting and taking shelter from the sun; in reality because the triumphant presence of Lucienne was torture to him. And yet he knew nothing of the conversation which his uncle had had in the morning with M. Bastian. The thought of Odile returned to his unhappy mind and he drove it out that he might remain master of himself, for soon he would require all his powers of judgment and all his strength. At other moments he gazed vaguely at the hop-pickers and tried to interest himself in their work and their talk; often he thought he heard the sound of a carriage, and half rising, he remembered the promise he had made, to be at home when M. von Kassewitz arrived.

Juliette's voice rose in decidedly spirited tones.

"What does this Prefect of Strasburg want to come to Alsheim for? We get on so well without the Germans."

"They have sworn to make themselves hated," quickly added the farmer's elder son, who was giving out the hops to the women who had no more. "It seems that they are prohibiting the speaking of French as much as they possibly can."

"A proof—my cousin, François Joseph Steiger," said little Reine, the tailor's daughter. "A gendarme said he had heard him shout 'Vive la France!' in the inn. Those were, I believe, the only French words my cousin knew. That was enough—my cousin got two months in prison."

"Your cousin called out more! But at Alberschweiler they have forbidden a singing society to execute anything in the French tongue."

"And the French conjurer who came the other day to Strasburg? Do you know? It was in the newspaper. They let him pay the tax, hire the hall, print his advertisements, and then they said: 'You will do it in German, my good friend—or you will go!'"

"What happened to M. Haas, the house-painter, is much worse."

"What then?"

"He knew that he could not paint an inscription in French on a shop any more. M. Haas would never—I know it—have painted a stroke of a brush in contravention of the law. But he thought he could at least put a coat of varnish on the sign he was painting, where he had painted a long time ago the word '*Chemiserie*.' They made him appear and threatened to take proceedings against him, because he was preserving the inscription with his varnish. Why, that was last October!"

"Oh, oh, would not M. Hamm be pleased if the rain, the wind, and the thunder threw down the sign of the inn here, which is called: 'Le Pigeon blanc' as happened to 'La Cigogne.'"

It was old Josephine the bilberry-picker who said to the farmer's wife, who at this moment appeared on the threshold of her house:

"Sad Alsace! How gay she was when we were young! Wasn't she, Madame Ramspacher?"

"Yes. Now—for nothing—evictions, lawsuits, and prison! The police everywhere."

"You had better keep silence!" said Ramspacher in a reproachful tone.

The younger son Francis took his mother's side.

"There are no traitors here. And then, how can one keep silence? They are too hard. That is why so many young men emigrate!"

From his corner in the shadow, Jean looked at these young girls who were listening—with flashing eyes, some motionless and erect, others continuing to bend and rise over their work of stripping the hop-plants.

"Work then—instead of so much chattering!" said the master's voice.

"One hundred and seventy unsubdued, and condemned by the tribunal at Saverne, in a single day, last January," said Juliette with a laugh that shook her hair. "One hundred and seventy!"

Francis, the great careless boy, who was close by Jean Oberlé at this moment, turned a basketful of hops on the shelf, and bending towards him said:

"It is at Grand Fontaine that one can easily get over the frontier," he said in low tones. "The best crossing, Monsieur Oberlé, is between Grande Fontaine and Les Minières. The frontier is opposite, like a spur. That is the nearest part, but one has to take care of the Forest Guard and the Custom officials. Often they stop people to ask where they are going."

Jean trembled. What did that mean? He began:

"Why do you speak to...?"

But the young peasant had turned away, and was going on with his work. Doubtless he had spoken for himself. He had trusted his plan to his melancholy and silent countryman, whom he would amuse, astonish, or sympathise with.

But Jean had been touched by this confidence.

A clear voice called out:

"There is the carriage coming into the town. It is going to pass M. Bastian's avenue!"

All the hop-pickers raised their heads. Little Franzele was standing up near the pillar which kept the door open—leaning the top of her body over the wall, her curly hair blown by the wind. She was looking to the right, whence came the sound of wheels. In the yard the women had stopped working. She murmured:

"The Prefect, there he is—he is going to pass."

The farmer, drawn from his work by the women's sudden silence as much as by the child's voice, turned towards the yard where the hop-pickers were listening motionless to the noise of the wheels and the horses coming nearer. He commanded:

"Shut the cart-door, Franzele!"

He added, muttering:

"I will not let him see how it is done here—in my place!"

The little girl pushed-to one of the sides of the door, then curious, having stuck her head out again:

"Oh, how funny. Well, he cannot say that he saw many people. They have not disturbed themselves much on his account! There are only the German women of course. They are all there near 'la Cigogne.'"

"Will you shut that door?" replied the farmer angrily.

This time he was obeyed. The second side of the door shut quickly against the first. The twenty persons present heard the noise of the carriage rolling in the silence of the town of Alsheim. There were eyes in all the shadowy corners behind the windows—but no one went outside their doors, and in the gardens the men who were digging the borders seemed so entirely absorbed in their work as to have heard nothing.

When the carriage was about fifty yards past the farm, their imaginations were full of what it would be like at the Oberlés' farther on at the other end of the village, and taking up a handful of hop-stalks, the women and girls asked each other curiously what the son of M. Oberlé was going to do—and they looked stealthily towards the barn. He was no longer there.

He had risen, that he might not break his word, and having run all the way, and pale in spite of his having run, he arrived at the gate of the kitchen garden at the very moment when the Prefect's carriage, on the other side of the demesne, was passing through the park gates.

All the household was ready. Lucienne and Madame Oberlé were seated near the mantelpiece. They did not speak to each other. The factory owner, who had returned from his office half-an-hour ago, had put on the coat he wore to go to Strasburg, and a white waistcoat—with his arms behind his back he watched the carriage coming round the lawn.

The programme was carried out according to the plans arranged by him. The official personage who was just entering the grounds was bringing to M. Oberlé the assurance of German favour. For a moment of inflated pride which thrilled him M. Oberlé saw in imagination the palace of the Reichstag.

"Monica," he said, turning round as breathless as after a long walk, "has your son returned?"

Seated before him in the yellow chair near the fireplace, looking very thin, her features drawn with emotion, Madame Oberlé answered:

"He will be here because he said so!"

"The fact that he is not here is more certain still. And Count Kassewitz is coming—and Victor? I suppose he is at the steps to show him in, as I told him?"

"I suppose so."

M. Joseph Oberlé, furious at the constraint of his wife—at her disapproval, which he encountered even in this submission, crossed the room and pulled the old bell rope violently, and opening the door which led to the hall saw that Victor was not in his place.

He had to draw back, for the sound of footsteps coming up were mingled with the sound of the bell.

M. Joseph Oberlé placed himself near the fireplace facing the door—near his wife. Footsteps sounded on the gravel, on the granite of the steps. However, some one had come in answer to the bell. The door was pushed open the next moment and the Oberlés perceived at the same time that the old cook Salomé, white as wax, her mouth set, was opening the door without saying a word, and M. von Kassewitz close behind her was coming in.

He was very tall, very broad shouldered, and clad in a tight-fitting frock-coat. His face was composed of two incongruous elements, a round bulging forehead, round cheeks, a round nose, then standing straight out from the skin in stiff locks, eyebrows, moustache, and short, pointed beard. This face of a German soldier composed of points and arches was animated by two piercing lively eyes, which ought to have been blue—for his hair was yellow—but which never showed clearly through the shadow of the spreading eyebrows, and because of the man's habit of screwing up his eyelids. His hair, sparse on the top, was brushed up well from the occiput to just above the ears.

M. Joseph Oberlé met him and spoke in German.

"M. Prefect, we are very greatly honoured by this visit. Really to have taken this trouble!"

The official took the hand that M. Oberlé held out, and pressed it. But he did not look at him and he did not stop. His steps sounded heavily on the thick drawing-room carpet. He was looking at the thin apparition in mourning near the fireplace. And the enormous man bowed several times very stiffly.

"The Count von Kassewitz," said M. Oberlé—for the Prefect had never been introduced to the mistress of the house.

She made a slight movement of the head and said nothing. M. von Kassewitz drew himself up, waited a second, then playing his part and affecting good humour, which perhaps he did not feel, he greeted Lucienne, who had blushed, and was smiling.

"I remember having seen Mademoiselle at His Excellency the Statthalter's," he said. "And truly Strasburg is some distance from Alsheim. But I am of the opinion that there are some wonders which are better worth the journey than the ruins in the Vosges, M. Oberlé."

He laughed with a satisfied air, and sat on the yellow couch with his back to the light, facing the fireplace. Then turning to the factory owner, who was seated near him he asked:

"Is your son away?"

M. Oberlé had been listening anxiously for a minute. He was able to say:

"Here he is."

The young man came in. The first person he saw was his mother. That made him hesitate. His eyes, young and impressionable, gave a nervous twitch as if they were hurt. Quickly he turned to the sofa, took the hand which the visitor offered him, and gravely but less embarrassed than his father, and with greater coolness he said in French:

"I have just been for a walk. I had to run not to be late, for I promised my father I would be here when you came."

"You are too kind," said the official, laughing. "We speak German with your father, but I am able to carry on a conversation in another tongue besides our national language."

He went on in French, laying stress on the first syllables of the words.

"I admired your park, Monsieur Oberlé, and even all the little country of Alsheim. It is very pretty. You are surrounded, I believe, by a refractory population—almost invisible; in any case, just now as I came through the village I hardly saw a living soul."

"They are in the fields," said Madame Oberlé.

"Who is the Mayor, then?"

"M. Bastian."

"I remember them: a family very much behind the times."

His look was questioning, and he moved his heavy head towards the two women and Jean. Three answers came at once.

"Behind the times, yes," said Lucienne—"they are, but such good people."

"They are simply old-fashioned folk," said Madame Oberlé.

Jean said:

"Above all very worthy."

"Yes, I know what that means."

The Prefect made an evasive gesture.

"Well, provided they go straight."

The father saved the situation.

"We have but few interesting things to show you, but perhaps you would like to see my works? They are full and animated, I assure you. There are one hundred workmen, and machines at work—pines sixty feet long under the branches, are reduced in three minutes to planks, or cut up as rafters. Would you care to see them?"

"Yes, certainly."

The conversation, thus turned in another direction at once became less constrained. The origin of the Oberlés' works, the Vosges woods, the comparison between the German manner of felling, by the Government, and the French system, by which the owners of a portion of a forest may fell the trees themselves under the supervision of the foresters—all these questions gave each a chance to speak. Lucienne became lively, Madame Oberlé, questioned by her husband, answered. Jean also spoke. The functionary congratulated himself on having come.

When her father made a sign, Lucienne rose, to ring for the footman and to ask that some refreshment might be served. But she had not time to make a single step.

The door opened, and Victor, the servant who had not been at his post a short time ago, appeared, very red, very embarrassed, and lowering his eyes. On his left arm, holding himself as erect as possible, was the grandfather, M. Philippe Oberlé.

The five persons talking were all standing. The servant stopped at the door and withdrew. The old man came in alone, leaning on his stick. M. Philippe Oberlé had put on his best clothes belonging to the time when he was in good health. He wore, unbuttoned, the frock-coat which was still decorated by the ribbon of the Legion of Honour. Intense feeling had transfigured him. One would have said that he was twenty years younger. He came forward taking short steps—his body bent a little forward, but his head held stiffly erect, and he looked at one man only, the German official standing by the side of the couch. His heavy jaw trembled and moved convulsively as if he were articulating words they could not hear.

Was M. Joseph Oberlé mistaken, or did he wish to put him on the wrong scent? He turned to where M. von Kassewitz was standing, astonished and on his guard, and said:

"My father has surprised us by coming down. I never expected he would take part in this."

The eyes of the old deputy, rigid under their heavy lids, did not cease looking at the German, who kept his countenance and remained silent. When M. Philippe Oberlé was three feet from M. von Kassewitz he stopped. With his left hand, which was free, he then drew his slate from the pocket of his frock-coat, and held it out to the Count von Kassewitz: on it two lines were written. The Count bent forward and then drew himself up haughtily.

"Sir!"

Already M. Joseph Oberlé had seized the thin sheet of slate, and read these words, traced with remarkable decision:

"I am in my own house, sir!"

The eyes of the old Alsatian added:

"Leave my house!" and they were no longer looking down, nor did they leave the enemy.

"This is too much!" said M. Joseph Oberlé. "Father, how could you come downstairs to insult my guests? You will excuse him, sir; my father is old, over-excited, a little touched by age."

"If you were younger, sir," said M. von Kassewitz in his turn, "we should not stop at this. You will do well to remember that you are also in my home, in Germany, on German territory, and that it is not well even at your age to insult authority."

"Father," said Madame Oberlé, hastening to the old man to support him, "I beg of you—you are doing harm to yourself—this emotion is too much for you."

An extraordinary thing happened. M. Philippe Oberlé, in his violent anger, had found strength to stand upright. He appeared gigantic. He was as tall as M. von Kassewitz. The veins on his temples swelled—the blood was in his cheeks, and his eyes were living once more. And at the same time the half-dead body was trembling and using up in involuntary movements its fragile and factitious life. He signed to Madame Oberlé to stand aside, and not to hold him up.

Lucienne, grown pale, shrugged her shoulders and went towards M. von Kassewitz.

"It is only an act in one of our family tragedies, monsieur. Do not take any notice of it and come to the works with us. Let me pass, grandfather."

The Count took no notice, and she passed out between M. Philippe Oberlé and the functionary who said:

"You are not responsible, mademoiselle, for the insult that has been offered to me. I understand the situation—I understand."

His voice came with difficulty from his contracted throat. Furious—half a head taller than any one there except M. Philippe Oberlé—M. von Kassewitz turned on his heel and went towards the door.

"Come, I pray you," said M. Joseph Oberlé, standing aside to let the Prefect pass.

Lucienne was already outside. Madame Oberlé, as ill from emotion as the old man, who refused her assistance, feeling her tears choke her, ran into the hall and up to her room, where she burst into sobs.

In the drawing-room Jean was alone with the old chief, who had just driven out the stranger. He drew near and said:

"Grandfather, what have you done?"

He wanted to say: It is a terrible insult. My father will never forgive it. The family is completely broken up. He would have said all that. But he raised his eyes to the old fighter, so near the end, still showing fight. He saw now that the grandfather was gazing fixedly at him; that his anger had reached its height; that his chest was moving violently; that the face grimaced and twisted. And suddenly, in the yellow drawing-room, an extraordinary voice, a hoarse voice, powerful and husky, cried out in a kind of nervous gallop:

"Go away! Go away! Go away! Go away!"

The voice rose to a piercing note. Then it broke, and with his mouth still open, the old man reeled and fell on the floor. The voice had sounded to the inmost recesses of the house. This voice that no one ever heard now, Madame Oberlé had recognised it, and through the open door of her room she had been able to catch the words. It was only a cry of rage and suffering, or the contrary to M. Joseph Oberlé, when the terrible sound of the words, which could not be distinguished or guessed at, reached him down two-thirds of the garden path. He had turned for a moment, with a frown—while the foremen and German workmen of the factory greeted M. von Kassewitz with their cheers—then he went on towards them.

Madame Oberlé was the first to run to the drawing-room, then Victor, then old Salome, as white as a sheet, crying with uplifted hands:

"Was not that M. Philippe I heard?"

Then the coachman and the gardener ran in, hesitating to come forward but curious to see this distressing scene. They found Jean and his mother kneeling near M. Philippe Oberlé, who was breathing with difficulty, and was in a state of complete prostration. His effort, his emotion, and his indignation had used up the strength of the old man. They raised him up, and sat him in a chair, and each one tried to revive him. For a quarter of an hour there was going and coming between the first floor and the dining-room. They fetched vinegar, salts, and ether.

"I was afraid that master would have an attack; he has been beside himself all the morning. Ah, there he is moving his eyes a little. His hands are not so cold.

Across the park there came a cry of "Long live the Prefect!" It entered the drawing-room wafted on the warm breeze, where such words had never been heard before. M. Philippe Oberlé did not seem to hear them. But after some minutes he made a sign that he wished to be taken to his room.

Some one came up the steps quickly, and before coming in asked:

"What, again! What are those cries? Ah! my father!"

He changed his tone and said:

"I thought it was you, Monica—that you had a nervous attack. But then who screamed like that?"

"He!"

"He?" said M. Oberlé; "that is not possible!"

He did not dare to ask the question again. His father, now standing, supported by Jean and by his servant, trembling and wavering, moved across the room.

"Jean," said Madame Oberlé, "see to everything. Do not leave your grandfather; I am coming up."

Her husband had kept her back. She wished to get Jean away from this. As soon as she was alone with M. Oberlé on the staircase they heard the noise of footsteps and the rustling of materials, and voices saying:

"Hold him up—take care in turning."

"What did he call out?" asked M. Oberlé.

"He called out: 'Go away! Go away!' Those are words that he often uses, you know."

"The only ones he had at his disposal to show his hatred. Did he say nothing else?"

"No. I came down at once and I found him on the floor. Jean was near him."

"Happily M. von Kassewitz did not witness this second act. The first was enough. In truth, the whole household was leagued together to make this visit—such an honour for us—an occasion of offence and scandal: my father; Victor, who was not ashamed to be an accomplice of the delirious old man; Jean, who was impertinent; you———"

"I did not think you could have had to complain of me!"

"Of you the very first! It is you who are the soul of this resistance, which I *will* overcome. I shall overcome it! I answer for that."

"My poor friend," she said, clasping her hands; "you are still set on that!"

"Exactly."

"You cannot overcome everything, alas!"

"That is what we are going to see."

Madame Oberlé did not answer and went upstairs quickly. A new anxiety, stronger than the fear of her husband's threats, tortured her now.

"What did my father-in-law wish to say?" she asked herself. "The old man is not delirious. He remembers; he foresees; he watches over the house; he always thinks things out carefully. If only Jean did not understand it as I understand it!"

At the top of the stairs she met her son, who was coming out of the grandfather's room.

"Well?"

"Nothing serious, I hope—he is better—he wishes to be alone."

"And you?" questioned the mother, taking her son's hand, and leading him towards the room he used. "And you?"

"How? I?"

When he had shut the door behind her, she placed herself before him, and her face quite white in the light of the window, her eyes fixed on the eyes of her child:

"You quite understood—did you not—what grandfather wished to say?"

"Yes."

She tried to smile, and it was heart-breaking to see this effort of a tortured soul.

"Yes. He cried: 'Go away!' It is a word he often used to say to strangers. He was addressing M. von Kassewitz. You do not think so?"

Jean shook his head.

"But, my darling, he could not 'address others so!'"

"Pardon; he meant it for me."

"You are mad! You are the best friends in the world, you and your grandfather."

"Just so."

"He did not wish to turn you out of the room?"

"No."

"Then?"

"He was ordering me to leave the house."

"Jean!"

"And for all that, the poor man was delighted to see me come back to it."

Jean would not look at his mother now, because tears had gushed from Madame Oberlé's eyes, because she had come close to him, because she had taken his hands.

"No, Jean, no; he could not have meant that, I assure you; you do not understand. In any case, you will not do it! Say that you will never do it."

She waited for the answer, which did not come.

"Jean, for pity's sake answer me! Promise me that you will not leave us! Oh! what would the house be without my son now? I have only you—you do not think I am miserable enough then? Jean, look at me!"

He could not wholly resist her. She saw the eyes of her son looking at her tenderly.

"I love you with all my heart," said Jean.

"I know it; but do not go away!"

"I pity you and respect you."

"Do not go away!"

And as he said no more she moved away.

"You will promise nothing. You are hard—you also are like——"

She was going to say "Like your father."

Jean thought: "I can give her some weeks of peace; I owe them to her." And trying to smile in his turn said:

"I promise you, mamma, to be at St. Nicholas's Barracks on October 1st—I promise you. Are you pleased?"

She shook her head. But he, kissing her on the brow, not wishing to say anything more, left her in haste.

The town of Alsheim was occupying itself with the scene which had taken place at M. Oberlé's. Through the torrid evening heat, amidst the fertile dust of the cut wheat, of the pollen of flowers, of dried moss which was blown from one field to another, the men came home on foot; the children and young people came on horseback, and the tails of the horses were gold, or silver, or black, or fire-coloured in the burning light which the setting sun cast over the shoulder of the Vosges. Women were waiting for their husbands on the thresholds, and when they drew near, went to meet them in their haste to spread such important news.

"You do not know what has happened at the works. They will speak about it for a long time! It seems that old M. Philippe found his voice in his anger, and that he drove the Prussian out!"

Many of the peasants said:

"You will speak of that at home, wife, when the door is shut!"

Many remarked with anxiety the agitation of their neighbours, and said:

"This will end in a visit from the gendarmes!"

At M. Bastian's farm the women and young girls were finishing their hop-picking. They were chattering, still laughing, or anxious, according to their age. The farmer had forbidden them to reopen the door looking on to the village street. He went on, always prudent in spite of his seeming joviality, to spread out the baskets of hop flowers, shining with fresh pollen. The oxen and the horses, passing near the yard, breathed in the air and stretched their necks.

And one at a time the women got up, shook their aprons, and weary, stretched their youthful arms, yawning at the freshness of the cool puffs of air which came over the roof, then started on their more or less distant way to home and supper.

At the Oberlés' house the dinner-bell rang. The meal was the shortest and the least gay that the wainscoting and delicately tinted paintings had ever witnessed.

Very few words were exchanged.

Lucienne was thinking of the new difficulty in the way of her projected marriage and of the violent irritation of M. von Kassewitz; Jean, of the hell that this house of the family had become; M. Oberlé, of his ambitions probably ruined; Madame Monica, of the possible departure of her son. Towards the end of dinner, at the moment when the servant was about to withdraw, M. Oberlé began to say, as if he were continuing a conversation:

"I am not accustomed, you know, my dear, to give in to violence: it exasperates me, that is all. I am then resolved to do two things—first to build another house in the timber-yard, where I shall be in my own home, then to hasten on Lucienne's marriage with Lieutenant von Farnow. Neither you nor my father nor any one can stop me. And I have just written to him about it."

M. Oberlé looked at each of them—his wife, son, and daughter—with the same expression of defiance. He added:

"These young people must be allowed to see each other and to talk to each other freely, betrothed as they are."

"Oh," said Madame Oberlé, "such things——"

"They are so!" he answered, "by my will, and dating from this evening. Nothing will alter it, nothing. I cannot let them meet here, unfortunately. My father would plan some fresh scandal—or you," and he pointed to his son; "or you," and he pointed to his wife.

"You are mistaken," said Madame Oberlé. "I suffer cruelly on account of this arrangement, but I shall make no scandal which will nullify what you have decided upon."

"Then," said M. Oberlé, "you have the chance to prove your words. I was not going to ask you to do anything, and I had decided to take Lucienne to Strasburg to the house of a third person, who would have let them meet in her drawing-room."

"I have never deserved that."

"Will you then agree to accompany your daughter?"

She thought for a moment, shut her eyes, and said:

"Certainly."

There was a look of surprise in her husband's eyes, and in Jean's, and also in Lucienne's.

"I shall be delighted; for my arrangement did not quite suit my fancy. It is more natural that you should take your daughter. But what rendezvous do you intend to choose?"

Madame Monica answered:

"My house at Obernai."

A movement of stupefaction made the father and son both straighten themselves. The house at Obernai? The home of the Biehlers? The son at least understood the sacrifice which the mother was making, and he rose and kissed her tenderly.

M. Oberlé himself said:

"That is right, Monica—very right. And when will it be convenient to you?"

"Just the time to let M. de Farnow know about it. You will fix the day and the hour—write to him when he answers you."

Lucienne, in spite of her want of tenderness, drew closer to her mother that evening. In the little drawing-room, where she worked at crochet for two hours, she sat near Madame Oberlé, and with her watchful eyes she followed, or tried to follow, the thoughts on the lined face so mobile and still so expressive. But often one can only partly read what is passing in a mind. Neither Lucienne nor Jean guessed the reason which had so quickly prompted Madame Oberlé's act of self-sacrifice.

CHAPTER XIII
THE RAMPARTS OF OBERNAI

Ten days later, Lucienne and her mother had just entered the family house where Madame Oberlé had spent all her childhood, the home of the Biehlers, which lifted its three stories of windows with little green panes, and its fortified gable above the ramparts of Obernai, between two houses of the sixteenth century—just like it.

Madame Oberlé had gone upstairs, saying to the caretaker:

"You will receive a gentleman presently who will ask for me."

In the large room on the first floor which she entered, one of the few rooms which were still furnished, she had seen her parents live and die; the walnut-wood bed, the brown porcelain stove, the chairs covered with woollen velvet which repeated on every seat and every back the same basket of flowers, the crucifix framed under raised glass, the two views of Italy brought back from a journey in 7, all remained in the same places and in the same order as in the old days. Instinctively in crossing the threshold she sought the holy water stoup hanging near the lintel, where the old people, when they went into the room, moistened their fingers as on the threshold of a holy abode.

The two women went towards the window. Madame Oberlé wore the same black dress she had put on to receive the Prefect of Strasburg. Lucienne had put on a large brimmed hat of grey straw, trimmed with feathers of the same shade, as if to cover her fair hair with a veil of shadow. Her mother thought her beautiful—and did not say so. She would have hastened to say so if the betrothed had not been he whom they expected, and if the sight of the house, and the memory of the good Alsatian folk who had lived in it, had not made the pain she already felt greater.

She leant against the windows and looked down into the garden full of box-trees clipped into rounded shapes, and flower borders outlined by box, and the winding, narrow paths where she had played, grown up, and dreamed. Beyond the garden there was a walk made on the town ramparts, and between the chestnuts planted there one could see the blue plain.

Lucienne, who had not spoken since the arrival at Obernai, guessing that she would have disturbed a being who was asking herself whether she could continue and complete her sacrifice, came quite close to her mother, and with that intelligence which always took everyone's fancy the first time they heard it, but less the second time:

"You must suffer, mamma," she said. "With your ideas, what you are doing is almost heroic!"

The mother did not look up, but her eyelids fluttered more, and quickly.

"You are doing it as a wifely duty, and because of that I admire you. I do not believe I could do what you are doing—give up my individuality to such an extent."

She did not think she was being cruel.

"And you wish to be married?" asked the mother, raising her head quickly.

"Why, yes; but we do not now look upon marriage quite as you do."

The mother saw from Lucienne's smile that she would be contending with a fixed idea, and she felt that the hour for discussion was badly chosen. She kept silence.

"I am grateful to you," continued the young girl. Then after a moment of hesitation:

"Nevertheless, you had another reason besides obeying my father when you agreed to come here—here to receive M. von Farnow."

She let her eyes wander round the room, and brought them back to the woman with smooth hair—that worn-out and suffering woman—who was her mother. There was no hesitation.

"Yes," she said.

"I was sure of it. Can you tell me what it is?"

"Presently."

"Before M. von Farnow?"

"Yes."

Keen annoyance changed the expression of Lucienne's face; it grew hard.

"Although we do not agree with each other very well, surely you are not capable of trying to turn my betrothed against me?"

Tears appeared in the corners of Madame Oberlé's eyelids.

"Oh Lucienne!"

"No, I do not believe it. It is something important?"

"Yes."

"Does it concern me?"

"No; not you."

The young girl opened her mouth to continue, then listened, became a little pale, and turned completely towards the door, while her mother turned only half-round in the same direction. Some one was coming upstairs. Wilhelm von Farnow, preceded by the caretaker, who accompanied him only as far as the landing, saw Madame Oberlé through the opening of the door, and as if on a military parade, he drew himself up and crossed the room quickly, and bowed his haughty head first to the mother, then to the young girl.

He was extremely well dressed in civilian clothes. His face was drawn and pallid with emotion. He said gravely in French:

"I thank you, madame!"

Then he looked at Lucienne, and in his unsmiling blue eyes there was a gleam of proud joy.

The young girl smiled.

Madame Oberlé felt a shudder of aversion, which she tried to repress. She looked straight into the steel-blue eyes of Wilhelm von Farnow, who stood motionless in the same attitude he would have taken under arms and before some great chief.

"You must not thank me. I play no part in what is happening. My husband and my daughter have decided everything."

He bowed again.

"If I were free I should refuse your race, your religion, your army—which are not mine. You see I speak to you frankly. I am determined to tell you that you owe me nothing, but also that I harbour no unjust animosity against you. I even believe that you are a very good soldier and an estimable man. I am so convinced of it that I am going to confide to you an anxiety which tortures me."

She hesitated a moment and continued:

"We had at Alsheim a terrible scene when Count Kassewitz came to the house."

"Count Kassewitz told me about it, madame. He even advised me to give up the idea of marrying your daughter. But I shall not do that. To make me give her up nothing short of——"

He began to laugh—

"Nothing short of an order from the Emperor would make me! I am a good German, as you say. I do not easily give up what I have won. And Count Kassewitz is only my uncle."

"What you do not know is that my father-in-law, for the first time for many, many years, in his exasperation, in the excess of his grief, has spoken. He cried out to Jean: 'Go away! Go away!' I heard the words. I ran quickly. Well, sir, what moved me most was not seeing M. Philippe Oberlé senseless, stretched upon the floor; it was my son's expression, and it is my conviction that at that moment he resolved to obey and to leave Alsace."

"Oh," said Farnow, "that would be bad."

He cast a glance at the fair Lucienne, and saw that she was shaking her blond head in sign of denial.

"Yes, bad," continued the mother without understanding in what sense Farnow used the word. "What an old age for me in my divided house—without my daughter, whom you are going to take away; without my son, who will have gone away. You are astonished, perhaps, that I should tell you an anxiety of this sort?"

He made a gesture which might mean anything.

"It is because," the mother continued more quickly, "I have no one to advise me; no help to hope for—under the circumstances. Understand clearly. To whom shall I go? To my husband? He would be furious? He would start to work and we should find that by his influence Jean would be incorporated in a German regiment in a week's time—away in the north or the east. My brother? He would rather insist on my son leaving Alsace. You see, monsieur, you are the only one who can do anything."

"What exactly?"

"But much. Jean has promised me that he will join the regiment. You can arrange that he shall be received and welcomed, and not discouraged. You can assure him protection, society, comrades—you have known him a long time. You can prevent his giving way to melancholy ideas, and stop him if he were again tempted to carry out such a plan."

The lieutenant, much disturbed, frowned, and the expression of his face changed at the last words. Then he said:

"Up to the first of October you have your son's promise—after that I will look after him."

Then speaking to himself, and again occupied with an idea, which he did not express entirely:

"Yes," he said, "very bad—it must not be."

Lucienne heard it.

"So much the worse," said she. "I betray my brother's secret, but he will forgive me when he knows that I betrayed him to calm mamma. You can be easy, mamma, Jean will not leave Alsace."

"Because?"

"He loves."

"Where then?"

"At Alsheim!"

"Whom?"

"Odile Bastian."

Madame Oberlé asked absolutely amazed:

"Is it true?"

"As true as we are here. He told me everything."

The mother closed her eyes, and, choking with halting breath:

"God be praised. A little hope rises in my heart. Let me cry—indeed I must!"

She pointed to the room, which was also open on the other side of the landing and was lighted by a large bay window, through which a tree could be seen.

Farnow bowed, showing Lucienne that he was following her.

And the girl moved on ahead, passing through the room where her ancestors had loved Alsace so much.

Madame Oberlé turned away; sitting near the window she leaned her head against the panes where as a child she had seen the sleet and the ice form into ferns, and the sun, and the rain, and the vibrating airs of summer-time, and all the land of Alsace.

"Odile Bastian! Odile!" repeated the poor woman. The bright face, the smile, the dresses of the young girl, the corner of Alsheim where she lived— a whole poem of beauty and moral health rose in the mother's mind; and with an effort she held to it jealously, in order to forget the other love-affair on account of which she had come here.

"Why did not Jean confide in me?" she thought. "This is a kind of compensation for the other. It reassures me. Jean will not leave us, since the strongest of ties binds him to the country. Perhaps we shall succeed in overcoming my husband's obstinacy. I will make him see that the sacrifice we are making, Jean and I, in accepting this German———"

Meanwhile laughter came from the next room, unfurnished except for the two chairs on which Lucienne and Farnow were sitting. Lucienne, with an elbow on the balustrade of the open window, the lieutenant a little behind gazing at her, and speaking with an extraordinary fervour; sometimes there was laughter. This laughter hurt Madame Oberlé, but she did not turn round. She still saw in the changing blue of the Alsatian fields the consoling image evoked by Lucienne.

Wilhelm von Farnow was speaking during this time, and was using to the best advantage this hour, which he knew would be short, in which he was permitted to learn to know Lucienne. She was listening to him as if dreaming, looking out across the roofs, but really attentive, and accentuating her answers with a smile and a little grimace. The German said:

"You are a glorious conquest. You will be a queen among the officers of my regiment, and already there is a woman of French family, but born in Austria, and she is ugly. There is an Italian, and some Germans, and some Englishwomen. You unite in yourself all their separate gifts—beauty, wit, brilliancy, German culture, and French spontaneity. As soon as we are married I shall present you in the highest German society. How did you develop in Alsheim?"

Her nature was still proud rather than tender, and these flatteries pleased her.

At this hour, profiting by the absence of M. Joseph Oberlé at Barr, M. Ulrich had gone up to see his nephew Jean. The days were drawing near when the young man would go to the barracks. It was necessary to tell him about the unsuccessful meeting with Odile Bastian's father. M. Ulrich, after having hesitated a long time, finding it harder to destroy young love than to start for a war, went to see his nephew and told him everything.

They talked for an hour, or rather the uncle talked in monologue, and tried to console Jean, who had let him see his grief, and had wept bitterly.

"Weep, my dear boy," said the uncle. "At this moment your mother is assisting at the first interview between Lucienne and the other. I confess I do not understand her. Weep, but don't let yourself be cast down. Tomorrow you must be brave. Think, in three weeks you will be in the barracks. They must not see you crying. Well, the year will soon pass, and you will come back to us—and who knows?"

Jean passed his hand over his eyes and said resolutely:

"No, uncle."

"Why not?"

At the same place where in the preceding winter the two men had talked so joyously of the future, they were once more seated at the two ends of the sofa.

Outside, daylight was fading away and the air was warm. M. Ulrich found suddenly on Jean's sorrowful face the energetic expression which had so forcibly struck him on the former occasion, and had so delighted him. The Vosges-coloured eyes, with brows close together, were full of changing gleams of light, and yet the eyes were steady.

"No," said Jean; "it is necessary that you should know—you and one other to whom I will tell it. I shall not do my military service here."

"Where will you do it?"

"In France."

"How can you say that? Are you serious?"

"As serious as it is possible to be."

"And you go away at once?"

"No; after I have joined the corps."

M. Ulrich lifted his hands:

"But you are mad. It will be the most difficult and most dangerous thing to do. You are mad!"

He began to walk up and down the room—from the window to the wall. His emotion found vent in emphatic gestures, but he took care to speak gently for fear of being heard by the people of the house.

"Why after? For, after all, that is the first thing that comes into my mind in face of such an idea, and why?"

"I had intended to go away before joining the regiment," said the young man quietly. "But mamma guessed at something. She made me swear that I would join. So I shall join. Do not try to dissuade me. It is unreasonable, but I promised."

M. Ulrich shrugged his shoulders.

"Yes; the question of time is a serious point, but it is not only that. The serious thing is the resolution. Who made you take it? Is it because your grandfather called out 'Go away!' that you have decided to go?"

"No; he thought as I think, that is all."

"Is it the refusal of my friend Bastian which decided you?"

"Not more than the other. If he had said yes I should have had to tell him what I have told you this evening—I will live neither in Germany nor in Alsace."

"Then your sister's marriage?"

"Yes; that blow alone would have been enough to drive me away. What would my life be like at Alsheim now? Have you thought about that?"

"Be careful, Jean. You forsake your post as an Alsatian!"

"No; I can do nothing for Alsace! I could never gain the confidence of Alsatians now: with my father compromised, and my sister married to a Prussian."

"They will say you deserted!"

"Let them come to tell me so then, when I shall be serving with my regiment in France!"

"And your mother—you are going to leave your mother alone here?"

"That is the great objection, after all, the only great one, for the present, but my mother cannot ask me to let my life be sacrificed and made useless as hers has been. Her next feeling later on will be one of approval, because I have freed myself from the intolerable yoke which has lain so heavily on her. Yes, she will forgive me. And then——"

Jean pointed to the jagged green mountains.

"And then, there is dear France, as you say. It is she who attracts me. It is she who spoke to me first!"

"You child!" cried M. Ulrich.

He placed himself before the young man, who remained seated, and who was almost smiling.

"A nation must be fine indeed who, after thirty years, can evoke such a love as yours! Where are the people one would regret in the same way? Oh! blessed race which speaks again in you!"

He stopped a moment.

"However, I cannot leave you in ignorance of the kind of difficulties and disillusions you are going to encounter. It is my duty. Jean, my Jean, when you have passed the frontier and claimed the qualification of Frenchman according to the law, and finished your year's military service.—What will you do?"

"I shall always be able to earn my bread."

"Do not count too much on that. Do not think that the French will welcome you with favour because you are Alsatian. They have perhaps forgotten that we——In any case, they are like those who owe a very old pension. Do not imagine that they will help you over there more than any one else."

His nephew interrupted him:

"My mind is made up—whatever happens. Do not speak to me about it any more, will you?"

Then Uncle Ulrich—who was caressing his grey, pointed beard as if to get out his words spoken against the dear land, words that were coming out with such difficulty—was silent, and looked at his nephew a long time with his smile of complicity, which grew and spread. And he finished by saying:

"Now that I have done my duty and have not succeeded, I have the right to acknowledge, Jean, that sometimes I had this same idea. What would you say if I followed you to France?"

"You?"

"Not immediately. The only interest I had in living here was in seeing you growing up and continuing the tradition. That is all shattered. Do you know what will be one of the best means of insuring yourself against a cold welcome?"

Jean was too agitated by the gravity of the immediate resolution to take up time in talking about future plans.

"Listen, Uncle Ulrich, in a few days I shall want you. I have told you about my decision precisely that you might help me."

He rose, went towards the library, which was by the entrance-door, took a staff officer's map and came, unfolding it, towards the sofa.

"Sit down again by me, uncle, and let us do some geography together!"

He spread on his knees the map of the frontier of Lower Alsace.

"I have made up my mind to go this way," he said. "There will be a few inquiries to be made."

Uncle Ulrich nodded his head in sign of approval, interested as if it were some plan for a hunt, or an approaching battle.

"Good place," he said, "Grande Fontaine, les Minières. It seems to me that that is the nearest frontier line to Strasburg. Who told you this?"

"François Ramspacher's second son."

"You can rely on it. You will take the train."

"Yes."

"Where to?"

"As far as Schirmeck, I think."

"No; that is too near the frontier, and it is too important a station. In your place I should get out at the station before that, at Russ Hersbach."

"Good! There I take a carriage ordered beforehand—I go to Grande Fontaine—I dash into the forest."

"We dash, you mean?"

"Are you coming?"

The two men looked at each other, proud of each other.

"Really," said M. Ulrich, "this astonishes you? It is my trade. Pathfinder that I am, I am going first to reconnoitre the land, then when I shall have done the wood so thoroughly that I can find my way through it even by night, I will tell you if the plan is a good one, and at the hour agreed upon you will find me there. Be careful to dress like a tourist: soft hat, gaiters, not an ounce of baggage."

"Quite so."

M. Ulrich again scrutinised this handsome Jean who was leaving for ever the land of the Oberlés, the Biehlers, and all their ancestors.

All the same, how sad it is, in spite of the joy of the danger.

"Bah!" said Jean, trying to laugh, "I shall see the Rhine at both ends—there where it is free."

M. Ulrich embraced him.

"Courage, my boy, we shall meet soon. Take care not to let any one guess your plan. Who is it you are going to tell?"

"M. Bastian."

The uncle approved, and already on the threshold, pointing to the next room which M. Philippe Oberlé never left now:

"The poor man! There is more honour in his half of a human personality than in all the others together. Good-bye, Jean!"

Some hours passed and Jean went to the office of the works as usual. But his mind was so distracted that work was impossible. The employees who wished to speak to him noticed it. One of the foremen could not help saying to the clerks in the writing department, Germans like himself:

"The German cavalry is making ravages here: the master looks half mad."

The same patriotic feeling made them all laugh silently.

Then the dinner bell rang. Jean dreaded meeting his mother and Lucienne. Lucienne held her brother back as she was entering the dining-room, and in the half-light tenderly embraced him, holding him closely to her. Like most engaged people, it was probably a little of the other she was embracing without knowing it. However, the thought at least was for Jean. She murmured:

"I saw him at Obernai for a long time. He pleases me very much, because he is proud, like me. He has promised me to protect you in the regiment. But do not let us speak of him at dinner. It will be better not to. Mamma has been very kind—the poor thing touched me. She can do no more. Jean, I was obliged to reassure her by telling her your secret, and I told her that you will not leave Alsace, because you love Odile. Will you forgive me?"

She took her brother's arm, and leaving the hall went into the dining-room, where M. and Madame Oberlé were seated already—silent.

"My poor dear, in this house every joy is paid for by the sorrow of others. Look! I alone am happy!"

The dinner was very short. M. Oberlé immediately after led his daughter into the billiard-room because he wanted to question her. The mother remained a moment at the table near her son, who was now her neighbour. As soon as she was alone with him, the constraint fell like a veil from her face. The mother turned towards her child, admired him, smiled at him, and said in the confidential tone she knew so well how to use:

"I can do no more, my dear. I am completely done up and must go to bed. But I will confess that amidst my suffering a while ago I had one joy. Imagine that till just then I believed most firmly that you were going to leave us."

Jean started.

"I do not believe it now; do not be afraid! I am reassured. Your sister has told me in secret that I shall have some day a little Alsatian for a daughter-in-law. That will do me so much good. I understand that you could not tell me anything yet, while so much has been happening. And then it is still new—isn't it? Why are you trembling like that? I tell you, Jean, that I ask nothing from you now, and that I have entirely lost my fears—I love you so much."

She also embraced Jean. She also pressed him to her breast. But she had no tenderness in her soul except that which she was expressing.

She remembered the child in the cradle, nights and days of long ago, anxieties, dreams, precautions, and prayers of which he had been the object, and she thought:

"All that is nothing compared with what I would always do for him!"

"When she had disappeared, and he had heard the noise she made opening the invalid grandfather's door, to whom she never missed wishing good night, Jean rose and went out. He went through the fields to the trees which surrounded the Bastians' house, went into the park and, hidden there, remained some time watching the light which filtered through the shutters of the large drawing-room. Voices spoke, now one, now another. He recognised the tone but could not distinguish the words. There were pauses between the slowly spoken words, and Jean imagined that they were sad. The temptation came to him to go round those few yards of frontage and enter the drawing-room boldly. He thought: "Now that I have decided to live out of Alsace; now that they have refused me because of my father's attitude and because of Lucienne's marriage, I have no longer the right to question Odile. I shall go away without knowing if she also suffers as I suffer. But can I not see her in her own home for the last time, in the intimacy of the lamplight which brings the three of them together? I will not write to her. I will not try to speak to her, but I must see her; I shall carry away a last look of her—a last remembrance, and she will guess that at least I am deserving of pity."

He hesitated however. This evening he felt too unhappy and too weak. From now to the first of October, would he not have the time to return? A step came from the garden side. Jean looked again at the thin blade of light which escaped from the room where Odile was sitting, and cut the night in two; and he withdrew.

CHAPTER XIV
THE LAST EVENING

The last evening had come. Jean was to take at Obernai a night train for Strasburg, so as to be in the barracks of St. Nicholas the next morning at seven o'clock, the regulation hour. His uniform, ordered of a Strasburg tailor, as was usual for the one-year service men, was waiting for him, blue and yellow, folded on two chairs, in the room which a month ago Madame Oberlé had taken, facing the barracks of St. Nicholas, about the middle of the rue des Balayeurs. After dinner he said to his mother: "Let me go out alone, so that I can say good-bye to the Alsheim country I shall not see again for a long time."

She smiled. M. Joseph Oberlé answered:

"My dear fellow, you will not see me again; I have bills falling due to-morrow, and I must work in my office. And besides, I do not care about useless sentiment. Well, perhaps you will not find it easy to get leave before two months. I dare say not, but that will only make you the better pleased to come home. Come! Good-bye."

More affectionately than he would have believed it possible he embraced him, and with a word from Lucienne in her clear, young voice, "Soon," he went out.

The night air was laden with moisture to a remarkable degree: not a cloud. A crescent moon, stars in thousands; but between heaven and earth a veil of mist was spread which allowed the light to penetrate, but dispersed it in such a manner that there was no object really in shadow, and none which showed brightly. Everything was bathed in a pearly atmosphere. It was warm to breathe. "How sweet my Alsace is!" said Jean, when he had opened the door of the kitchen garden, and found himself behind the village houses, facing the plain, on which the moonlight was sleeping, blotted here and there with the shadows of an apple-tree or a walnut. An immense languor escaped from the soil, into which the first rains of autumn had sunk. The perfumes of stubble and ploughed land mixed with the odours from all kinds of vegetation come to their fullness of growth and aroma. The mountain was sending out gently to the valley the odour of pine pollen on the breeze, and the mint and the dying strawberries and bilberries, and its juniper berries crushed by the feet of passers-by and flocks. Jean breathed in the odour of Alsace; he thought he could recognise the exquisite perfume of that little mountain which is near Colmar, called Florimont, where the dittany grows, and he thought, "It is the last time. Never again! Never again!"

There were no glittering points of light on the roofs; he followed the line of them on the left of the path: they seemed to have joined fraternal hands round the church, and under each Jean could picture a face known and friendly. Such were his thoughts for a while as he walked on. But as soon as he saw, grey in the middle of the fields, the big clump of trees which hid M. Bastian's house, every other thought fled. Arrived at the farm where the younger son had said to him, "It is by Grande Fontaine that you must cross the frontier," he went into the cherry avenue, and he still remembered and found the white gate. No one was passing. Besides, what did it matter? Jean opened the lattice gate, went in, and walked on the grass border, even with the great trees, to the window of the drawing-room, which was lighted, then going round the house, came to the door which opened on the side opposite the village of Alsheim.

He waited an instant, went into the vestibule, and opened the door of the large room where the Bastian family sat every evening. They were all there in the light of the lamps, just as Jean had imagined. The father was reading the paper. The two women on the other side of the brown table laden with white linen unfolded, were embroidering with initials the towels which were going into the Bastian linen press. The door had opened with no other noise than that of the pad brushing against the parquet. However, all was so calm round the dwelling and in the room, that they turned their eyes to see who was coming in. There was a moment of uncertainty for M. Bastian, and hesitation for Jean. He had fixed his gaze first of all on Odile. He had seen how she also had suffered, and that she was the first, the only one who recognised him, and how she grew pale, and that in her anguish, her raised hand, her breath, her glance, were arrested. The linen Odile was sewing slipped from her hands without her being able to make the slightest movement to lift it up.

It was perhaps by this sign that M. Bastian recognised the visitor. Emotion seized him immediately.

"What?" he asked gently, "is it you, Jean? No one showed you in. What have you come for?"

He slowly put his paper down on the table without ceasing to scrutinise the young man who was standing in the shadow, on the same spot, a step or two from the door.

"I have come to say good-bye," said Jean.

But his voice was so full of pain that M. Bastian understood something unknown, tragic, had entered his house. He rose, saying, "Why, yes, to-morrow will be the first of October. You are going to the barracks, my poor boy. No doubt you wish to speak to me?"

Already M. Bastian had advanced, had held out his hand, and the young man, drawing him back into the darkest corner of the room, had answered in a very low voice, his eyes looking into the eyes of Odile's father. Madame Bastian gazed into the shadow, where they made an indistinct group.

"I am leaving," Jean murmured, "and I shall never come back, M. Bastian; that is why I took the liberty of coming."

He felt the rough hand of the Alsatian tremble. There was an exchange of secret and rapid dialogue between the men, while the two anxious women rose from their chairs, and with their hands leaning on the table, bent forward.

"What do you say? You will come back in a year?"

"No, I am going to join the regiment because I promised to. But I shall leave it."

"You will leave it?"

"The day after to-morrow."

"Where are you going?"

"To France!"

"For ever?"

"Yes."

The old Alsatian turned aside for a moment. "Talk on, you women, talk on; we have business to discuss."

They moved away, whilst he, breathless as though with running, cried: "Be careful what you do; be prudent; don't let yourself be caught."

He placed both hands on Jean's shoulders. "I must stay: that's my way, you see, of loving Alsace; there is no better. I live here, and here I die. But for you, my boy, things are different, I understand—don't let the women guess; it's too serious. Does any one know at your home?"

"No."

"Keep your secret," and then, lowering his voice, "You wanted to see her once more. I don't blame you, since you will never meet again."

Jean nodded as though to say "Yes, I had to see her once more."

"Look at her a minute, and then go. Stay where you are—look over my shoulder."

Over M. Bastian's shoulder Jean could see that the troubled look in Odile's eyes had grown to terror. She met his gaze fearlessly; she had no thought but for the dialogue which she could not hear, the mystery in which she felt she had some part, and her face betrayed her anguish.

"What are they saying? Is it bad news again? Is it better? No; not better, they are not both looking my way."

Her mother was still paler than her daughter.

"Farewell, my boy," said M. Bastian in low tones. "I loved you.... I could not act differently ... but I think highly of you; I will remember you."

Overcome by emotion, the old Alsatian silently pressed Jean's hand and let it fall. As to Jean, trembling and dazed, he walked to the door, looking back for the last time. He was going then—in one minute he would be gone, never to return to Alsheim.

"Au revoir, madame," he said.

He would have liked to say au revoir to Odile, but sobs prevented the words.

He gained the shadow of the corridor; they heard him hurrying away.

"What does it mean?" demanded Madame Bastian. "Xavier, you are hiding something from us."

The old Alsatian sobbed aloud; he threw precaution to the winds—she had guessed.

"Odile," she cried, "run and say good-bye to him."

Odile was already across the room; she caught Jean up at the corner.

"I beg of you to tell me why you are so miserable," she cried.

He turned, determined to be silent, to keep his vow. She was quite close to him; he opened his arms; she threw herself into them.

"Oh God," she cried, "you are leaving; I know it—you are going."

He kissed her hair tenderly, a lifelong farewell, turned the corner, and fled from her.

CHAPTER XV
JOINING THE REGIMENT

At a quarter to seven, Jean Oberlé, wearing a jacket and round cap, walked by the stable of the old French barracks of St. Nicholas, built on the site of a convent, now called by the Germans "Nikolaus Kaserne." He reached the iron gate, saluted the officer, exchanged a few words with him, and advanced towards a group of about a dozen young men, volunteers for a year's service, who were standing at the end of the courtyard, under the clock. Cavalry men in undress—light blue tunic with yellow braid, black trousers, and flat caps—moved here and there over vast, level, dusty grounds. A detachment of cavalry, lance at shoulder, had taken up their station to the left by one of the stables, waiting their officer's command to take the road.

"Herr Sergeant," said Jean, approaching the non-commissioned officer, carefully dressed, but of vulgar appearance, who, with a protecting and pretentious manner, was waiting for him by the group of volunteers. "I am one of the volunteers for the year."

The sergeant, who had very long black moustaches, which he never ceased twirling between the thumb and first finger, asked his christian and surname, and compared them with the names and surnames on the list he held in his hand.

Meanwhile, secretly intimidated by the supposed wealth of those he received, eager to please them, but anxious lest they should discover it, the sergeant looked the volunteer up and down, as though seeking some physical defect, anything in fact which might make this Alsatian civilian ridiculous in the eyes of a non-commissioned officer.

"Join the others," he said, when his examination was finished.

The others were for the most part Germans, who, judging by the different types, had come from all parts of the Empire. They had dressed carefully, so as to show their comrades, volunteers like themselves, and the soldiers in the barracks, that in civil life they were men who belonged to wealthy families.

They wore patent leather shoes, kid gloves, yellow or tan, elegant ties, valuable neck-pins. Each man introduced himself to his future comrades. "Allow me to introduce myself: my name is Furbach, my name is Blossmann." Jean knew none of them. He merely bowed without giving his name. What did it matter to him who was to be their comrade for this one day only?

He took his place to the left of the group, his mind far away from the St. Nicholas barrack, while the whispered question, "Who is he—an Alsatian?" went the round of his comrades.

The easy-going smiled amiably, others put themselves on the defensive, and with the rivalry of racial instinct, drew themselves up and fixed their hard blue eyes upon the new-comer with an unflinching stare.

Two other volunteers arrived, and the sergeant, as the clock struck, preceded the fifteen young men up the staircase, and marshalled them into a room on the second floor, where the medical examination was to take place. At eight o'clock the volunteers were again in the courtyard, no longer grouped as the fancy took them, but drawn up in two files, the sergeant in attendance. They were awaiting the colonel. Jean's neighbour was a tall, beardless youth, son of a manufacturer of Fribourg, with bright eyes, and smooth cheeks, which bore, however, two scars, one near the nose, and one under the right eye, souvenirs of his duels as a student. Seeing Jean Oberlé's dreamy, reserved look, he put it down to timidity caused by his new surroundings, and took upon himself the office of guide.

Whilst the Alsatian, his arms behind his back, his pale, strong face turned to the gate, watched the people of Strasburg crossing the street in the October sun, his companion endeavoured to arouse his interest in the inhabitants of the barracks.

"You were wrong not to do as I did: I got introductions to several officers, and even know several of the chief quartermasters. There, do you see the *wachtmeister* coming out of the stable; that's Stubel, hard drinker, great eater, good sort; that other one who is watching us from the end of the courtyard, the man with a little red moustache, do you see? That's Gottfried Hamm—a bad sort."

"You know him?"

"Yes."

"Attention!" called the sergeant. "Eyes right!", He himself marched ten quick steps forward, halted with head erect, his arms hanging straight at each side, his left hand gripping his sabre below the guard. He had caught sight of an officer advancing towards them with deliberate step, wrapped in his grey cloak, the mere sight of whom had scattered some twenty hussars, who had been leaning against the walls sunning themselves. The colonel stopped before the first file of young men, the hope of the German reserve army. He was sanguine, bustling, and energetic, a very good cavalry-man, broad-shouldered, with thin legs, hair almost black, and eyes fierce in the interests of the service.

"These, Colonel," said the sergeant, "are the volunteers for a year's service."

The colonel frowned immediately, and fixing his eyes on each of these young men in turn, said severely:

"You are privileged. You are dispensed from more than a year's service. Be worthy of it. Be an example to the soldiers; remember that you will be their chiefs later. No breaking of rules, no larking, no wearing of civilian dress. I shall punish severely."

He asked for the list of volunteers. Seeing Jean's name he mentally connected it with Lieutenant von Farnow's.

"Volunteer Oberlé," he called out.

Oberlé stepped out of the ranks. Without relaxing the severity of his expression, the colonel fixed his eyes for a few moments on the young man's face, thinking to himself that here was the brother of the Lucienne Oberlé whose hand he had allowed Lieutenant Farnow to ask in marriage.

"That's right," he said; and saluting rapidly he walked away, his grey cloak swelling with the north wind.

As he disappeared, a lieutenant in the 1st regiment, adjutant-major of the Rhenish Hussars, a well-made, distinguished-looking man, bearing himself in the correct military style, a perfect man of the world, came towards the group of volunteers, and read an order assigning to each one his appointed place in such and such a company and squadron. Jean was to join the 3rd company of the 2nd squadron.

"No luck," murmured his neighbour: "that's Gottfried Hamm's company."

Henceforward the fifteen volunteers were part of the army; each one had his allotted place in that well-disciplined multitude, their responsible chiefs, the right to demand a uniform from such and such a depot, a horse from such and such a stable. To this they now turned their attention. Jean and his chance companion, son of a librarian of Leipzig, made their way to the top floor of the barrack, entered the clothing-stores and received their uniforms, leaving behind various articles, such as cavalry cloaks and pairs of boots, which the *kammer-sergeant* was pleased to accept for himself as a token of welcome, or undertook to remit to certain non-commissioned officers of the company. It was a long business, and did not finish till past ten. Then there was a visit to the principal brusher's room, where there was the little wardrobe of white wood, used henceforth in common by the volunteer and the soldier; and there was still the visit to the stable sergeant, whose duty it was to assign to each his horse and second brusher; then another to the regimental tailor; it was past midday when Jean was able to leave the barracks and lunch hastily.

For this first day the volunteers were dispensed from returning to barracks at one o'clock. It was only after the horses had been groomed that they made their appearance simultaneously as arranged between themselves, radiant in their shining new uniforms, before the curious gaze of the cavalry, and the jealous scrutiny of the non-commissioned officers who examined, as they passed, the cut and quality of their uniforms, the style of their collars and braid, the lustre of their shining boots. Among the young men there was only one who remained a stranger to the self-complacency of the others. He was thinking of a telegram which he should have received by now, of which the terms of the pre-arranged code floated before his eyes all the afternoon. This was his only thought. Anxiety at not hearing news of his uncle Ulrich's departure, nervousness mixed with a certain defiance which, in anticipation of the morrow, he mentally hurled at the authority to which he at present bowed, prevented the young man from feeling fatigue. It was half-past eight before the exercises for man and horse were concluded, and then some of the volunteers were so tired that they sought their beds, supperless. Jean did likewise, but for a different reason. He went at once to the Rue des Balayeurs.

The landlady met him at the door:

"There is a telegram for you, M. Oberlé."

Jean went to his room, lit a candle, and read the unsigned telegram awaiting him:

"All is well."

This meant that all was ready for next day, that M. Ulrich had made all necessary preparations. The dice were cast; on the 2nd October, in a few hours, Jean would leave the barracks of Alsace. Although he never hesitated for a moment, yet, upon reading the words which settled his fate, the young man was overcome by emotion. The reality of separation entered his soul more bitterly, and being physically weary, he wept.

He had thrown himself on his bed fully dressed, his face buried in his pillow; he thought of all his friends who remained behind in Alsace, whilst he was an exile for ever; he could hear their exclamations of pity or indignation when the news reached Alsheim; he saw the girl he loved, the radiant Odile of Easter Eve, become the despairing woman who had clung to him in the moment of farewell, guessing all, yet begging for an answer he could not give. All this was necessary, irreparable. The night passed slowly. Silence reigned in the streets. Jean realised that he would soon need all his moral energy, and endeavoured to lay aside vain visions and regrets, repeating to himself over and over again the plans settled between himself and his uncle at their last interview, which he was to carry out in every detail to-day.

Yes, to-day, for the neighbouring cocks were beginning to crow. It was not possible to leave by an early train. The rendezvous at the barracks was fixed for four o'clock, while the first train for Schirmeck left Strasburg at 5.48; he would not reach Russ-Hersbach until after seven, and to take it was a great risk. The absence of a volunteer would be noticed in less than three hours, and the alarm given. Uncle Ulrich and Jean had come to the conclusion that the most sure means of crossing the frontier without arousing suspicion was to take the train which left Strasburg at 12.10 a.m., that is to say, whilst the volunteers were at lunch.

"I have been over the ground to make sure," said M. Ulrich: "I am sure of my calculations. You will reach Russ-Hersbach at twenty-one minutes past one, a trap will take us to Schirmeck in a quarter of an hour. We turn to the right and reach Grande Fontaine half an hour later. There we leave the trap, and, thanks to our good legs, we can reach French ground by two forty-five or fifty. There I leave you and return."

It was important to catch the 12.10 train, which would be an easy matter, as the volunteers were usually free by eleven.

Jean fell asleep at last, but not for long. Before four in the morning he was again at the barracks.

The short repose he had taken had restored his strength of will. Like most energetic people, Jean was nervous beforehand, but when the moment of action came difficulties vanished. While the horses were being groomed, and during the exercises, which lasted till close on eleven, he was perfectly calm. His attitude was even less reserved and detached than on the previous day, and his Saxon comrade remarked upon it.

"Already at home?" he inquired.

Jean smiled. He looked upon buildings, officers, and soldiers, all the pomp of the German army, with the same feelings as a school-boy set at liberty looks on the professors and pupils of his college. He already felt detached from his surroundings, and observed with a certain amused curiosity the scenes he would never see again.

About eleven he saw at the head of a detachment of Hussars, Lieutenant Farnow ride into the barracks, superb in his youth and military splendour. The horses were splashed with mud from their ride, and the men, tired out, only awaited the signal to halt, that they might curse the day's exercises. Not in the least weary, Farnow rode into the courtyard with as much pleasure as though he had been invited to a hunting party, and was expecting the signal to start. "There's my sister's future husband," thought Jean; "we shall never see one another again, and if war breaks out, he is my enemy."

He saw the vision of a tall cavalry chief, charging across a dusty plain, rising in his stirrups, nostrils distended, shouting out orders. Farnow, not suspecting the distraction he was causing the young volunteer, just let his blue eyes linger a minute on the latter's face. He moved off, followed by his men, to the farther side of the courtyard. A brief word of command was heard, then the clashing of arms, and silence. The exercises were prolonged another half hour, to satisfy the instructor's zeal. At half-past eleven Jean was rushing up the staircase, knowing that there was barely time to catch the train, when one of the men of his company called out:

"There's no time to go out; we have a review at midday: it's the captain's orders."

Jean continued on up the stairs, not paying the slightest attention to this obstacle raised at the last minute. His mind was made up. He was going to leave. He would meet his uncle at Russ-Hersbach, who would be waiting there with a carriage. Jean's one thought was to reach the station. He changed hurriedly, and mixing with a group of men belonging to other companies, and who had no reason to remain in barracks, he had no difficulty in getting away. When he was in the street, some yards away from the guard-house, on the pavement of the rue des Balayeurs he began to run. The clock stood at seventeen minutes to twelve. Was there time to run the three hundred yards which lay between him and his apartments, change into civilian dress and catch the 12.10? It was some distance to the station. On the other hand there was great risk in attempting to cross the frontier in uniform. While he was running Jean thought it would be simple to change in the train or at Russ-Hersbach. Entering the hall, he called breathlessly to his landlady:

"I am in a great hurry. Will you call a cab? I will be down in a minute."

Three minutes later he ran down carrying a bag into which he had thrown his civilian clothes, which he had left ready on his bed. He jumped into the cab, giving as address, "Rue de la Mésange," but at the next corner he called out: "Drive with all speed to the station, coachman."

He reached the station a minute before the time, got his ticket for Russ-Hersbach, and jumped into a first-class compartment, which contained two other passengers. A minute later the train had entered the tunnel under the fortifications, reappeared, and steamed away to the west, across the plains of Alsace.

At the same moment the captain, who was holding the review in the courtyard, caught sight of one of the volunteers attached to his company, and turning to the *wachtmeister* said: "Where is the other?"

"I have not seen him, Captain," Hamm replied, and turning to the young Saxon, Oberlé's comrade: "Do you know where he is?"

"He went out after the exercises, sir, and has not returned."

"I won't punish him this time," growled the captain; "no doubt he misunderstood, but speak to him in my name when he returns, Hamm; don't forget."

There was no immediate alarm, but when the men again assembled at one o'clock for the grooming of the horses, which went on every afternoon from one to two o'clock, Jean's absence could not fail to be noticed. The whole length of the wall outside the stables, horses tethered to iron rings were being brushed down by men, amongst whom were the volunteers receiving a lesson in the art. The sergeants looked on nonchalantly when the *wachtmeister* of the 3rd Company came out of his office, and made his way to the south side of the court, where Oberlé should have been. He bit his red moustache as his eyes wandered up and down the ranks.

"Oberlé has not come back?" he asked. The same man as before replied:

"When he left the barracks he ran towards his apartments."

"Did you see him in the mess-room?"

"He did not lunch with us."

"That'll do," said the *wachtmeister*.

Hamm turned away briskly. The expression of his face and eyes showed that he considered the situation serious. Serious for Oberlé, but equally serious for himself. Neither the captain nor the lieutenant was in barracks at the moment. If there was trouble the captain would not fail to ask why he had not been warned. Hamm crossed the courtyard, thinking over what he ought to do, and recalling a remark of the brigadier of Obernai. When Gottfried was at Obernai a fortnight before, he had said to him: "You are going to have Oberlé's son in your regiment. Keep an eye on him. I shall be surprised if he does not create some disturbance. He is the counterpart of his grandfather, a madman who hates Germans, and who is quite capable of any folly."

But before taking zealous action it was necessary to know some details. This was easy: the rue des Balayeurs faced the gateway. Hamm brushed his blue tunic with his hand, left the barracks, and made his way to a large house on the left with green shutters.

"Left in a cab, before midday, carrying a bag," was the answer Jean's landlady gave him.

"What address did he give?"

"Rue de la Mésange."

"Any number?"

"I don't know; anyway I heard none."

Hamm's suspicions became more definite. The *wachtmeister* no longer hesitated. He hastened to the captain's quarters in the Herderstrasse.

The captain was out.

Disappointed and warm from his sharp walk, Hamm took a short cut to the barracks, through the University gardens. He suddenly remembered that close by in the rue Grandidier, lived Lieutenant Farnow. It is true the lieutenant did not belong to the 2nd squadron, but Hamm knew of his engagement. It had been talked of among the officers. He made his way to the superb stone house and mounted to the first floor.

"The lieutenant is dressing," replied the orderly to his question.

Von Farnow in shirt and trousers was dressing before paying certain calls, and going to the officers' casino. In trousers and shirt he was leaning over his toilet-table with its bevelled glass, washing his face. The room was perfumed with eau-de-cologne, brushes and manicure set were strewn round him. He turned as the door opened, his face all wet.

"What is the matter, Hamm?" he cried, seizing a towel.

"I took upon myself to call upon you, lieutenant, as the captain is not there, and Oberlé——"

"Oberlé? What has he done?" Farnow interrupted nervously.

"He has not put in an appearance since half-past eleven this morning."

Farnow, who was drying his face, threw down the towel violently on the table, and approached the non-commissioned officer. He remembered Madame Oberlé's fears. "He thinks as I do," thought Hamm.

"Has not come back? Have you been to the rue des Balayeurs?"

"Yes, lieutenant; he left the house in a cab at ten minutes to twelve."

The young lieutenant felt as though death's icy hand was on his heart. He closed his eyes for a moment, and with a violent effort regained his composure.

"There is only one thing to do, Hamm," he said. He was deadly pale, but not a muscle of his face quivered. "You must warn your captain, and he will do what is prescribed in such cases."

Farnow turned calmly, and looked at the ornamental clock on his desk.

"One-forty—you must be quick."

The *wachtmeister* saluted and withdrew.

The lieutenant ran to the adjoining study, and asked to be connected with the Strasburg station. Ten minutes later the telephone bell rang, and he learnt that a volunteer of the 9th Hussars, in uniform, had reached the station at the last moment with a valise portmanteau and taken a first-class ticket to Russ-Hersbach.

"It's impossible," exclaimed Farnow, throwing himself on to the sofa; "there must be some mistake Russ-Hersbach is almost on the frontier. Jean would not desert—he is in love; he must be at Alsheim—he must at least have wanted to see Odile again. I must find out."

"Hermann," he called, rapping with his knuckles on the mahogany table.

The orderly, a stolid German, opened the door.

"Saddle my horse and yours immediately."

Farnow was soon ready; he hastened downstairs, found the horses waiting, crossed Strasburg, and once past the fortifications, spurred his horse to a sharp trot.

As he neared Alsheim, Jean's desertion seemed to him more credible. Every detail of his conversation with Madame Oberlé came back to him, and other reasons as well for believing the calamity against which his imperious will was fighting desperately. "He does not understand Germany; he was glorying in it at Councillor Brausig's. And then his disunited family—a disunion increased by my engagement. But then he is himself engaged, or almost; and characters like his, French characters, must be dominated by love. No; I shall find him there—or have news of him."

It was warm; the long dusty road stretched from village to village, without shade, a thin line between the fields, now bare of their crops. The sky hung over them like brass, on the horizon banks of motionless clouds rose above the Vosges, throwing out rays of light. The horses, covered with sweat, continued to gallop. Under the scattered walnut-trees, among the stubble, children raised their switches and shouted as the riders passed them.

"Is the lieutenant crazy?" thought Hermann; "he is going faster and faster."

Farnow's anguish increased as he drew nearer his destination. "If I do not find him," he murmured, "supposing he has———"

Obernai was passed on the right. A sign-post at the cross roads pointed to Alsheim, and soon the blue roof of the Oberlés' house appeared among the green.

"Lucienne, Lucienne, Lucienne!"

The house seemed to slumber in the heavy heat of the autumn day, the silence being broken only by a feeble, monotonous voice. Seated near grandfather Oberlé's chair, in the room which the invalid could never hope to leave, Madame Oberlé was reading aloud the *Journal d'Alsace*, which the postman had just delivered.

Through the open window her voice could be heard murmuring as though engaged in the rhythmic recital of the rosary. In the billiard-room above, that which was still called Jean's room, M. Joseph Oberlé was dozing behind the curtain, on his knees lay several letters, and a copy of the *Strasburger Post*. At the end of the room Lucienne could be seen writing at a Louis XVI. desk.

"Monsieur? Monsieur Oberlé?"

Joseph Oberlé jumped up and threw open the door, which was ajar, meeting the concierge running towards him.

"Why do you call me; you know I don't like———"

He remained speaking with the man for a minute, and returned smiling.

"My Lucienne, Herr von Farnow is waiting for you at the park gate."

She rose, blushing.

"Why doesn't he come in?"

"It appears that he is on horseback, and in a great hurry. Perhaps he dares not. Go and fetch him, my darling; tell him from me that there shall be no disturbance, that I will prevent any further scenes."

With a gesture he implied that he would bolt all the doors sooner, especially that of the room whence came the monotonous voice reading the paper.

She looked in the glass, arranging her hair. He repeated:

"Run, my treasure; he is asking for you. If you don't return quickly I'll come for you."

She nodded, and ran down the steps two at a time. She walked rapidly down the avenue, happy, yet troubled, her mouth slightly open, her eyes seeking Farnow.

At the end of the avenue she caught sight of the two steaming horses on the road held by the orderly, and almost at the same moment the lieutenant came towards her.

Farnow's usually pale face was flushed, his expression troubled; he hastened, but with no sign of joy, towards Lucienne, who came half running to meet him, trying to laugh.

"How are you, Wilhelm? What a nice surprise!"

The lieutenant raised his hat, but made no reply. He took her hand, and drew her aside; he did not raise it to his lips; no accustomed words of admiration came from him; his eyes were hard and feverish, and he drew her near the wood-yard close by.

Lucienne continued to smile bravely, though her heart was heavy with painful dread.

"Where are you taking me? Who is this churlish friend, who won't even say good day? You, so particular——"

"Come, we shan't be seen here," he said; he drew her behind a pile of wood into a kind of retreat formed by three unequal piles of planks. Farnow dropped Lucienne's hand.

"Is Jean here? Be careful; is he at Alsheim?"

His eyes expressed his anguish, his manner an imperious will struggling against calamity.

"No; he is not here," replied Lucienne simply.

"You expect him, then?"

"No."

"Then we are lost, mademoiselle, lost!"

"Mademoiselle?"

"Yes; if he is not here he has deserted."

"Ah!" The young girl recoiled, supporting herself against the wood, her eyes haggard, her arms outstretched.

"Deserted? Lost? Can't you see that you are killing me with such words? Do you really mean Jean? Deserted! Are you sure?"

"Since he is not here, I am convinced of it. He took a ticket for Russ-Hersbach—do you understand, Russ-Hersbach? He must be across the frontier. He left Strasburg more than three hours ago." He laughed harshly, angrily, beside himself with misery.

"Don't you remember? He swore to your mother he would go to the barracks. He did go. To-day the time for his promise expired, and he deserted. And now...."

"Yes ... now?"

Lucienne asked no proof. She believed it. Her bosom heaved; she let go her hold on the wood, and joined her hands beseechingly. She was obliged to repeat her question; Farnow stood motionless, grief-stricken. "What shall you do now, Wilhelm?"

Farnow drew himself up in his dusty uniform; his brow was contracted.

"I must leave you," he said in a low voice."

"Leave me, because my brother has deserted?"

"Yes."

"But this is madness!"

"It is my duty as a soldier."

"Then you do not love me?"

"Love you. Ah!... But honour forbids me to marry you. I cannot become the brother-in-law of a deserter. I am an officer, a von Farnow!"

"Well, cease to be an officer and continue to love me," cried Lucienne, holding out her arms to the rigid figure in blue. "Wilhelm, true honour consists in loving me, Lucienne Oberlé, in keeping the promise you made me! Leave my brother to go his own way, but don't spoil our two lives."

Farnow could scarcely speak; the veins of his neck were swollen with his efforts for self-control.

"There is worse to come," he said at last, "you must know the truth, Lucienne. I must denounce him."

"Denounce him? Jean? You cannot. I forbid you!" cried Lucienne with a gesture of horror.

"I must do so. Military law compels me to do so."

"It is not true!—it is too cruel."

"I will prove it to you. Hermann!"

Hermann came forward in amazement.

"Listen. What is the article of the law relating to any person who has knowledge of a plan of desertion?"

The soldier collected his thoughts, and recited:

"Any one who shall have credible knowledge of a plan of desertion, when there is still time to frustrate it, and who does not give information thereof to his superiors, is liable to be imprisoned for ten months, and during war for three years."

"Quick! To horse!" cried Farnow. "We must start.

"Farewell, Lucienne."

She ran forward and seized his arm.

"No, no, you must not go; I shall not let you."

He gazed a moment on her tear-stained face, where ardent love and sorrow were mingled.

"You must not go! Do you hear?" she repeated.

Farnow lifted her from the ground, pressed her against his breast and kissed her passionately. By the despairing violence of his kiss, Lucienne realised it was indeed farewell.

He put her from him brusquely, ran to the gate, leapt to the saddle, and galloped away in the direction of Obernai.

CHAPTER XVI
IN THE FOREST OF THE MINIÈRES

Night was falling, but Jean was still on German soil. He was sleeping, worn out with fatigue; he lay stretched upon a bed of moss and fir cones, while M. Ulrich watched, on the look out for fresh danger, still trembling from the danger he had just escaped. The two men had crept into a space between two stacks of branches left by the wood-cutters, who had been thinning the fir-tree plantation. The branches, still green, stretched from one stack to the other, making their hiding-place more secure. A storm of wind blew across the mountain, but otherwise no sound could be heard upon the heights.

Two hours must have passed since Jean and his uncle had taken refuge in their hiding-place.

When the train reached Russ-Hersbach, M. Ulrich had at once seen and said that the moment for Jean to change his uniform had passed. Even such a little thing as that would have excited too much attention in that frontier province, peopled by visible and invisible watchers, where the stones listen and the fir-trees are spies. He threw the valise to the coachman of the landau engaged three days previously at Schirmeck.

"Here's some useless luggage," he cried, "fortunately it's not heavy. Drive quickly, coachman."

The carriage crossed the poverty-stricken village, reached the town of Schirmeck, and quitting there the principal valley turned to the right into the narrow winding valley leading to Grande Fontaine. No suspicious glances followed the travellers, but witnesses of their passing increased. And this was serious. Although Jean was sitting with his back to the driver, partially hidden by the blinds and partially by the cloak which M. Ulrich had thrown over him, yet there was no doubt the uniform of the 9th Hussars had been seen by two gendarmes in the streets of Schirmeck, by workmen on the road, and by the douanier who was smoking and had continued to smoke his pipe so tranquilly, sitting under the trees on the left of the first bridge by which one entered Grande Fontaine.

Every moment M. Ulrich thought, "Now the alarm will be given! Perhaps it has been already, and one of the state's innumerable agents will come up, question us, and insist upon our following them whatever we may say."

He did not tell Jean of his anxiety, and the young man, excited by the spirit of adventure, was quite different to the Jean of yesterday.

In spite of the steepness and stoniness of the path by the mountain stream, the horses made good headway, and soon the houses of Grande Fontaine came into sight. The beech-wood of Donon, all velvety and golden and crowned with firs, rose in front of them. At 2.15 the carriage stopped in the middle of the village, in a kind of sloping square, where a spring of water flows into a huge stone trough. The travellers got out, for here the carriage road ended.

"Wait for us at the inn of Rémy Naeger," said M. Ulrich; "we will go for a walk, and return in an hour. Drink a bottle of Molsheim wine at my expense, and give the horse a double portion of oats."

M. Ulrich and Jean, leaving on the right the path which mounts to Donon, immediately took the path to the left, a narrow road with houses, gardens, and hedges on either side, which connects Grande Fontaine with the last village of the upper valley, that of the Minières.

They had scarcely gone two hundred yards when they caught sight of the keeper of Mathiskop coming out of his house, in his green uniform and Tyrolese hat, descending towards them. Seeing that the man would be obliged to pass them on the road M. Ulrich was afraid.

"There is a uniform, Jean, which I don't care to meet at present. Let us go by the forest."

The forest was on the left. They were the fir woods of Mathiskop, and farther on those of the Corbeille, thickly wooded slopes rising higher and higher, where a hiding-place would be easy to discover. Jean and his uncle jumped the hedge, crossed some yards of meadow, and entered the shadow of the fir wood. It was none too soon; the military authorities had given the alarm; warning had been telephoned to all the different posts to keep a look out for the deserter Oberlé. The keeper they had seen had not yet received the warning, and passed out of sight, but M. Ulrich, by means of his old field-glass of Jena days, could see that there was excitement in the usually quiet valley, where a number of douaniers and gendarmes could be seen hurrying about. They also hurried to the Mathiskop forest, and the chase commenced.

M. Ulrich and Jean were not captured, but they had been sighted; they were tracked from wood to wood for more than an hour, and were prevented from reaching the frontier, to do which they would have been compelled to cross the open valley. M. Ulrich had the happy idea of climbing to the top of a stack of wood and letting himself down into the opening between two stacks, Jean followed his example. This had been their salvation, the gendarmes beat about the wood for some time, and then made off in the direction of Glacimont.

Night was falling, and Jean slept. Banks of clouds rose before the wind, and hastened the darkness. A flight of crows crossed their hiding-place, brushing the tree tops. The flapping of their wings woke M. Ulrich from the reverie into which he had fallen while contemplating his nephew dressed in the uniform of a German soldier, lying stretched on Alsatian soil. He rose and gingerly climbed to the top of the stack.

"Well, uncle," asked Jean, waking up, "what do you see?"

"Nothing, no gendarme's helmet, no douanier's cap," whispered M. Ulrich. "I think they have lost the scent; but with such persons one cannot be sure."

"And the valley of the Minières?"

"Appears to be deserted, my friend. No one on the roads, no one in the fields. The keeper himself must have gone home to supper—there is smoke coming from his chimney. How do you feel, boy—valiant?"

"If we are pursued, you'll soon see."

"I don't think we shall be. But the hour has come, my boy."

He added after a short interval, whilst he pretended to listen: "Come up whilst we lay some plan of campaign."

"You see below the village of the Minières?" asked M. Ulrich, as Jean's head appeared above the branches and turned towards the west.

"Yes."

"In spite of the mist and the darkness, can you make out that on the other side the mountain is covered partly with fir- and partly with beech-trees?"

"I guess it."

"We are going to make a half circle to avoid the gardens and fields of the Minières, and when we are just opposite that spot, you will only have to descend two hundred yards and you will be in France."

Jean made no answer.

"That's the spot I marked out for you. See that you recognise it. Over there round Raon-sur-Plaine, the Germans have kept all the forests for themselves; the barren lands they have left to France. On the opposite side, facing us, there is an extensive strip of meadow land which is French territory. I even saw a deserted farmhouse, abandoned before the war, I suppose. I'll go first."

"Excuse me, I'll go first."

"No; I assure you, my boy, that the danger is equally great behind. I must be guide. I go first; we'll avoid the pathways, and I will lead you carefully to a point where you have only one thing to do: go straight ahead and cross a road, then a few yards of underwood, and beyond is French soil."

M. Ulrich embraced Jean silently and quickly; he did not wish to lose control of himself, when all depended on calmness.

"Come," he said.

They commenced the descent under cover of the tall fir-trees which commenced just there. The slope was strewn with obstacles, against which Jean or his uncle frequently stumbled, moss-covered stones, fallen and rotten trunks, broken branches, like claws stretched out in the darkness to bar the way. Every moment M. Ulrich stopped to listen and would frequently look round, to make sure that Jean's tall form was close behind him—it was too dark to see his face.

"They'll be checkmated, uncle," whispered Jean.

"Not too fast, my Jean; we are not yet safe."

Still under cover, the fugitives reached the meadows of the Minières, and began to ascend the mountain opposite, but without quitting cover.

When M. Ulrich reached the summit he stopped and sniffed the wind, which blew more freely through the young trees.

"Do you smell the air of France?" he murmured, in spite of the danger of talking.

A plain stretched in front of them, but was invisible; they could distinguish the trees, which seemed like stationary smoke below, and above were the scurrying clouds. M. Ulrich cautiously began the descent, listening eagerly. An owl flew by. They had to make their way a short distance through a prickly undergrowth which clung to their clothes.

Suddenly a voice in the forest called:

"Halt!"

M. Ulrich stooped, his hand on Jean's shoulder.

"Don't move," he whispered quickly. "I'll call them off, by turning towards the Minières. As soon as they follow me, get up, run off, cross the road and then the little coppice—it's a straight line in front of you. Adieu."

He rose up, took a few steps cautiously, and then made off quickly through the woods.

"*Halt! Halt!*"

A report rang out, and as the noise died away under the branches M. Ulrich's voice, already some distance off, called:

"Missed."

At the same moment Jean Oberlé made a rush for the frontier. Head lowered, seeing nothing, his elbows squared, his chest lashed by the branches, he ran with all his might. He passed within a few inches of a man lying in ambush. The branches were pushed aside, a whistle was blown, Jean redoubled his efforts. He reached the road unawares; another report rang out on the edge of the wood. Jean rolled over on the edge of the copse. Cries arose:

"Here he is! Here he is! Come."

Jean jumped up instantly and dived into the wood. He thought he had stumbled over a rut. He leapt into the copse. But his legs shook under him. He felt with anguish a growing faintness overcoming him. The cries of his pursuers rang in his ears, everything swam before his eyes. He came upon an open space, felt the fresh wind on his face and lost consciousness.

Late at night he came to his senses. A storm was raging over the forest; he saw that he was lying on a bed of green boughs, in an empty room of the disused farm, lit by a small lantern. A man was bending over him. Jean realised that it was a French keeper. His first sensation of fear was dissipated by the man's welcome smile.

"Were other shots fired?" he inquired.

"No, no others."

"So much the better; then Uncle Ulrich is safe—he accompanied me to the frontier. I was in the army, but I have come to be a soldier in our own land."

Jean saw that his tunic had been taken off and that there was blood on his shirt. It hurt him to breathe.

"What's wrong with me?" he asked.

"You were hit in the shoulder," said the man, who would have wept if he had not been too ashamed to do so. "It'll heal; fortunately, my comrade and I were making our rounds when you stumbled into the field. The doctor will be here at break of day—don't be alarmed, my comrade has gone to fetch him. Who are you?"

Half conscious, Jean Oberlé replied: "Alsace———" but he could scarcely speak.

Rain was falling heavily; it hammered upon roof and doors, upon the trees and rocks surrounding the house. The tops of the trees shook and twisted in the storm like seaweed tossed upon the bosom of the ocean. The murmur of a million voices rose in harmony over the mountains, and thundered upon the night.

The wounded man listened—in his weakened state what did he hear? He smiled:

"It is France," he murmured; "she sings to me," and he fell back with closed eyes awaiting the dawn.

Milton Keynes UK
Ingram Content Group UK Ltd.
UKHW040509120324
439192UK00006B/463